SUMMER MAGIC

THE THORNE WITCHES BOOK 1

T.M. CROMER

COPYRIGHT

To Deb
You've made the journey into paranormal fun.
Thanks for all the late-night brainstorming sessions.
"Did you just sniff me?"

ALSO BY TM CROMER

Books in The Thorne Witches Series:

SUMMER MAGIC

AUTUMN MAGIC

WINTER MAGIC

SPRING MAGIC

REKINDLED MAGIC

LONG LOST MAGIC

FOREVER MAGIC

Books in The Stonebrooke Series:

BURNING RESOLUTION

THE TROUBLE WITH LUST

A LOVE TO CALL MINE (coming soon)

THE BAKERY

EASTER DELIGHTS

HOLIDAY HEART

Books in The Fiore Vineyard Series:

PICTURE THIS

RETURN HOME

ONE WISH

Look for The Holt Family Series starting January 2020!

FINDING YOU

THIS TIME YOU

INCLUDING YOU

AFTER YOU

THE GHOST OF YOU

THE THORNE WITCHES

THE THORNE FAMILY TREE

PRESTON
THORNE

M.

RUBY
SMYTHE

ALASTAIR
THORNE
BOOK 6

TRINA
GILLESPIE

PRESTON
THORNE

M.

AURORA
FENNELL

RYKER
GILLESPIE

M.

GIGI
THORNE
BOOK 7

NASH
THORNE
BOOK 8

HOLLY
THORNE
BOOK 5

SUMMER
THORNE
BOOK 1

AUTUMN
THORNE
BOOK 2

WINTER
THORNE
BOOK 3

SPRING
THORNE
BOOK 4

THE THORNE WITCHES

THE CARLYLE FAMILY TREE

CARLYLE

TRISTAN CARLYLE — M — GLORY ASHBROOKE

PHILLIP CARLYLE — M — KIERA PALMER

ROBERT KNOX

MARIANNE CARLYLE

ZANE CARLYLE
BOOK 3

KEATON CARLYLE
BOOK 2 — M — DIANE MARSHALL

COOPER CARLYLE
BOOK 1

KNOX CARLYLE
BOOK 1

CHLOE CARLYLE

"We've got a problem, C.C."

Cooper Carlyle, in the process of cooking breakfast, hung his head, appetite gone. "Please don't tell me it's that damned elephant."

"Okay, I won't." Keaton swiped two bacon strips in passing.

Coop's head came up. "Really? It's not the Thorne beast?"

His brother laughed. "Oh, no. It *is*, but I won't tell you he's in our pool again if you don't want to know."

With a litany of curses, Coop threw down the spatula, turned off the burner, and stalked to the deck. What he saw triggered another long series of swear words. Eddie The Elephant was the most recent rescue of one Summer Thorne, his all-around pain-in-the-butt neighbor to the west. Since she'd petitioned and freed the elephant from a miserable life of performing on command, the ginormous beast had been nothing but a menace to the Carlyle estate. When he wasn't leaving massive amounts of gag-worthy crap all over the lawn, he was making himself at home in the Olympic-sized swimming pool off the back deck.

Today, Eddie was already underwater and using his trunk as a snorkel. Periodically, he would peek over the edge of the pool toward the rear of the property where the Carlyles' prized horses grazed.

The longer Eddie stared at the mares, the angrier and more creative Coop's language became. The damned elephant thought he was going to make time with the mares. It didn't matter that they were two different species.

"Get her on the phone," Coop bit out.

"Sorry, man. No can do. Duty calls. There's a permitting issue I need to address before ten. But hey, have fun with that." Keaton gestured to the backyard with his thumb.

"Coward!" he hollered after Keaton's retreating back.

"Yep!"

Coop mentally ran through every removal scenario. Short of a crane, he didn't know how to get the two-ton Tom out of the pool.

How had Summer done it in the past? The last time it happened, he had received a call that Eddie was in his pool only to return home and find his nemesis trudging down the road with her elephant in tow.

A mental rundown of various techniques proved futile.

As he pondered options, he detected movement from the corner of his eye. His training kicked into gear, and he laid a hand on the firearm at his side. Or where the firearm should've been.

Shit!

He hadn't yet put on his service belt today. His lack of attention to his attire went to show how damned aggravated he was over finding Summer's elephant in his pool.

Sunlight shimmered off bright golden-blonde hair. The glimpse of his intruder had him easing back into the shadows of the porch and ducking behind a stone pillar.

Summer Thorne.

Coop fought the instinct to run and hide. Hell, technically he *was* hiding. He wasn't ashamed. Heck, no!

The woman was almost as much of a nuisance as the droves of animals she cared for. More so, if he thought back over all the years he'd known her. Her last name was certainly appropriate; she'd been a *thorn* in his side for as long as he could remember.

It all started fifteen years ago when Summer and her sisters had moved to Leiper's Fork. From the first day she'd laid eyes on him, Coop had become Summer's sole obsession. During high school, anywhere he turned, there she was. Her big blue eyes were as bright as the sky and stared at him as if he were a gift from the gods directly to her. The adoration and borderline stalking had unnerved him and made him the butt of his friends' jokes.

After six months of her shadowing his every step, Coop had had enough and arranged to crush her affections. He'd planned it down to the last detail.

Step one: Ask her to prom.

Step two: Show up late—*without* a corsage.

Step three: Continually leave her alone to go off with friends.

Step four: Get caught kissing the gorgeous Rosie McDonough.

His plan had worked brilliantly.

What he hadn't expected was to feel like the worst sort of asshole for what he'd done. He'd only wanted her to stop trailing around after him. But seeing her bent double, tears pouring from her eyes, had made his stomach ache.

She hadn't even confronted him that night. Just backed away and caught a ride home from the dance. Never again did she dog his footsteps or turn those overly brilliant eyes in his direction. If they ran into each other in the hallways of school, she always took care to avert her face as if he didn't exist.

To this day, eleven years after he'd tricked her, her large, teary eyes still haunted him.

Now, whenever possible, they steered clear of one another.

He imagined *her* reasoning was some prolonged sense of embarrassment. But he'd been the one who was ashamed. They'd become frenemies of a sort whenever they were in public. And privately, they avoided each other like the plague.

Exhibit A: Currently, she crept through the shrubbery.

Exhibit B: Here he was, attempting to make himself skinnier than a column. Which was nearly impossible. That's what he got for all those hours of manual labor in his barn and regular workouts at the gym.

"Dammit, Eddie!" she muttered. "How the hell am I supposed to get you out of that pool without help? Levitation?" She sneezed and glanced up. "What do you think, Saul?"

3

Coop squinted, unsure if his eyes were deceiving him. Nope, they weren't.

A scurry of squirrels lined a branch over Summer's head. They chattered among themselves as if having a discussion about the removal of Eddie from the pool. One furry rodent got particularly aggressive. If Coop didn't know better, he'd say it was enthusiasm for its plan. In its fervor for the subject, the head squirrel took a misstep and plunged to the ground.

Summer's reflexes bordered on the supernatural as she held out a hand and caught the animal mid-air. With a stroke of one finger over its furry head, she whispered words only known to the animal and tossed the creature back up to the branch where four other squirrels were leaned over, watching their companion plummet towards certain death.

"You're welcome, Saul," Summer said to the ringleader. "Think nothing of it." Distracted, she faced forward and appeared to contemplate the bigger problem at hand.

Who the hell was this woman? Dr. Doolittle?

"Whatcha doin'?"

The deep voice behind him nearly had Coop coming out of his skin.

"Jesus, Knox! That's a great way to get shot," he scolded in little more than a whisper.

"Except you aren't wearing a gun," his cousin stated the obvious. "And I happen to live here."

"Is that my bacon?"

Knox grinned around a bite of the perfectly cooked meat. "Don't know. It was sitting on the counter, waiting to be devoured."

"Shhh! Lower your voice, or she'll hear you."

"*She?*" asked the voice of an outraged female.

He closed his eyes and sighed. Fighting to keep the sickly look off his face, he spun around. "Oh, hey, Summer."

The spitting-mad female in question narrowed her eyes and refused to speak.

In an effort to change the subject and not allow himself to think about how much this one female terrified him, Coop pointed to Eddie. "Your damned elephant is in my pool—*again*! Want to tell me what plan you and the Squirrel Mafia came up with to get him out?"

4

She sucked in air so sharply, she choked. Face an alarming shade of crimson, she attempted to hack up a lung.

If he took delight as he pounded a little too hard on her back, well, he had to take his pleasure where he could get it.

Knox handed her his bottle of water, and the grateful look she shot his cousin's way had Coop bristling.

At six-two and a hundred ninety-five pounds, Knox had a lean, muscular build designed to turn a woman's head. Added to the superb physique, the man's sun-bleached blond hair and laughing sapphire eyes cemented his status as town heart-throb. He had only to show that uber-white smile, and panties dropped left and right.

Summer didn't appear immune to his cousin's charms either.

Why the idea of her drooling over Knox bothered him, Coop couldn't say. After being the recipient of her blatant crush, he should be happy someone else was now the focus of her attention. Except he wasn't.

"You all right, gorgeous?" Knox asked, the picture of concern.

Coop's gag reflex triggered. "Laying it on thick, aren't you, man?"

Both Knox and Summer ignored him.

She ran a shaky hand under her weepy eyes and thanked Knox ever-so-sweetly for his assistance.

"What about my assistance?" Coop asked.

Why the hell was he getting offended? He had absolutely no interest in her. If he never saw her or a member of her personal zoo again, he'd be ecstatic.

Her eyes rolled back in her head, and she scoffed, "I'll send you the bill for the chiropractor."

A bark of laughter escaped Knox.

"C.C.! *Help!*" Keaton's shout spurred him into a dead run around the side of the house, Knox and Summer fast on his heels.

The sight of a bat-wielding chimpanzee halted them all dead in their tracks. The primate stood on the hood of Coop's police cruiser, swinging like an MVP for the New York Yankees.

"What the fu—!"

"Morty, no!"

Summer's and Coop's yells canceled each other out.

5

"Shoot him!" screamed Keaton as the ape wound up to take another swing.

"Don't you dare!" she screeched.

As Summer moved to intercede, Coop grabbed her and yanked her out of harm's way.

"Are you crazy?" he barked. "Do you know the strength of that animal? He can crack your head like a walnut."

"Morty wouldn't hurt me."

"Says every victim of a chimpanzee attack," muttered Knox.

"He wouldn't," she stressed. "He has post-traumatic stress disorder. I've been counseling him."

And with that comment, Summer cemented why everyone in the county thought she was certifiable. Coop included.

"Knox," he said quietly. "Get my gun."

"No!" She fought like a woman possessed.

Morty picked up on her distress and became more agitated by the second. The tip of the aluminum bat made a sharp clank as it dented the hood of the cruiser.

"Summer, I need you to calm down. The chimp is—"

Keaton's scream rent the air.

If it came to a choice between his brother or Summer's monster pet, it was no contest. Coop would shoot the animal like a rabid dog. "Knox, hustle your ass!"

Knox cast a regretful glance at Summer and ran for the house.

"Cooper, if you shoot him, I will never forgive you." Her eyes shimmered with unshed tears. If anything, they looked larger, more heart-wrenching than ever.

His gut clenched. He'd only ever seen her cry the one other time, and the remembered sight of her silent sobs still made him sick.

"He's dangerous, Summer. Normally, I would try a tranquilizer, but the tranq gun is in the Ford. What do you suggest I do?" he asked impatiently.

"Give me a chance to talk to him. I can make him see reason."

Incredulous, he blurted, "You're crazy!"

. . .

SUMMER WINCED. SHE HAD NO ILLUSIONS AS TO HOW THIS TOWN VIEWED her. It didn't matter that she'd gone to college and earned her degree as a Doctor of Veterinary Medicine; she'd always be the strange woman who kept to herself and collected exotic animals.

Had she held out any hope that Cooper Carlyle might have viewed her in a different light, that was now gone. Later, when she returned home, she would examine why, after all this time, his words still had the power to hurt.

Shoving back her shoulders, she cleared her throat. "I'm perfectly sane, Sheriff. Morty was used for animal testing and was abused by one of the lab techs. Some days, he has flashbacks. But he's never hurt a single living being."

"Then why is he swinging a freaking bat at my head?" Keaton hollered from where he was trapped between the two vehicles.

"Because he doesn't know you, Keaton," she replied. What was obvious to her wasn't necessarily obvious to others. "Now everyone just calm the fuck down!"

Her hand flew up to cover her mouth and nose. *Oops!* Abruptly, she sneezed. A squeak sounded to her right, but she refused to look in that direction. She didn't dare draw attention to the rodents lining up along the sidewalk. Because consequences like the town's soon-to-be increased mouse population tended to be more than she cared to think about, she kept her swearing to a minimum.

With any luck, Coop and Keaton wouldn't notice their new mice infestation.

The sound of the bat smashing into the Ford's windshield caused Summer's eyes to close in pain.

As if she didn't have enough expenses with the feeding of one perverted elephant, one chimp with PTSD, a blind owl, three flatulent dogs, about ten-too-many kleptomaniac cats, five mischievous squirrels, and seventeen pigmy goats—not to mention her mobile clinic. Bribing a few officials to get permits for the lame lion she had slotted to come home this week was going to have to wait until she talked to her finance manager.

"Morty, come to Mama, sweet boy. Come on," she urged. She'd have gone to him, but Coop still had a death grip on her arm.

Her beloved chimp narrowed his eyes on Coop and curled back his lips to bare his teeth. In a gesture of intimidation, he rose up to his full height. Once again, he raised the bat and brought it down on what remained of the windshield. The crackle and subsequent sound of shattering glass filled the air.

Crap!

Morty tended to be possessive of her attention. She had her reservations about his tolerance should she bring a man home. But in a small town of less than one thousand people, her chances of a relationship were nil anyway. No one wanted to date the crazy chick.

"Morty, no! That's not the way we deal with our anger. Remember?" she said softly, careful to keep her tone soothing.

"Oh. My. *God!*" She could hear the grinding of Coop's teeth. "Are you serious right now?"

His aggression triggered Morty's, and the ape slammed his bat on the hood of the vehicle and screamed his rage.

"Morty, baby, you have to behave or no lemon Tastykakes!" It was a last-ditch effort, but Summer was desperate.

The string of curses emitting from Coop made her cringe.

The lure of lemon Tastykakes did the trick. Morty lowered the bat, cocked his head to the side, and let out a questioning meep.

"Yep, lemon. Your favorite. But only if you come to Mama right now." Summer jerked free of Coop and squatted with her arms wide.

Morty was halfway to her when she heard the cocking of a gun. Horror resulted in the speed of her heart ratcheting into high gear.

That damned trigger-happy bastard intended to shoot her chimp!

"No!" She stood, whirled about, and effectively placed herself between the barrel of the gun and Morty. Tempering her voice due to the upset shriek behind her, she said, "No, Coop. You'll have to shoot me first."

He looked tempted as if he contemplated doing just that.

Maybe she shouldn't have put the idea in his head.

Summer swallowed hard and closed her eyes. The long-term ramifications of him shooting her chimp didn't bear thinking about. She'd never be able to look at Coop in the same way again. While she needed a way to squash her unrequited feelings for him, this was not it.

The love she'd harbored for him would never be reciprocated in her lifetime. Somewhere, a cosmic bookkeeper, who kept a tally of all the times she'd made cow eyes at him or secretly wrote Mrs. Summer Carlyle like a flighty teen girl, was laughing their butt off.

The bat clattered to the pavement, and a warm hand reached up to clasp hers. She sighed her relief and pivoted toward her pet. "Good boy, Morty."

He leaped at the same time she tugged. In her arms, he nuzzled into her hair. With an arch look in Cooper's direction, she said, "See? He's really sweet."

"He's psychotic. Permit or not, Summer, that animal isn't safe for you to have around. I'm going to petition that he be sent to a zoo."

"And I'll see you in Hell first, Sheriff," she snarled, any attempt at friendliness gone. She sneezed. The handful of mice in her periphery doubled. Summer couldn't worry about that now. She had to take care of her chimp.

Morty was her baby. She'd had him from a year old, and they'd spent every day for the last ten months together. Protecting him was second nature, like a mother bear with a cub.

Morty, sensing her fear and anger, pulled back to sign, *"Are you okay, Mama?"*

"Yes, sweet boy. Mama's fine. Let's get you home."

"What about the damned elephant in my pool?" Coop shouted.

"One crisis at a time. I need to bring Spring back with me. She has a way with Eddie."

As she strolled away, Summer could feel the eyes of all three men watching her back. She almost added extra sway to her hips, but she didn't want to be accused of trying to entice Coop. Over the years, she'd taken enough flack for her behavior during her Sophomore and Junior year.

"Summer!"

She glanced over her shoulder to see three sets of similar eyes watching her with varying degrees of disbelief.

Coop was the one she focused on.

With a nod toward the smashed windshield, he said, "Bring your checkbook with you when you come back."

"*S*pring?" Summer called upon entering Thorne Manor. "Sister? Where are you? I've got a serious nine-one-one here."

Cream cheese bagel in one hand and a cup of coffee in the other, Spring sauntered into the foyer. "Don't tell me. Eddie is in the Carlyle pool again."

Summer nodded. "I don't know how the hell we are going to remove him either. Three of the four Carlyle men are present."

If anyone discovered the Thorne women were witches in bum-fucked rural Tennessee, the bible belt of America, then gossip would spread, hell would break loose, and residents would line the drive with pitchforks. She suspected the locals would recreate the Salem Witch Trials.

Sure, there were a few open-minded individuals, but as a whole, people were content to go about their lives firmly entrenched in their belief systems. Any deviation tended to bring out the ugly. People hated change as much as they swore they didn't. The idea of witchcraft in this little town would blow their ever-loving minds.

Her thoughts circled back to Cooper. He'd be the first one tying her to the stake just to be rid of her.

"We could go with the distraction routine like the last two times.

Baked goods and a bikini," her sister suggested, chowing down on her bagel. "I have cinnamon buns in the oven."

"I'm game for that plan. If it ain't broke, don't fix it," Summer agreed as she snagged the coffee mug and took a sip. Once she handed it back, she said, "But you have to be the bikini model this time. I don't think I could stand it if Coop believed it's another ruse to get his attention."

"Can't be me. I have to levitate that damned elephant."

"Then we need to come up with another plan." Summer shuddered as she remembered the coldness in Cooper's steel blue gaze. "One that doesn't involve me appearing like a pathetic attention-seeking virgin in front of Coop."

"You could always let your goats loose in the town square." Both sisters turned toward the cool voice at the top of the stairs. Their oldest sister, Autumn, shrugged and descended the steps as if she didn't care one way or another if they accepted her suggestion. "I would be willing to assist Spring with elephant retrieval. But you'd owe me one—to be collected at a later date."

Agreeing would be like making a pact with the Devil, because Autumn's favors usually involved Summer getting caught in a humiliating situation. However, she didn't see where she had a choice. "But how do I round up the goats after the fact? If I whistle and they all fall in line, the jig will be up."

With a flick of her auburn hair over her shoulder, Autumn spaced her words as if Summer were dull witted. "That's what Coop and his department are for. Let them round the goats up."

A quick look showed Spring thought this was a fine idea. Whatever, Summer would go with the majority rule.

"Okay. I'll load up Gertie and her sixteen siblings. You two change into bikinis in case we need a backup plan. Once I've released the goats in town square, I'll text you." She swallowed her self-contempt and asked, "Do you think when this is all done, one of you could, you know, make Coop forget the whole incident? I'd hate to be on his radar any more than I already am."

The twin looks of pity caused her to die a little inside. Why did she have to be the family failure in their little sisterly quartet? If one freaking spell worked properly for her, she'd faint from the sheer shock.

Unable to handle the shame, she averted her eyes.

"I'll take care of it," Autumn assured her. "Now go."

"Oh, and I need a check to cover the damage to Cooper's police cruiser," she hedged.

"What happened to his cruiser?" her two sisters asked in stereo.

"Morty had an episode. Tried to use Keaton's head for batting practice."

Delighted, Autumn clapped her hands and laughed. "Remind me to give Morty an extra banana with his Cheerios. And I've got you covered on the check. I just wish I could've seen Keaton's face."

"He screamed like a terrified little girl."

They all broke into laughter at the thought of the studly Keaton emitting a high-pitched scream of terror.

Autumn took extra pleasure. The two had dated in the past, and while her sister never confessed what happened to destroy their relationship, they hadn't ended it amicably. Within the span of three months, Keaton married another woman, and Autumn became a full-fledged, card-carrying member of the Grudge Club.

Spring sobered first. "Go, before Coop calls animal control. We'll head over shortly."

With a nod of thanks, Summer headed out to the animal barn.

It took a bit of encouragement, but Gertie led the way into the small trailer. Where Gertie went, so did her sisters. Not dissimilar to Summer and her own sisters.

Of course of the four of them, Autumn was usually the one who led the other three by their noses straight into trouble. It had been that way since they were small. Probably because she was the oldest of the four, she tended to be the bossiest. Not that Spring, Summer, or their other sister, Winter—affectionately called Winnie—minded. Autumn's schemes were always great fun.

A short while later, Summer eased into the parking lot behind the Leiper's Fork church close to the center of downtown. A quick peek around showed the lot to be empty. Now was the time to strike.

"Okay, Gertie. Do you know what to do?"

"Do those animals really answer you?" a soft voice asked, nearly causing Summer to shed her skin.

The owner of that young voice was none other than Chloe Carlyle, Keaton's eight-year-old daughter.

Freaking great! Kids were notorious for spilling the beans, and this one was the daughter of the mayor and niece to the sheriff. Where she'd come from in the seconds since Summer scanned the area was anyone's guess.

"Uh, in a manner of speaking," Summer hedged. "Where's your dad?"

The dirty, dark-haired tomboy eyed her with suspicion. "Why?"

"Maybe because you're eight years old and too young to be gallivanting all over town by yourself? Keaton should keep better track of you."

"You know what I think, Miss Summer? I think you were about to let those goats loose."

Panic wrapped its big fat fingers around her throat and squeezed. Called out by a kid. "That's a dang lie!" Why was *she* the one sounding like a defensive child?

A smirk appeared and reminded Summer that Chloe was indeed part of the smartass Carlyle clan. "If you don't tell me what you're doing with the goats, I'm going to scream for my dad. He isn't too happy with you right now."

The Morty Incident.

Yeah, had Summer nearly been on the receiving end of a bat, she might not look too favorably on the owner of the chimpanzee swinging it. Keaton Carlyle had to be ready to string the Thorne sisters up.

"Fine. I was about to let them loose. They need to stretch their legs. I thought I'd let them run around the parking lot since it's deserted."

Chloe lifted a brow. "Wrong."

Red faced, Summer challenged the little tyrant. "What makes you the authority on goat herding?"

"You're trying to cause trouble. Uncle Coop said you specialize in trouble."

"Your Uncle Coop is an as—"

"Don't say anything you're going to regret, sister."

Saved by Winnie's arrival, Summer took a deep breath and counted to ten.

"Everybody knows you are in love with him," Chloe continued to taunt.

Temper rattled, Summer lifted her hand.

"We don't zap small children," Winnie warned in a whisper as she grabbed Summer's wrist and squeezed. "Even if the little shits deserve it." With a flick of her fingers, Winnie sent Chloe on her way.

"I am going to assume she won't remember we were here?" Summer asked, throwing back the bolt to the trailer door.

"Not a second of it. Why didn't you cloak the area when you pulled up?"

Summer cast her sister an exasperated glance. "Oh, I don't know. Probably because I'd encase the town in smog or something equally as awful?"

"Point taken."

It was no secret in the Thorne family that Summer's magic was hit or miss on a good day. When emotions ran high, the results were almost always in the miss column.

"How did you know I was here?"

"Spring called, said you might need help. Wonderful sister that I am, I thought I'd pop over. Not a second too soon."

In the process of swinging the door open, Summer paused. "You *popped* over?"

With a dismissive wave of her hand, Winnie snorted. "No one saw me. *I* made sure to cloak myself."

Her sister's superior skill in all things magic pissed Summer off most days. Why couldn't the juju be spread out evenly? She'd be satisfied to master one freaking spell.

The ability to conceal her actions would be nice. To hide behind an optical illusion? Yeah, she could've used that more than once during high school. But better she didn't possess the ability. She'd have been tempted to spy on Coop in the locker room showers.

Wait! *Did her sisters get away with doing that?*

"Did you ever use your cloaking ability for nefarious purposes?" she demanded.

"Define nefarious."

Clearing her throat, she relayed her thoughts.

Winnie's grin was answer enough.

"You saw Coop in the altogether?" Summer demanded in outraged.

"Not Coop. Zane. And damn, was it amazing!"

"It being *it*?" At her sister's nod, curiosity got the better of her. "How big?"

Hands spread close to nine inches apart, Winnie giggled.

"Day-ng. Maybe I lusted after the wrong Carlyle back then."

"Back then?" Winnie snorted. "Still."

"Not hardly."

Winnie duplicated Chloe's skeptical look.

"Shut up and help me release Gertie and her crew. We have work to do."

"SHERIFF CARLYLE."

Coop placed his coffee mug on the deck rail to press the transmit button on the radio attached to his hip. "Go ahead."

"We have a problem."

Didn't they always if his dispatch was calling? "What's up, Lil?"

"The town has been overrun with goats."

"Goats?"

"Yes, sir. Goats."

He cast a contemplative glance at Eddie. "Whose goats?"

"I believe they may belong to Summer Thorne."

Coop wanted to cuss and kick the nearest object. That woman's menagerie was going to be the death of him.

"Where's Aimes? He's supposed to be on patrol in town."

"He's on scene. But he says they aren't normal goats."

"Uh huh. What's so abnormal about them?"

"He didn't say. Only to tell you to get downtown STAT."

"I'm on my way, Lil. Tell him to stay put."

The time had come to do something about Summer and her varmints.

"And, Lil? Set up an emergency board meeting tonight. First thing on the agenda is shutting down Summer Thorne's personal zoo."

"Yes, sir."

Did he detect censure in Lil's tone? "She's a menace, Lil."

"She?"

"Uh, her animals."

"Ten-four."

Yep. He definitely detected censure, in addition, a liberal sprinkling of knowing in the word "she".

He threw the remains of his tepid coffee into a nearby bush and cast one last backward glance at the giant Don Juan in his pool.

As if Eddie knew he was in the clear for a bit, he grinned and shot up water from his trunk.

Coop pinned the elephant in place with a glare and shouted, "Stay away from my mares!"

A trumpeted call was Eddie's response.

Displeased with the whole mess, Coop stalked to his cruiser. Correction, his smashed up cruiser.

Sonofabitch!

He'd forgotten about the windshield. No way could he drive that vehicle. Looked like he was driving Keaton's old Ford today. With any luck, the junker would get him to the station to pick up another squad car.

One more thing to lay at Summer's door.

As he climbed into the cab, he studied the woods along the West side of his property. A prickle along his spine told him someone was lurking about.

He flipped open his phone and dialed Knox. "Hey, man. I'm heading to town. Do me a favor and keep an eye on that elephant and the horses, will you? Also, be sure to lock up tight."

"Another feeling?"

"Yeah, call me crazy, but..."

"No need to explain, Coop. We all know your intuition is usually spot on."

He chuckled as he backed out of the driveway. "Usually?"

"Well, I'd only call into question your judgment on one thing."

"Oh, what's that?"

"Summer Thorne. That chick is smoking hot and clearly adores you."

"Not this again." Coop sighed his disgust.

"I'm just sayin'."

"Enough about Summer Thorne. She's the reason I'm heading to town. Her and her damned animals."

"Then you'll have no problem with me asking her out?"

The steering wheel jerked in his hands. An oncoming driver honked his concern when Coop crossed the dotted line.

Sweat beaded on his forehead. Did he have a problem with Knox dating Summer? Why did the idea of his cousin hooking up with Summer cause Coop's pulse to kick into high gear? It didn't bear thinking about.

"What are we talking here, Knox? Your standard quick lay or something more meaningful?" His voice came across more gruff than usual, but it couldn't be helped. *He* may not want a relationship with Summer, but he didn't care to see her hurt.

"Summer's a good girl, Coop. I'm not planning to hit it and quit it."

Irritable and out of sorts, he punched the dash.

"What was that? Coop? You okay?"

"Yeah, I'm fine," he lied. "I have no problem with you asking Summer out. She means nothing to me."

"Good. I didn't want to step on any toes if you were interested."

"Nope. No toes to step on."

"I didn't think so. I mean, it isn't like she's ever forgiven you for that bonehead move at prom."

And she never would.

"You have your answer, Knox. Just go check on her damned elephant, will ya?"

On the drive to town, he examined why the idea of his cousin in a relationship with Summer bothered him. Perhaps his shame played a major role. Or maybe, because he was bound to see her more often than he already did if she started dating Knox, it would bring up all the old crap from the past. It certainly wasn't because he was interested in her himself.

Knox was correct in one thing, Summer did indeed have a smoking hot body. All delicious curves meant for long, steamy nights of wild monkey sex. He imagined her thick mane of hair fisted in his hand as he slammed into her.

In his sexual daydream, Coop nearly missed the turn for town. He shook his head at his own stupidity. Never going to happen. If he'd had a chance with Summer, it had long-since passed.

The sight that greeted Coop when he arrived downtown was pure chaos. Intersection traffic was blocked as well as the entrance to multiple side streets.

What appeared to be miniature goats ran about hairy scary—until a horn blared or some driver shook their fist with a yell. Then, like an in-sync water ballet, all the goats would tip over on their sides, legs straight out as if they'd gone belly up for good.

Curses could be heard over the din. All of them directed at a flustered Summer Thorne.

Their eyes connected across the road between them.

Hers quickly dropped to the pavement and a slight pink blush lit her cheeks.

God, she was beautiful with her bright blonde curls and her flashing blue eyes. Her smooth complexion was marred only by a light dusting of freckles across her nose.

Not that he could see her freckles from this distance, but there wasn't an inch of her face he hadn't memorized the day he'd tore her heart from her chest. His gaze swept the length of her curvy figure, and his mouth watered. His fantasies all came flooding back.

Yep, he was an idiot eleven years ago for chasing her away, and again today for giving Knox the green light to pursue her.

With a heavy sigh, he started forward. "Summer!"

A mass bleating echoed off the brick buildings, then all the goats toppled where they stood.

"*For the love of*—." He bit off the curse and hurried to her side. "Care to tell me why your herd is in the middle of downtown when you should be getting that pervert out of my pool?"

Titters of laughter sounded around them, and he glared his response.

Pedestrians scurried away with the occasional backward glance. Where Summer went, drama was sure to follow.

Her chin shot up and challenge lit her gaze. "I told you, Spring needed to remove Eddie."

"Uh, huh. So why this?" He waved his arm to encompass the entire street.

Her delectable mouth opened and closed twice—*he knew because it was all he could focus on*—and she frantically glanced about as if looking for something or someone to save her.

"Summer, start talking."

"Maybe we could shelve this for another time, Sheriff." Winnie sashayed up and wrapped a slender arm around her sister's shoulders. "I think the important thing is to help round up these goats."

"Care to enlighten me how we go about doing that?" He shot a sharp glance at a suspiciously quiet Summer. "If I'm not mistaken, these are fainting goats. Any sudden movement and they drop."

The sisters shared a secretive look.

His anger began on a low simmer. They were playing him.

Summer chose that moment to comment. "Exceedingly skittish fainting goats. They were rescued from—"

His temper erupted. "I don't give a rat's ass where they were rescued from or why the hell they are 'exceedingly skittish', Summer." One finger tipped up her chin as he leaned in to relay his point. "You have five minutes to get them off the streets, or I take matters into my own hands. Are we clear?" A tap of his gun holster clarified his threat. Not that he intended to shoot her pets, but she didn't need to know that. If it got her butt in gear and got the animals in hand, he'd use whatever bluff he needed to.

"You're evil," she whispered hoarsely, emotion choking off the tail end of her accusation.

God, please don't let her cry. A woman's tears ripped his insides out. Who was he kidding? *This* woman's tears ripped his insides out.

"Yeah, no one could accuse me of being an angel. But the law is the law, and you're breaking it. Shall I tally the offenses?" His thumb caressed the soft skin of her jawline and was at direct odds with his words.

Damned if her skin wasn't like silk to the touch. His eyes followed the movement of his thumb. Was the rest of her equally soft and smooth? And why was his mind suddenly preoccupied with thoughts of a naked Summer Thorne? He shifted closer.

"Sheriff Carlyle?"

He ignored the summons behind him, lost to the beating pulse of Summer's throat. The tan column begged his lips to—.

"Uh, Coop?" the person behind him persisted.

"What?" he snapped, bringing his head around.

"Keaton's old Ford is on fire," Deputy Aimes informed him.

3

*S*ummer stood shell-shocked and helpless against Coop's touch. How many times had she longed for him to wake the hell up and notice her as a woman?

Too many to count.

Now that it happened—granted in the middle of a busy downtown—she froze like a pathetic loser.

He swore and hurried toward the blazing vehicle, leaping over the goats that toppled left and right.

"Wow. The whole town witnessed that little display. Think Coop was making his interest known?" Winnie asked as she came to stand shoulder to shoulder with her.

Because coherent sentence forming was impossible, Summer blinked and shrugged. What *was* that all about?

Autumn joined them on the sidewalk. "Mission accomplished. Eddie is safely back home. Way to distract Coop, Summer. I didn't think you had it in you."

She didn't, but Summer didn't intend to tell her sister otherwise.

"Where's Spring?" Winnie asked.

"She stayed behind to taunt Knox." A flash of white teeth indicated

Autumn's amusement. "She was forced to resort to the bathing suit distraction. Or that's what she'll swear happened."

"The poor bastard doesn't stand a chance," Winnie mumbled.

The other two nodded their heads in agreement.

"That was Keaton's old red Ford, right?" The glee in Autumn's voice was suspicious.

Summer nodded and raised a questioning brow. "Please tell me you're not the one responsible for the fire."

"Pfft. Who, *me*? I will say Granny Thorne's concealment spell works fabulously well though."

Summer and Winnie groaned.

Autumn's Grudge Club ticket had just been validated.

"Time to get the heck outta here before Coop comes back. He doesn't look happy." Summer let loose a sharp whistle.

Gertie and her posse jumped to their feet and formed a line. Like an army of four-legged soldiers, they trotted in two rows of single formation toward the church parking lot.

"Oh, shit."

Summer's head whipped to where Autumn pointed.

Disbelief warred with outrage on Coop's countenance as he stared at her perfectly behaved herd. When his fury-filled gaze touched on her, Summer shivered. She needed to get a move on. The last thing she wanted was to wind up in a cell at the sheriff's department.

"You're in big trouble," Winnie sang.

"Well, I'm not waiting around to deal with his temper. Can't you, ya know..." Summer wiggled her fingers behind her hand. "... make everyone forget we were ever here? Like you did Chloe."

"That was the initial plan, but there are too many people. I'm not sure a simple finger-wave is going to cut it."

Autumn agreed with Winnie. "It's going to take a stronger spell."

"What are we supposed to do? Sneak in and dump a potion in the town's water supply?" Summer desperately suggested. The guilty looks from her sisters sparked her outrage. "This is exactly what I need; another strike against me. This town is going to run me out on a rail!"

"Overdramatic much?" Autumn laughed.

"The freaking goats were *your* idea!"

"If I told you to jump off the Brooklyn Bridge, would you?"

A swan dive off the Brooklyn Bridge sounded great right about then. It didn't take a genius to recognize the dirty scowls directed her way meant Summer was the most hated individual in town at the moment.

She pointed a finger at Autumn. "You suck!"

"Never on the first date and only if he—"

Winnie's hand over Autumn's mouth stemmed their sister's retort. "Let's get a move on. The lynch mob is forming, and with the way our sheriff looks at the moment, I'm of the belief he might assist instead of have them desist."

The three sisters beat a hasty retreat. They raced around the corner of the building, laughing like a pack of wild hyenas. Once in the parking lot, Winnie spun about and waved her hands. The air around them pulsed once then solidified to a normal appearance.

"Let's get you loaded, ladies," Summer said to the goats.

The rapid pounding of soles on the pavement caught the sisters' attention. Everyone froze. Even the goats paused to witness Coop approach. When he stopped short, ten feet away, they all exhaled a collective breath.

Like a bewildered beast, he swung his head back and forth in his search for the Thorne sisters.

Summer sidled up to Winnie, licked her lips, and whispered, "Can he hear us?"

"No. The spell cloaks sound as well. Or mostly it does." Winnie offered up a delicate shrug. "I imagine if there is horrendous banging or screaming, it might be a different story."

"Yeah, none of this is suspicious at all." Autumn snorted and snapped her fingers. Gertie and crew loaded into the trailer with minimal noise.

As her hungry eyes devoured Coop, Summer said, "I really need to perfect this particular spell."

"So much for not lusting after the sheriff," Winnie snickered.

Summer flipped her off. "Shut up and get in the van."

"This is how every bad abduction starts." Autumn inserted.

"There's such a thing as a good abduction?" Winnie asked as she climbed through the side door.

"Why couldn't I have been an only child?" Summer complained although she didn't mean it. She wouldn't trade her sisters for anything in the world.

With a quick crank of the engine, they were on their way.

Coop grew smaller in the rearview mirror until he disappeared.

Why couldn't her obsessive thoughts of him go the same route?

COOPER HAD TO BE LOSING HIS MIND. THERE WAS NO OTHER explanation. How else did three women and a herd of roughly twenty fainting goats disappear in less than two minutes?

Luckily, he knew Summer's ultimate destination.

*Un*luckily, he had no transportation to get to said destination.

He turned and stalked back the way he'd come. As he approached the smoldering Ford, Coop caught his brother's angry vibe.

That POS Ford had been Keaton's favorite toy. Keaton and his daughter, Chloe, had invested their time trying to restore the 1950s F1 to its former glory.

In Coop's opinion, the old rust bucket was a money pit. Parts needed to be custom made and took weeks, sometimes months, to get. Still, it gave his brother and niece a project to bond over.

"I'm sorry, Keaton. I needed to get to town and the cruiser wasn't safe to drive in that condition." Coop rested a hand on his brother's shoulder. "I'll pay for the damage."

"Was Autumn here?"

He frowned and nodded. "Yeah, but not *right* here. She was across the street."

"Uh huh."

"You think this is her fault?"

"Oh, I don't *think*, I *know*."

"Keaton, don't make accusations you can't back up."

Keaton ignored him and studied the neighboring buildings. Apparently, he found what he was looking for because a triumphant, evil grin spread across his face. "Bingo."

Coop followed the line of sight to an exterior security camera.

The brothers shared a questioning look and lifted their brows.

That camera, if working, would provide the evidence they both needed. Coop had no doubt Summer's little fiasco with the goats was staged. He just didn't know why. The video footage might give him an idea.

"Come on. Let's see what Old Man Harkins caught on tape." He checked both ways before leading the charge to the hardware store.

The recording proved nothing except Old Man Harkins was a crotchety pain in the ass who refused to cooperate until threatened with a court order, and the Thorne sisters were piss-poor goat herders. It could be said they weren't trying very hard to gather the animals, but no definitive proof of mischief could be detected.

Keaton muttered about sneaky witches and their desire for revenge.

While Coop didn't feel the women warranted being called names, he did mull over the revenge factor.

Perhaps Keaton was right. Maybe the Thornes had it in for the Carlyles. After all, the Thorne estate had been in the women's family for generations, and before they moved to town, their grandfather, Preston Thorne, resided there. It was no secret Grandpa Carlyle and Preston had hated each other.

Coop had thought the ridiculous feud died out with his grandparents' generation, but perhaps it hadn't. Maybe the sisters and their father, the current Preston Thorne, kept it alive and well.

Had Coop and Keaton reactivated old grievances with their romantic slights to Summer and Autumn? What was the saying? Hell hath no fury like a woman scorned?

His cousin Knox needed to be warned. If he truly intended to date Summer, he could be walking into a minefield. Coop wasn't about to let that happen. Or that's what he told himself. If he had other reasons to prevent Knox from asking her out, Coop refused to acknowledge them.

"I heard you called an emergency meeting tonight."

Keaton's words startled Coop. He'd been lost in thought and forgotten he was in the middle of downtown.

"Uh, yeah. I thought we should address Summer Thorne's animal issues. You know, the Babe Ruth of chimps, Marty."

"Morty," Keaton corrected absently with a glance at his watch.

"Whatever. Between him and that Casanova of an elephant, we have a problem."

"C.C., she is going to hate you if try to take away her pets."

"Those 'pets' are out of control, Keaton. What if it was Chloe that chimp raged on this morning? She'd be dead right now." He sighed and shook his head, secure in his decision. "And Eddie is making eyes at our breeding stock. If he decided to do anything other than show off his swimming prowess, he could injure one of the mares. We can't afford the risk."

Keaton ran his hands through his dark hair, spiking the thick strands in his irritation. "Look, I get it. But you'd better be prepared for the fall-out. My F1 was a casualty of Autumn's rage—*nearly nine years later!* You've already got a strike against you with Summer. You do this, and man, I don't want to be in your shoes."

With a point of his finger at the charred vehicle, Coop scoffed at Keaton. "You don't know this was Autumn's doing. Let's deal with one issue at a time."

His brother glanced at his watch a third time in as many minutes.

"What's the deal, man? You have somewhere to be?"

Keaton nodded. "Yeah. City Council meeting. As Mayor, I'm required to attend, but Diane is late picking up Chloe. It's her week to have her."

"Where is Chloe, anyway? I'd have thought she'd have gotten a kick out of the goats."

"She's with her friends at the park."

"Look, if you need to run, I can wait on the tow truck. I need to be here to take statements from a few of the bystanders. When I'm done with that, I'll check on Chloe."

"Thanks, C.C.. Will you text me with the time of the meeting tonight?"

Coop watched his brother hurry away toward the city building before he phoned Lil to send the next tow truck driver on rotation.

"Yes, sir. The meeting to discuss Summer's rescue is on the agenda for tonight at six. I've notified all parties involved."

A sick dread built inside him. All parties involved meant she'd already placed a call to Summer. "How did she take it?"

"She had a few creative choice words for you, Sheriff."

When Lil resorted to calling him Sheriff, she was displeased.

"Why do I feel like she has a sympathetic ear in you, Lil?"

"Because she does. I think you're wrong, but I'm just the hired help."

A snort of disbelief escaped. Lil was no more the hired help than Morty was a sweet baby. She practically ran the entire town on her own.

"Will you be there tonight?"

"Yes, Sheriff. I'll be there in support of Summer. She's doing a wonderful thing for those poor animals."

"Lil," he groaned. "How will it look if you support her? You're supposed to be on the side of public safety."

Her tone changed from frosty to frigid. "I have never once not looked out for the welfare of this town in all my fifty-eight years, Cooper Neal Carlyle. I resent you insinuating differently."

Crap. As his mother's life-long best friend, Lil was practically his second mom. Everyone knew when a mother used a middle name you were in deep shit.

"You happen to be wrong because you can't see straight where that gal is concerned."

He almost asked what gal, when she clarified.

"You could do a whole lot worse than Summer Thorne. In fact, you have."

When did this become about his love life? "Let's keep on track with the reason for this phone call, Lil. My love life is not up for discussion."

Her humph told him that he'd offended her greatly. Freaking awesome. The next month of his work life would be hell.

"Six o'clock, city hall, *Sheriff*."

She hung up before he could apologize.

"Was that about Miss Summer, Uncle Coop?"

He glanced around to see Chloe and two young boys roughly her same age perched on the edge of their bike seats, one leg out to the side to balance their ride.

"Why do you ask, midget?"

Her lips formed a grimace at the endearment. Oops, he'd forgotten she didn't care to be called the nickname in front of friends. Another female he'd pissed off today. He was three for three.

Surprisingly, she answered. "Because you get that funny look on your face when you talk about her."

Funny look?

He hadn't realized the question popped out until she answered.

"Yeah, like you sucked on a lemon."

The boys laughed, and Chloe took delight in his discomfort.

Her expression changed in an instant, a look of horror replacing the smugness. "Is that Daddy's truck?"

"I'm sorry, midg—uh, Chloe. There was a bit of an accident."

Tears pooled in her wide brown eyes, and he wanted to vomit. *Why did females have to cry?*

"Daddy's going to be so mad."

"He knows already." He squatted in front of her and smoothed the sides of her dirt-smudged shirt. "Look at it this way, you and your dad can start over from scratch. You already have the experience under your belt. The second time around will go faster. Not only that, but this lets you draw out the project."

She nodded, but didn't appear one-hundred percent convinced.

"Why don't you and the boys head over to Monica's Cafe? Get an ice cream? Tell Monica I said put it on my tab."

"Okay, Uncle Coop." She lifted her leg and spun the crank arm until the right pedal was on top for perfect takeoff position. With a frown she asked, "Did Miss Summer do this?"

"The Ford? No, honey. She had nothing to do with the truck." Not directly anyway. Her ape on the other hand…

4

"*T*hat side-winding snake in the grass!"

"Summer, calm down."

"That two-timing, yellow bellied, low-life scum sucker!"

"Summer—"

"I'll turn that turd into a toad! That's what I'll do!"

"Sister—"

"He'll be pissing blood for a week when I kick him in those grapes he calls 'nads!" She spun around and faced her three sisters, who all struggled to hide their amusement. "It's not *funny*! That asshole has humiliated me for the last time."

She sneezed but didn't stop to worry about the results of her swearing.

All humor was wiped from their faces as they realized the deeper meaning here. Not only was Coop trying to take away all Summer loved, he'd set out to do it publicly and rub her nose in it along the way.

"Everyone knows what you are trying to do here, sister. They'll be on your side." Autumn stood and smoothed the wild gold curls back from Summer's face. "Hell, you've treated or taken in everyone's rejects at one time or another, and that includes the people."

Tears welled, and she was powerless to prevent them from falling.

"Why does he hate me so much? What have I ever done to him?" She sniffed. "I wasn't even home before the call came through. Not ten minutes before he'd been acting as if he w-wanted..." She halted, unable to continue.

No sense going there. Obviously she misread his intent when he'd touched her earlier. The little caress that sent her heart into orbit hadn't even caused his to lift off. *Because he doesn't have a heart!*

Her sisters' expressions ranged from bewildered to helpless. They had no answers for Coop's behavior either.

Winnie rose to her feet. "Come, sisters. It's time we cast a spell."

"We doing this? Turning Coop into a toad?" Spring asked, half serious.

"No. We are going to make sure the meeting tonight ends in Summer's favor," Winnie informed her as she wrapped Summer in her warm embrace. Her nature was in direct odds with her name. Winter was the warmest, most loving of the four Thorne sisters.

"Uh, Winnie, magic on our own behalf is a big no," Summer said.

"We aren't doing it on *your* behalf. We are doing it on behalf of those poor animals in need of help. The Goddess will approve of us taking care of her creatures."

Summer couldn't fault Winnie's logic. What she could fault was her own abilities. "Should I sit this one out so it doesn't backfire?"

"Absolutely not," her three sisters replied in unison.

"You are one of the four, sister. You—"

A banging on the front doors interrupted Spring's speech. The group shared a wary glance.

"Autumn Thorne, get your ass down here!" Keaton yelled from his place on the porch.

For once, Autumn's expression was devoid of humor. Pale and shaky, she said, "He knows I torched his truck."

"How? How could he know?" Winnie asked, the voice of reason.

"I don't know *how*, but he does."

Summer had to agree with her sister's assessment of the situation. Keaton sounded over-the-top angry. Only his child or his beloved truck could be the cause for such a mellow guy to lose his cool.

The banging started again. "I know you're in there. Open up."

Four faces crowded the window and craned to see below.

"This is all my fault. I'll go," Summer offered after another minute of listening to him slam his fist against the wood.

She stepped toward the bedroom door only to have Autumn place a hand on her arm and halt her progress.

"No. I'll own up to my actions."

Autumn was a braver soul than Summer. Had the situation been reversed, if Coop was pounding the doors down, she'd have gladly sent a mediator in her place.

"We'll all go," Winnie insisted, loyal to a fault.

As one, they headed to the foyer.

"Stop stalling. He's going to leave a dent," Summer finally said after another minute of Keaton's thumping against the solid mahogany and iron double doors. "Heads will roll if Dad comes home to a damaged door. That thing is an antique."

Their father, Preston Thorne IV, was an antiquities dealer who traveled the world looking for exotic pieces to add to his personal collection as well as to sell in his downtown shop. As such, he rarely remained in one place for any length of time. But the man would know if there was even the slightest nick on any one of his precious pieces.

"Pfft. He can't damage that thing. It's solid." Autumn, determined to stall, crossed her arms over her chest.

Another thud shook the door on its hinges. Summer raised a brow. "Uh, you were saying?" She stepped to the door and threw back the bolt.

"Autumn, you—" Keaton halted his charge when he noticed the wrong sister had answered and saw evidence of her upset. "Summer, what's wrong? Is everyone—" His eyes took in the four sisters. Only one of which had tear-stained cheeks. "Oh. Tonight's meeting. Look, I'm sorry about that. Coop…" He shrugged then turned his laser focus on Autumn. Angry lines bracketed his mouth. "You!"

With a false air of arrogance, Autumn crossed her arms under her breasts.

Keaton's eyes dropped to the ample cleavage displayed in the white tank top and his face grew flushed.

Score one for Autumn. The woman knew men.

Ah, to have that ability. Summer heaved an internal sigh. What couldn't she accomplish if she had full use of her powers and a playboy-pinup body like Autumn?

At five-ten, her sister was the perfect compliment to Keaton's six-three. She boasted a pair of high-sitting D cups, a trim waist, and a firm ass that made men's jaws unhinge and tongues dangle when she shook her money-maker down the street.

Summer wouldn't have been surprised to see big red hearts pulsing in place of the men's eyes.

With her blazing hair and challenging amber eyes, Autumn was a man's wet dream. Jessica Rabbit in human form.

Summer tamped down her envy.

Being gorgeous came with its own set of problems.

Rather than stay silent and watch the uncomfortable gawking, Summer intervened. "What's going on, Keaton? Why all the yelling?"

It took an act of congress, but he finally ripped his gaze from Autumn's chest. His expression turned ugly. "She set fire to my damned truck!"

"Me?" Autumn splayed her fingertips over the expanse of skin at her chest.

Her little-ol'-me act wasn't fooling anyone—especially Keaton. Although, his eyes did dip to where her fingers rested before snapping above chin level again.

"Why do you think she set fire to your truck? Couldn't it be the thing was an old piece of crap with crossed wires?" Winnie hedged.

Wrong thing to say. His already dark countenance blackened. "I have been painstakingly restoring that truck with my daughter for the last six months. Trust me, the wires were *not* crossed."

He took a step in Autumn's direction.

As one, the sisters took a step back.

He continued on his trajectory, not stopping until Autumn was backed against the foyer wall. His chest pressed to the one he'd been obsessed with since the ten-foot tall mahogany door opened.

"Why?" Had his tone been harsh instead of ragged, the sisters would've been on him like white on rice. But he genuinely seemed bewildered and hurt by Autumn's fire bombing.

"We needed the distraction." Autumn shrugged and portrayed an unfeeling wench. The sisters all knew differently. Inside she was still bruised by Keaton's defection years earlier.

If family lore was to be believed, once a Thorne found their one true love, their heart would never veer off the path of that love. It made for devastation and heartbreak when those affections weren't returned. Such was the case with Autumn. Such was also the case with Summer.

Both sisters tried to hide the fact they were suffering from unrequited love, but the truth was obvious to any who cared to see.

"Distraction? The goats weren't enough?" He nodded to encompass the group's guilty expressions. "Yeah, I knew what you were doing. But I'm here to tell you, your *distraction* has broken my daughter's heart," he ground out. "You owe her an apology."

Autumn snorted. "Not in this lifetime."

Oh, boy. Summer closed her eyes. Nothing like drawing a line in the sand for a man who wasn't afraid to cross it.

"You little bitch," he snarled. "I dodged a bullet nine years ago."

If he'd have slapped Autumn, it would've hurt her less. The challenge died from her eyes. Void of their spark, the amber turned to a murky brown. Pain radiated from her as if she could no longer contain the heartbreak. Each of the sisters physically felt the impact.

Autumn skirted sideways and presented her back to one and all as she moved toward the stairs. "I'll tell you what. I'll stop by, write a check for the damage, and apologize on my way out of town tomorrow. Is that good enough for you?" she threw over her shoulder.

"Out of town? Where are you going?" Keaton demanded.

"I'm sure it's none of your business. And honestly, I can't see why you'd care. Suffice it to say, I won't be around to destroy the truck once it's repaired. Good enough?"

She swept up the stairs with all the majestic grace of a queen, back straight, head held high.

"Autumn!"

When Keaton would've charged after her, Summer and her sisters blocked his path. "You should go. You've gotten what you came for."

After a long stare, he acknowledged Summer's words with a resigned nod.

"Oh, and Keaton, I'm sorry about Morty, but he's not going

anywhere. Be sure to tell your brother to bring his A-game tonight. I don't plan to lose my Sanctuary," she vowed.

After he'd gone, she turned to her sisters. "Let's cast that spell. But first, I need to check on Autumn."

As she crossed the threshold of her elder sister's room, Summer registered that Autumn was indeed packing.

"You're really going?"

"I am. I'm sick of this hick town. How the hell do you stand these self-righteous asshats?"

Her sister hadn't meant to be derogatory. The question was legit. Summer, because of her dealings with her mobile vet's office and the rescue center, had a lot more interactions with the residents of this town.

"Some of them aren't so bad."

"We're outcasts, sister. We always have been because of those fucking Carlyles."

Autumn dumped the whole of her underwear drawer into a cardboard box she conjured. Jean shorts and tank tops followed suit. In her rush to pack, she wasn't taking care to fold her clothing. It said a lot about her mental state because Autumn was the family's neat freak.

Seeing her so riled hurt. "Don't go."

"I have to get out of here. You, of all people, should understand why."

With an absent nod, Summer wandered over to the dainty vanity. The piece looked like it belonged in a museum. The color, a robin's egg blue, was distressed with hints of a soft blush pink paint bleeding through the cracks. The pulls had deep red tassels, and the top was a dark honey mahogany.

Summer ran her hand over the top. She'd always loved this piece.

"You can have it."

Spinning about, she faced Autumn. "No. Mom brought that piece home for you on her final trip. I know what it means to you." She hugged her sister. "Wherever you get settled, we'll see it delivered."

Uncharacteristically quiet, Autumn nodded her acknowledgement.

"I'm sorry about Keaton, Tums."

The nickname brought a ghost of a smile to her sister's face. Only Winnie still used hers. The rest of them had reverted back to their given name sometime during high school in an effort to appear more sophisticated.

"He broke up with *me* all those years ago."

The haltingly whispered words shocked Summer. Everyone always believed Autumn told Keaton to take a hike. Believed he'd found comfort in another's arms and gotten the other woman pregnant by accident. The resulting marriage had been for the baby's benefit. No one was surprised by his divorce four years later.

Never once had Summer suspected Keaton dumped Autumn. "What happened?"

Autumn's guilt-filled eyes rose to meet her steady gaze. "I confessed to being a witch."

Summer sat, missed the edge of the bed, and landed on her tailbone with a thud. "Shit!"

She sneezed.

Squeaking started mere seconds after she swore, and four little mice lined the baseboard by the door.

"I'm good, guys. Thanks." She waved off the rodents.

With a twitch of its whiskers, the largest of the mice led the others out of the room.

"If anyone knew you were the swearing Pied Piper of Leiper's Fork, you'd never live it down," Autumn laughed through her tears.

"I know." She grimaced and scrambled to her feet. "Why did you tell him, Tums? You had to know he wouldn't take it well."

"We were getting serious. I thought he loved me enough that he'd be okay with it." Autumn swallowed hard. "If the Goddess blessed us with children, they would be witches. He had to be forewarned."

She nodded. Autumn's reasoning made sense. "But he wasn't okay with it, was he?"

"No. Not at all. He accused me of putting him under a love spell. Demanded I remove it. Said it explained why he couldn't go a minute without thinking about me."

"Oh, Tums."

"Yeah. When I told him I hadn't—*couldn't*—because things didn't work that way, he flat out called me a liar." Autumn swiped at the new tears forming. Of the four sisters, she hated to show any weakness. "Goddess, I loved him. He was my everything."

"Past tense?"

"How can I love Keaton as he is today? He's angry and awful to me whenever we're in the same room."

"Did you tell him we were witches too?"

Autumn nodded regretfully. "I'm sorry."

"Don't be. He seems to have kept it a secret."

"That would be my doing. After his initial angry reaction, I *did* put a spell on him. I made it so he couldn't reveal what we are."

One thing bothered her, and Summer voiced it. "Why doesn't he treat the rest of us poorly? If he is afraid of you because of your powers, it would stand to reason that he would be afraid of us."

"You didn't cast a 'love spell' to bind him to you for all eternity," Autumn snarked, her bitterness at the unfairness of the situation bleeding through.

"But then neither did you. You know how this works better than any of us. You had Mom to teach you."

Silence reigned for a moment. Both reflected on what was lost when their mother had died.

Summer could scarcely recall the woman who had given them birth. Twenty years was a long time to try to keep only a handful of memories alive.

Autumn, on the other hand, had a few more years of guidance. Hers and Winnie's acceptance ceremonies within the coven had been orchestrated by their mother, Aurora.

Summer and Spring had missed out. Instead, they'd been sponsored in the ceremony by their Aunt GiGi a few years after their mother's passing.

She shrugged off the melancholy. "Where will you go?"

"Perhaps the Keys? I could always bartend in Key West."

"With that creamy skin? You'll look like a lobster in an hour."

"North then? I've always wanted to visit New England. Meet that branch of the Thorne tree."

"I don't want you to go," Summer said softly.

"None of us do," Spring piped in from the other side of the wall.

Autumn's bitter laugh caused their sisters to join them.

"You'd think after nine years of constant exposure, I'd be over Keaton and his stupidity. But I'm not. And I won't ever meet anyone as long as I'm here." Autumn softened her decision to leave with, "I need a break. If only for a little while. A year, two at the most."

"That's a lifetime without our big sister," Winnie croaked out.

"You'll have to be the big sister for a bit, Winnie. You can do it. Besides, I'm only a snap away." Their big sister hugged each of them in turn. "Now, let's get on that spell for protecting Summer's rescue animals. Packing can wait another day."

"No offense, Summer, but because you are the weak link here, you need to purify yourself. Autumn, I think you should do the same because of Keaton's angry energy. When you're both done, come to the attic. In the meantime, Spring and I can purify the space and prepare the circle."

"Well, look at you, taking charge and shit. It's like you're already stepping into the role of the elder, Win," Autumn teased with a light hug. "Thank you. A bath is just the thing."

Thirty minutes later, the sisters all utilized their specific element inside the circle. They called to the Goddess to ask for guidance and protection of Summer's sanctuary.

Through it all, an old raven perched in the rafters watching the proceedings. When the circle was closed, he cawed and swooped down on Summer's shoulder to nuzzle his head under her chin.

"Mr. Black approves of our work here today," she laughed and rubbed the head of Spring's familiar. "Thanks for the vote of confidence, Blackie Boy. Cooper Carlyle doesn't stand a chance against the Thornes."

*S*ummer walked into the town hall meeting with her sisters, Winnie and Autumn, at her back. She reminded Coop of a queen with her ladies-in-waiting. Her head was held high and her chin jutted out. Regal and ready to remove heads from shoulders. Probably Coop's.

Lil directed the Thorne sisters to a set of chairs and settled in beside them. No mistake as to where *her* loyalties lie.

A buzz filled the room as townsfolk poured in and the panel took their places behind the desk at the head of the room.

"You should talk to her, Coop," Knox said. Neither man was in doubt as to whom he referred to.

Coop shoved down the urge to do just that. "Why? What point would it solve?"

Knox sighed his disgust. "You're a stubborn ass. You know that?"

"Because I believe those wild animals need constant, professional supervision?" he asked, angry that he'd been painted the bad guy in this scenario.

"No. I was there this morning. However, she calmed him in nothing flat." His cousin shoved off the wall and leaned in to emphasize his point. "You're an ass for not going about this in a different manner. If you sat down and addressed your concerns in a reasonable, concise way, she'd listen. But you had to go behind her back and call in the town heavyweights for this fight. Like I said, you're an ass."

After Knox stormed away, Coop headed for Summer. Perhaps he did owe her an apology. His intent was short lived. The meeting was called to order, and Coop was directed to state his case.

He recited the dates and times the elephant had escaped its enclosure and ended up in his pool. He also stated the labor involved in cleaning up after the animal in question.

Out of the corner of his eye, he saw Summer whipped around to glare at Autumn. Whispering ensued between the two sisters.

"Are you two done? May we continue?" he asked pointedly.

Autumn sat back with a grin. Summer ignored him entirely and stared straight ahead.

Coop returned to the microphone and addressed the morning's incident with Morty. Keaton and Knox both stood in acknowledgment.

"And finally, the goats in the square this morning, as many of you witnessed firsthand. It is my belief, Summer Thorne is ill-equipped to handle the demands of Summer's Sanctuary in addition to her mobile veterinary unit," Coop stated. He cast a regretful glance in her direction.

Her face was a frozen mask. The sister on either side of her each held one of her hands in their grasp. They were a beautiful family unit. But not one able to deal with the rigors of caring for wild animals. As if she sensed his regard, Summer lifted her expressive eyes to meet his gaze. Betrayal shone back at him.

Coop cleared his throat.

"It is my further belief, only the animals deemed wild, such as the elephant and chimpanzee, should be taken from her care and placed in a zoo or other facility better suited to handle those types of animals."

Summer rose and approached the podium.

With his palm, he covered the microphone. "I'm sorry, Summer. Truly."

"Go to the Devil, Sheriff," she spat and shoved his hand from the mic.

"First, I'd like to beg your indulgence for a moment." She gestured toward the rear of the room. "My sister, Spring, has brought one of the animals in question. It's my aim to show you exactly how docile he is."

The double doors at the back of the room opened, and Spring entered holding the hand of a smartly attired ape. Morty wore a blue suit with a pale yellow silk tie. As he walked by where Coop sat next to Keaton, the chimp tugged Spring to a halt.

Damned if the beast didn't stare them down with reproof in his large brown eyes. Morty focused his attention on Summer and his hands flew about in a flurry of movement.

She bit her lip, as if in an attempt to stem laughter, and nodded. "Yes, sweet boy. I quite agree. Come."

Morty and Spring continued to the podium where Spring then handed the chimpanzee off to Summer.

"What did he say, Dr. Thorne?" Councilman Chambers questioned.

"He expressed an apology to Coop and Keaton. He said he was out of line this morning and that it wouldn't happen again."

Coop snorted his disbelief. "Right."

Both Summer and Morty faced him. Their twin expressions, raised eyebrows and challenging stare, were a sight to behold.

"If you don't mind, Sheriff Carlyle, you've had your turn to speak. Now it's mine," Summer said. Having dismissed him, she faced the panel. "May I bring Morty forward?"

Two of the four council members appeared nervous. The other two seemed enchanted by Morty.

"You're going to lose, C.C. She's wrapping them around her finger with this stunt," Keaton murmured in an aside.

"This is Sir Mortimer, and he says he's happy to make your acquaintance." To the ape, she said, "How do you introduce yourself, Morty?"

The damned the little charmer lifted Councilwoman Moore's hand to place a kiss on her knuckles before he graced all the members with a grin.

"Morty has flashbacks to a time when he was abused. However, I am licensed to treat him and can medicate him when needed. He's in no better hands than mine. I am also willing to implant him with a microchip for tracking purposes and to alert us when he crosses the boundaries of our property." Summer opened the folder in her hand and passed a single sheet to each of the council members. "The black outline shows our property's boundary. There is a red line within that border. This is the new restricted area I am proposing for Morty's tracking device. We will know instantly if he's crossed the line."

"How long will this take to put into place?" Councilwoman Moore asked.

"It's being completed as we speak, ma'am."

Moore nodded as if pleased.

Keaton was correct, Coop's cause appeared lost.

Coop stood to state his objection. "First, her idea seems to be little better than an invisible fence used for dogs. Second, we haven't addressed the issue of his anger issues. Chimpanzees are easily twice as strong as the average human."

"I'm likely to be more dangerous than Morty, Sheriff," Summer protested.

"Lastly, the elephant has escaped and ended up on my property on no less than five separate occasions. I have prime breeding stock, and he can easily injure one of my mares."

"Eddie would never go after your mares. He watches them from afar."

"Like you watch Coop, Summer?" a female heckled from the back of the room.

Fiery red surged up Summer's neck and into her cheeks.

"Rosie McDonough, if you know what's good for you, you'd shut your mouth," Autumn called. "By the way, how are those genital warts clearing up?"

Titters and full-blown laughter resounded.

"Let us stay focused on the issue," Councilwoman Moore chided. To Coop, she asked, "Have there been any documented incidents in the time Dr. Thorne has provided shelter for these animals?"

Coop hung his head. "No. I didn't feel the need to write her up."

"Without anything on record, Sheriff, I feel we cannot rule on this matter. Summer's Sanctuary permits are in order, even for the monkey and the elephant." Moore shuffled the papers in front of her. "However, I'm willing to grant you a concession, Sheriff. Dr. Thorne, you have thirty days to make the necessary changes to the property and animal enclosures to keep them secure. If, during that time, we have another incident, the council will reconvene to address the issue."

Councilwoman Moore went down the panel one by one for objections. All the council members were in accord.

"Sheriff, we will put you in charge of ensuring the Sanctuary is in compliance."

"Why can't you put Deputy Aimes or someone else in charge?" Summer asked.

Coop noted Summer's sickly expression and suppressed a grin. "I have no problem with that, Councilwoman. Thank you for taking the time from your schedule this evening to address this issue. I have little doubt we'll be back here within thirty days."

IN THE PARKING LOT, SUMMER PACED BESIDE HER VAN. "YOU CALL THAT a win? Now Coop will be on my butt twenty-four-seven, waiting for me to screw up."

Spring shrugged. "I'm just saying you didn't lose."

"Next time we cast a spell, we might want to tweak it a bit. Like count me out. I'm sure it went sideways because of my involvement," Summer said. "As a matter of fact—"

"Incoming," Winnie muttered.

Summer glanced up to see Cooper bearing down on their group. "Shit."

She sneezed. Squeaking and scurrying feet sounded behind her.

To keep him from seeing the mice, she met him halfway. "You may think you've won, but—"

"No. I don't. I wouldn't call that a win at all," he countered. "But I have no doubt you'll fuck up again. I intend to write up a report on all three incidents for today. I can guarantee, if any of your animals gets out to cause mayhem again, you're done."

"Why are you doing this?" She swallowed her hurt. After all this time, she should be immune to his antagonistic attitude and personal vendetta against her, but she wasn't. "What have I ever done to you,

Coop?" If her last words came out ragged and raw, she couldn't help it. She was feeling ragged and raw.

She'd done her best over the years to tamp down her feelings. Worked to always appear cordial without giving a clue one way or the other about her inner turmoil. But right now, she found her emotions impossible to disguise.

He frowned. "This isn't personal."

"I can't help but feel it is. Would you be hauling Rosie up in front of the entire town to defend her business?"

"Rosie works at the Pack'N'Ship, Summer. It isn't the same thing."

Her brain was going to explode. No doubt about it. The fury boiling in her chest would find its way to her head and blow the top right off. She could feel it building.

"Right." She pivoted on her heel ready to leave.

Coop halted her with a hand on her arm.

It was only the fifth time he'd willingly touched her. The first was at a pool party when he bumped her shoulder while flirting, the second was to escort her to his car on prom night, the third was this morning to stop her from rushing to Morty, and then there was the moment on the sidewalk. The one time she thought he was genuinely attracted to her. Each time, she'd experienced a sizzle, not dissimilar to an electrical current. How could he not feel it?

"The most a person could get at the Pack'N'Ship is a paper cut."

"Or the clap," she muttered.

His eyes flew wide and a bark of laughter escaped. "Summer Thorne! I didn't know you had it in you to be petty."

She yanked her arm free and glared. "Just stating the truth, Sheriff. If you're going to dip in *that* pool, you should probably make sure you're wearing a full wetsuit."

His intent gaze dropped to her lips then slowly rose. The heavy-lidded look had her lady parts on high alert.

"And how about you, Summer? Care to let me take a dip in your pool?"

The husky quality of his voice went straight for her g-spot. She feared she'd come at the mere suggestion of sex with him.

For a long moment, she stood, sucked into the tractor beam of his sexy, mesmerizing gaze. She didn't know where she found the strength to fight the pull, but she slowly shook her head until sanity returned.

"Not in this lifetime, Cooper Carlyle. If we're going with the whole water analogy, I'm going to say that ship has sailed."

He grinned. "In spite of what you think, I like you."

"Well, I don't like you," she retorted. "Now, if you don't mind, I have animals to feed."

6

"*H*as anyone seen my car keys?" Coop slammed through the kitchen, upending the sectioned basket of wallets and keys.

"Come on, man. If they weren't in your slot, they aren't there." Keaton complained as he sorted through the mess Cooper made. "Did you get the spare set back from the repair shop this morning?"

"Of course. I'm not a moron like some people."

"What the hell is that supposed to mean?"

Tensions at an all-time high, the brothers squared off.

Zane ambled in, took one look at the two of them, and turned back around. Their cousin avoided conflict at every opportunity, which was ironic because, as a lawyer, he made his living arguing his case.

Knox, on the other hand, was a born peace maker. His cool head always prevailed. He eased his tall frame into the closest seat. "Come on, guys. Chill."

Well, so much for words of wisdom. "Chill? That's all you've got?" snapped Coop.

Knox abruptly stood back up, his chair sliding back and creating a screech across the tile. "What's your problem? You've been an ass to everyone, even poor little Chloe, who doesn't deserve it. And Zane is ready to cut his visit short and head back to Nashville."

The brothers froze.

Their cousin *never* lost his temper. Not in the twenty-two years they'd known him. The man's picture was in the dictionary under the word Zen. He'd come to them as a silent, motherless seven-year-old. Not speaking or smiling. Over time, he opened up and became more of a brother than a cousin.

"Well? Aren't you going to deny it?" Knox demanded. "Ever since the meeting, you've been a complete jerk, snapping everyone's head off. Boo hoo, so you lost the vote to out Summer's Sanctuary. Get over it."

"You don't understand, Knox."

"Then explain it. Because while I get that your intent was safety, this pissy attitude is over the top."

And wasn't that the problem? Coop didn't know what exactly was bugging him. Or maybe he did.

Even after he'd crushed Summer's romantic dreams, she hadn't hated him. The disdain in her eyes, directed solely at him during the meeting, had stung. Hell, it still stung. He'd never seen such iciness coming from her in all the years they'd been acquainted.

Summer was warm and sunny like her name. To see her hard and devoid of emotion bothered him. Made him want to do whatever it took to make her smile again. But he couldn't. The residents of this town needed to be protected. Those animals of hers had real issues.

"You're right. I'm sorry. There's no excuse."

Knox gave a single abrupt nod and left.

"I've never seen him even raise his voice," Keaton said, staring in wonder at their cousin's retreating form. "That must mean you truly *were* an asshole."

"Screw you," Coop said with a scowl.

Knox was right. Coop didn't need to go around like a bear with a sore tooth. What he needed to do was head over to the Thorne estate and determine a solution to keep those animals better contained.

As he started for the exit, he stopped and turned back. "Ya know, I get that I've been an ass, but why are you upset?"

Shutters came down over Keaton's normally expressive eyes. "No reason."

"I'm here if you need to talk."

"Does that make us girlfriends? Are we going to share our feelings and write in our little pink diaries?"

"Whatever. I'm offering an ear to get whatever is bothering you off your chest. Don't want to talk, it's cool."

"I don't have anything bothering me. Life is good. Or haven't you heard Autumn left town?"

Now Keaton's restlessness and discontent made sense. Autumn Thorne had always been an open wound for him.

Because there were no words to make it better, Coop left Keaton to brood over his coffee.

"Coop?"

He poked his head back into the kitchen, brows raised in question.

"Thanks anyway. Check the ignition for your keys. You seemed distracted when you came in today."

Sure enough, his keys were already in the car. He groaned.

The situation with Summer had him scattered and out of sorts. It was imperative he resolve the issues between them. If only because, as sheriff, his job required he be in top form, both mentally and physically.

He pulled up to the Thornes' animal barn and parked. Through the newly installed windshield, he watched Summer halt the wheelbarrow.

They warily studied each other for a full thirty seconds, before he gathered his balls in hand and exited the cruiser.

"Hey."

"Sheriff." Her expression resembled nothing if not a woman less than thrilled to see him. "To what do I owe today's visit? All animals are present and accounted for as of two minutes ago, so I know it's not that."

"I thought we could work out a compromise."

"I don't believe I need to compromise. I won the vote last week, or have you forgotten?"

Snippy didn't suit her. "Cut the crap, Summer."

Her brows shot skyward.

Oh, hell. "I didn't mean it that way." He scrubbed a hand across his forehead. "Look, can we start over? On this issue at least? I know you can't forgive me for being a jerk all those years ago, but on this, I need you to see I wasn't doing it to be spiteful."

Did he imagine her expression softening?

He pressed his advantage. "As sheriff, I'm responsible for the safety of the residents of Leiper's Fork. I'm here to see what we can do to fortify the cages and pens so your animals stop roaming the countryside. Fair enough?"

WHEN COOPER TURNED THE FULL WATTAGE OF HIS WARM SMILE ON Summer, the coldness in her soul melted a good twenty degrees. Instead of being a frozen block, her heart was merely a melting popsicle.

"The cages and pens are fortified plenty, *Sheriff*," she stressed in an effort to remind herself his true reason for being there. It certainly wasn't any misplaced affection for her. "I happen to have a very mischievous set of squirrels on the property who like to unlock gates."

"Nothing a bullet won't take care of," he said with a smile.

Goddess preserve her! *He was serious!*

Overhead, Saul raised a ruckus and made his thoughts on Coop's suggestion known. The colorful language directed Coop as to where he could shove his gun. The head of her squirrel mafia leaned over as he warmed to his rant and promptly toppled off the beam.

Having been through this a time or two, Summer's reaction was second nature. She caught him mid-flight. With a kiss to the top of his head, she released him to scurry away. It wouldn't do to use magic to return him to his perch. Cooper would believe he was losing his mind.

"I don't think shooting my squirrels is an option, *Sheriff*."

This time the term was derogatory, and he knew it—as she intended.

Mouth compressed into a thin line and eyes narrowed, he stalked forward.

When he was two feet away, she held up a hand. "I think that's far enough."

The subtle shift of his expression warned her of his intent.

As she retreated, he pursued until she was pressed to the wood of the stall.

"What's the matter, Summer? Does my presence bother you?"

Hell, yes. "No," she gulped out the lie. "No more than any other overly aggressive guy trying to bully me."

His smirk disappeared and apology took its place. He backed a few steps. "Sorry. I thought…"

She knew what he thought. The same thing this whole freaking town thought; she was still crazy about him.

To hide the truth, she averted her face and moved to pass him.

His hand shot out and halted her in her tracks. Apparently her poker face sucked. That, along with her indrawn breath, must've provided a distinct clue to her true feelings.

His grip loosened. Like the morning downtown, his eyes traced the skin on her neck, finally coming to rest on her lips.

A riot of sensation shot straight through her nervous system, and her body went on high alert, eager and longing. Every cell chanted, *"Oh, please! Oh, please! Oh, please!"*

"Do you ever wonder about what would've happened had we met when we were older, Summer? Had I not been a stupid jock with a point to prove?"

Like a deer frozen in headlights, she stared up at him, glued in place. The oncoming wreck was going to smart. She had no doubt he toyed with her to prove another point, but she didn't have the will to stop him.

The pads of his fingers caressed the back of her neck and urged her closer. His other hand nudged her chin and angled her head into position to receive his kiss. *The kiss she'd dreamed of since she was a starry-eyed thirteen-year-old girl.* The kiss that, when it happened, would rock her world.

His dark-blond head blocked out the light, or maybe she closed her eyes. His breath against her lips caused her lungs to seize. Both hands came around to cup her jaw and hold her head. The back and forth motion of his thumbs on her cheeks relaxed her enough to open for him.

Once his tongue swept inside, she registered the taste of coffee and mint. A heady combination.

One of them moaned—*most probably her.*

The kiss went on forever and yet ended too soon.

As he drew away, he nipped her lower lip. Her body surged forward without any instruction from her. She craved more, needed to taste him again. Feel his seductive touch against her skin. To ride him like—!

Only Saul's scolding dragged her back to the real world.

Face flaming brighter than the sun, she stepped away.

"If I'd have known you kissed like that, I'd never have kissed Rosie that night." He punctuated his words with a soft chuckle.

However, with that careless statement, he brought back all the old embarrassment and anger. Sure he meant to be complimentary and flirty, but it stabbed her straight in the heart all the same. If the Goddess were looking down upon her, she was probably shaking her head at Summer's stupidity.

Coop was a player. He'd always be a player. Major league at that.

And Summer would be laughed out of the Minors.

"Yes, well, if you'd have had honest intentions instead of trying to make me look like a fool, you would've found out," she snapped as she busied herself with... *when the hell had she conjured up a bridle?* Oh! The thought of riding him. Damned wonky magic.

She flung the bridle down and scooted it to the side with her foot.

"We were kids, Summer," he said softly, stepping up behind her. His breath stirred the air around her. "I think we can both agree I was an idiot at the time."

"At the time?"

He cleared his throat. "I'm sorry. I don't know what I can do to prove to you I'm sincere."

Why was she fighting so hard? She just wanted him to leave. Maybe if she acknowledged his apology, he would go.

With a heavy sigh, she faced him. "I accept your apology, Coop. For what it's worth. Now, if you don't mind..." She waved a hand at the wheelbarrow. "...I have work to do."

"Want a hand?"

Her jaw dropped.

The man who would shut down her Sanctuary was now offering to help?

"*You* want to help *me* clean stalls? What's the catch?"

"No catch." He shrugged. "It's my day off. I've got nothing better to do."

Overhead, Saul sounded off again and caught Coop's attention.

"What's the deal with that squirrel? It's acting like your chaperone or something."

Her first real laugh in over a week escaped. If he only knew what Saul was saying, Coop would probably shoot her familiar for real.

"Saul is a bit opinionated."

"Opinionated, huh?" Coop picked up a nearby pitch fork and glanced around. "This place must keep you busy from dawn until dusk. Two of us will cut the work in half."

Even half a day in his company was half a day too much.

She made a grab for the fork, but he held it up and out of her reach. Short of climbing his six-foot body, she wasn't getting that tool. Irritated at his high-handed insistence, she said, "Seriously, it's fine. I'm used to it."

"You don't want me here. I get it. But it's nothing more than an offer of help. Call it penance for past mistakes." He smoothed the groove between her brows. In a low, deep voice, he urged, "Just say yes."

"Saying yes to you scares me."

She could've bitten off her tongue as soon as she said it.

His wicked grin sent her heart into overdrive.

If the Goddess was kind, the ground would open and swallow Summer. But she must've angered the deity in a previous incarnation, because nothing in life had ever been easy.

"Fine. Whatever. You're going to do what you want anyway." She pointed to the left row of stalls. "Those still need cleaning."

Wheels on the gravel drive caught her attention. When Knox stepped from behind the door of his SUV, she sighed.

The man should've been a model. He was the perfect eye candy for lonely, sex-starved women everywhere.

His warm, wide smile encouraged her matching smile.

"Summer."

"Hi, Knox."

She started forward only to be impeded when Coop shoved the wheelbarrow in front of her.

"Where should I dump the manure?"

Before she could respond, Knox replied. "Behind the silo. There's a compost pile."

The men eyed each other, and challenge crackled in the air between them.

Coop turned his keen gaze to study her. What he was looking for, she couldn't say.

Confused, her eyes darted from one man to the other. Why were they staring at her? "Knox has come over and helped out on occasion."

The tension in the moment was as thick as frosting on a cupcake.

She hadn't been aware she'd stopped her head ping-ponging to stare at Coop until Knox spoke. "Summer, may I speak with you?"

The blush started somewhere around her toes and worked its way up her neck. "Uh, yeah, sure."

She stopped long enough to grab three bottles of water from the cooler. She tossed one to Coop, before offering one to Knox and following him to his SUV.

"What's up, Knox?"

His bright blue-gray eyes focused over her shoulder and the beginning of a smirk played about his mouth.

"Knox?"

He turned his gaze to her. "Sorry." Clasping her hand in his, he closed the distance between them. "I was wondering if you would like to go to dinner one night this week."

"With you?" Her question came out in an incredulous gush.

They both winced.

"You find me objectionable?"

"Hell, no!"

She sneezed. Within seconds, squeaking started from behind her.

Based on her emphatic exclamation, she suspected an entire colony was gathered there.

Sure enough, his attention was caught by the noise. "Don't freak out, Summer, but you seem to have a rodent problem in your barn."

He lifted her and set her on the hood of his vehicle as if she were a skittish princess who'd faint at the sight of a mouse.

"Do you have rat poison?"

"No!"

She hadn't realized she'd screamed until Coop stormed from where he'd been hovering just inside the barn and Spring ran out of the house.

Coop looked as if he intended to tear Knox's head from his shoulders.

"Back away from her, Knox." The menace was unmistakable.

She grabbed onto Knox's shirt when he would've backed up. "No. It's not how it looks. He wasn't forcing himself on me."

Knox grinned and rested a hand on her hip.

She gulped.

The testosterone in the air was more than her sex-deprived body could handle. With an unconscious clenching of her fist, she balled up the material.

Coop's anger cut her. He cast her one last irate glare before he pivoted and stormed into the barn. Her eyes were caught on the full curve of his ass encased in his jeans. Again, her hand spasmed where it clutched Knox's shirt.

"So that's how it is, huh?" he asked softly.

"How what is?"

She avoided his kind, knowing gaze by glancing at her sister.

Hurt flashed across Spring's face but was gone in an instant. Without making her presence known to Knox, Spring retraced her steps back to the house.

"Summer?"

The deep, seductive baritone drew her back to the conversation at hand.

"The mice aren't hurting anything." Inane sure, but it was the best she could do.

"No mass extermination needed?" he teased.

"No. No mass extermination needed."

"Okay, you softie. Back to the reason I'm here; how about dinner?"

She wanted to say yes. If only to prove to one of them she wasn't a lost cause still pining for Cooper. But Summer couldn't ignore what she'd witnessed on her sister's face.

"It's probably not a good idea."

"Because of Cooper?"

"Because I come with more baggage than one guy should have to put up with in a lifetime."

"Why don't you let me worry about whether I'm willing or able to deal with baggage?" he suggested and dropped a kiss on her nose.

Nothing. Not even a small spark.

She sighed her disgust. Why did it have to be Coop who'd captured her heart? Here sat a perfectly nice guy, a stunning one to boot, and she experienced no attraction whatsoever.

"Your face says it all."

"It's not you, Knox. Believe me, it's definitely not you." She smoothed his shirt and patted his chest. "You're every woman's fantasy come to life; kind, considerate, hot as hell. But..."

"But you still want Coop."

Alarmed by his perception, she frantically shook her head and cast a wild look toward the barn entrance.

"Don't panic. He can't hear us. He's glaring at us from the paddock." He leaned in to murmur, "Your secret is safe with me."

Relief flooded through her, and she rested her head against his shoulder. "Thank you."

"Word of advice?"

She raised her head.

"Play hard to get. Everything has come easy to Coop. And he needs to work to earn your affections this time around. Okay?"

"Boy, are you wrong about his interest," she muttered. "Besides, I'm not sure I trust his motives in being here."

His half-smile had her silently questioning what he knew.

"Just remember what I told you." He helped her down from the hood of the SUV and tugged on her ponytail. "You're worth the effort, Summer Thorne. Don't let anyone convince you otherwise."

7

"*D*o you and Knox have something going on?"

Summer glanced up from the stall she'd been cleaning. "Excuse me?"

"I'm pretty sure you haven't lost your hearing in the last thirty minutes," Cooper snapped. It had taken him that long to work up to the question after his cousin left.

She took her time answering, and the seconds drew out into what felt like days.

Dread churned inside him. What was she doing to him? In the matter of a week, his whole world had been turned upside down.

Seeing her pressed against his cousin nearly caused the top of his head to explode. His blood pressure, which he'd always maintained at a healthy level, had to be in the life-endangering zone.

"We're friends."

Her softly spoken response didn't answer a damn thing. Friends slept together all the time. "As in friends with benefits?"

Shut the hell up, Coop!

"I can't see where that would be your business." She turned her back and continued to scoop.

He followed her into the stall and jerked the fork from her grasp. "It damn well is if you're kissing me while sleeping with him."

"You kissed me, Coop," she retorted. "You. Kissed. Me. Not the other way around."

"Well, you certainly weren't fighting me off or telling me no. Hell, you'd still be lip locked with me if I hadn't broken it off."

Her outraged gasp and chalky-white face told him he'd gone too far.

"You're something else, you know that? You…"

Whatever else she intended to say was lost as she looked beyond him. Eyes huge, she stilled.

He glanced over his shoulder.

The chimp. Murphy…Marty…no…Morty. That was it.

The rage on the beast's face made last week's near annihilation of the cruiser look like child's play.

Coop pivoted to shield Summer. "Stay behind me, sweetheart."

Her snort was derisive in nature. "Sweetheart, my ass," she scoffed then sneezed.

Nails on wood, followed by squeaks started on the other side of the stall wall.

What the hell *was* that? Another ape?

Standing on hind legs, fur puffed out like an enraged cat, the chimp screamed and clanged his latest weapon—a freaking *crowbar*—against the metal bars of the open stall door. His other arm swung wildly in a circle, with a periodic pound of a fist on his chest.

"Cooper, he thinks you're threatening me. Back into the corner behind me. Slowly."

"Not a chance. He's—"

The stubborn female darted under his arm to close the distance between her and the chimp.

Coop made a grab to pull her to safety.

She raised a hand and fisted it.

He halted his forward movement. Not because he wanted to, but because his will seemed to have taken a vacation from his body. He was literally a statue. Panic and a nightmarish sense of the unreal dominated his brain, and he struggled against the invisible bonds holding him in place.

He'd heard of paralyzed with fear, but this lent new meaning to the term.

Whatever force held him in check, also held Morty. The chimp seemed to be a tad bit more accepting of his locked status than Coop.

Summer stroked her fingers between the eyes of the chimp, whispering words foreign to Coop's ears. Whatever she said, Morty understood and his face relaxed as his expressive brown eyes turned to liquid pools of love for Summer.

"That's my sweet boy. That's my Morty," she crooned. "Will you give Mama the crowbar, sweet boy? That's right, relax your fingers."

And damned if the crazy ape didn't do just that. Morty relinquished his hold on the weapon without batting an eye, as if hypnotized.

Hypnosis. When Coop got home, he intended to google if apes were susceptible to hypnosis.

"I'm going to release you, Morty. You have to promise Mama you won't attack Cooper when I do. Mama will be very upset. Do you understand?"

The brown eyes shifted his way, and the soft light left Morty's gaze. Nostrils flared and lips curled.

"Morty, Cooper isn't the bad man."

Did Coop detect a subtle shift in expression?

Morty gave him one last sneer, shifted his attention to Summer, and pursed his lips.

Summer rewarded the chimp and bent down to place her lips against his.

Lucky chimp.

Gradually, feeling came back to Coop's body. Not unlike when blood flow returns to a limb. The pain and tingling caused him to shake his arms and legs. His voice took longer to return.

She scooped the chimp up and hugged him to her. "Sheriff, I'll assume you can show yourself out. Spring or Winnie can help me return the animals to their stalls later tonight." She cleared her throat. "Thanks for your help."

"That animal needs to be put down, Summer," he ground out.

Her grip tightened. "Don't even think about it."

Morty, sensing her upset, drew back his teeth and barked his displeasure at Coop.

As she strode away, a sly look passed over Morty's face. The hand hugging her back lifted straight out, middle finger extended.

That little con artist flipped him the bird!

After they'd disappeared into the house, Coop was left to wonder what the hell had just happened. Never in his life had he hesitated in a crisis. He acted with cool precision. Every. Single. Time. Had it been fear for Summer's safety?

Because he needed to work through the incident in his mind, he ignored Summer's dictate to leave the property and finished cleaning the barn. He returned the tools to their proper places, and with a double check of the posted feed schedule, added a scoop to all the various feeders.

A caw came from the darkened corner of the rafters. A subtle indication of movement was the only warning he received before three pounds of raven descended on him.

He held up his arm to protect his face.

He needn't have bothered. The raven perched on the wall beside him, its head cocked to one side as if making a study of him. After a quick internal debate on the possibility of losing a finger, Coop stretched a hand toward the bird.

Instead of inflicting a wound, the beautiful black bird ducked its head for the touch.

Coop smoothed the feathers in a downward direction. The sooty feathers around its neck puffed as the bird gurgled and released another call.

"Aren't you a gorgeous beastie?" Coop murmured.

The bird nodded as if in agreement with Coop's assessment of him.

And as he bonded with the raven, he had a better understanding of why Summer loved her misfits. The awe that came with the gained trust of a wild animal was a heady sensation.

"Thank you for helping me understand," he told the bird.

The raven once again nodded and spread its wings. Two flaps to gain purchase, and the bird took flight.

Coop shook his head in wonder. He must've lost his mind. Here he was, talking to the animals. Everyone would believe he was as looney tunes as Summer.

"Now you know why she does it."

The soft voice at the entrance of the barn grabbed his attention.

Spring Thorne.

Easily one of the loveliest women in Tennessee. With her hair the color of the Earth's richest soil, and her eyes the color of the Emerald Isle's lush fields, she lived up to her name. Spring wore no makeup. She didn't need to. She sported a peaches and cream complexion, with smooth, unblemished skin.

As he stared, a becoming pale pink blush found its way to her cheeks, enhancing her beauty. Yet in spite of her gorgeousness, he felt no desire for her. Not in the way he'd discovered he now felt for her sister.

"Now I know."

"She's not into Knox, ya know."

"Excuse me?"

"Summer. I know it looked damning before, but she's not into him."

"Has she told you this?"

A secretive smile lit her face. "She didn't need to. I know."

Oh-kay. Whatever that meant.

Because she'd paused like she required an answer, he nodded.

Spring strolled farther into the barn. Stopping alongside him, she gestured to the raven back on its perch in the darkened corner of the barn rafters. "I see you've meet Mr. Black. Or as we affectionately call him, Blackie."

"I have. He formally introduced himself a few minutes before you arrived."

She giggled, and damned if the sound didn't remind him of young females running through a field of violet and yellow flowers on a cool spring morning. The sound was pure joy.

"Why are you here, Coop?"

Because he couldn't explain the sudden desire that overtook him to discover more about Summer's life, even to himself, he shrugged. "The simple reason?"

She nodded.

"Look, I know she believes she's doing a great thing here, and she is. But even though the town believes her safety measures are enough, I still think differently." He shot her an imploring look. "Spring, her more wild friends are dangerous, whether any of you care to acknowledge it or not. My end goal is to make sure everyone is safe, your sisters included."

Disappointment and some other undefined emotion flashed in her eyes.

Had he said the wrong thing? What had she been hoping he would say?

"You're wasting your time trying to persuade her to get rid of any of her rescues."

"I'm finding that out," he replied dryly. From nowhere, the urge arose to make at least one of the Thornes see his side. "I'm not the bad guy here, Spring. I'm really not. But the elephant and the chimp are meant to be in the wild. They aren't house pets like dogs and cats. Morty especially is dangerous. I've seen him twice, and both times he's had a weapon that could crack Summer's head like a walnut."

"He'd never attack her."

Coop threw up his hands and growled. "How can I get through to any of you?" Hands on hips, he shifted to stare up into the rafters. He'd have better luck reasoning with Mr. Black. He sighed and faced her again. "Even if Morty would never attack her, it isn't to say he wouldn't attack you, Autumn, or Winnie."

"Me or Winnie. But no, he wouldn't do that either."

Curiosity got the better of him. "Why wouldn't he attack Autumn?"

"She's gone."

"That's right. Keaton mentioned it to me earlier. Want to tell me what happened?"

Spring's tear-bright eyes were luminous. "The day of the great fainting goat escapade, she decided it was time to go."

"Why?"

"That's her story to tell."

"According to you, she's not here to tell it. What happened, Spring?"

She glanced over her shoulder as if she worried about being overheard.

"It's probably not a state secret," he said dryly.

Amusement lit her eyes and a smile twisted her lips, then she became serious once again. "Keaton came here, yelling about his truck. He said she owed his daughter an apology and then added a few incredibly hurtful things. After that, she said she needed a change of scenery."

Well, shit on a stick! No wonder Keaton had been a feral beast this last week. "I'm sorry if his accusations were the reason she left."

"To be honest, we've all thought about relocating."

"All?" His gut clenched at the idea of Summer leaving, and he rubbed his hand across the planes of his stomach.

"Yeah. Somewhere we won't be known as the Weird Season Sisters." She shrugged as if to dismiss the hurtfulness of the name. "Summer's Sanctuary can be moved to any out of the way spot. Winnie's internet business won't take a hit. And me? I can open a florist shop anywhere. My flowers are award winning."

"But a Thorne has lived on this land for over two-hundred years." Christ, he sounded like an idiot. As if that little fact, which they all well knew, was going to stop their migration to another county or state.

"We won't sell. Dad still needs a home base, and the family cemetery is here. But we can all have a fresh start somewhere else."

"No."

Her brows shot up and her mouth opened with wonder. "No?"

"Yeah, no. There's no need for any of you to leave. If someone's giving you a hard time, I'll take care of it."

Spring's expression softened. "You've turned out to be a good man, Cooper Carlyle."

"Right. If he's so great, then why is he trying to shut down my rescue?" Summer stepped into the aisle, arms crossed and stubborn expression in place. She appeared angrier than when she left with Morty thirty minutes ago.

He could feel his own anger building. "I'm not. But a better place for Eddie and Morty would be a zoo with trained animal handlers." He moved to stand in front of her. "You are being deliberately obtuse about this."

"Uh oh," Spring muttered. "Now you've done it."

"Obtuse? *Obtuse?*" Summer seethed. "Oh, *I'm* the obtuse one?"

61

"I just said it, didn't I?" he snapped.

Spring waved a hand between their faces. "If you two want to work out your anger issues, there's a hay loft up those steps. I can promise you won't be disturbed for an hour or so."

The image of bending Summer over a hay bale hit fast and hard. The blood drained from the head on his shoulders and marched happily to his other head.

Neither of them could speak after Spring dropped her little sexual-encouragement bomb and left.

Summer took a step back and cleared her throat, looking anywhere but at him.

Suddenly, all he wanted was for her to see him. Not the jerk from high school. Not the sheriff, trying to take away her beloved animals. Him, the man.

"Summer."

HER NAME, SPOKEN IN A HUSKY WHISPER, CAUSED SUMMER'S STOMACH to tighten. She didn't dare look at Coop. Didn't care to witness the knowing smirk on his face.

Why had her sister done that to her? Why put it out there that Summer was lusting after him?

Summer struggled to remember the topic at hand... *Morty!* That was it.

Mouth drier than the Mojave Desert, she said, "The so-called professional animal handlers abused Morty. They tortured him in some form or another every day. He doesn't tolerate being caged because they would stick a cattle prod through the bars to shock him. Being contained brings flashbacks for him."

She ventured a peek in his direction. The heavy frown on his face and seriousness of his expression meant he finally heard what she was trying to relay. Or at least she hoped he had.

"Were they brought up on charges? At the... testing facility? Wasn't that what you told me last week? That he'd been abused there?"

"You remembered," she said, somewhat awed he cared enough to.

His light, teasing smile caused a rush of warmth to her private parts. "I remember everything about you, Summer Thorne."

Her heart rate shot to an alarming pace in less than a second. "I prefer to forget," she croaked.

Apology was written in every line of his rugged face. He shifted closer and wrapped an escaped curl around his index finger. "Is that why you want to leave town?"

Leave town? What the heck was he talking about? She never discussed leaving town. "Where did you hear that?"

"Spring said Autumn left because of Keaton, and that you all might relocate too." His mesmerizing gaze searched her face. Those incredible eyes stopped on her lips and his lids dropped to half-mast. The hooded expression spoke of his intent to kiss her.

"Don't."

His gaze flew to hers.

"Don't try to seduce me. It won't work." Right! It would *so* work. *Was* so working. Right now her lady bits were urging her toward disaster.

"It's been eleven years, Summer. People change."

"You humiliated me at the town meeting *last week*, Sheriff. Or have you forgotten?"

He growled his frustration and released her hair. "That wasn't an exercise in humiliation, Summer. That chimp missed my brother's head by less than a foot. He could've killed him."

"I wouldn't let that happen."

"In case you've forgotten, it *was* happening. You were in my back-yard, and Morty was swinging at Keaton. What if it was my niece? What if Keaton had been a little more sluggish or less alert?"

Her anger dissipated. To a degree, he was correct, but he didn't know her animals like she did. "Morty only ever postures. He's never hurt another living being." She took his hand. "Come on. I want to show you something."

His hand tightened and his fingers wove into hers. "Are we shelving the topic and heading for the hay loft? Because I'm down with that."

A laugh escaped. "No. You smell like the back end of a mule. It isn't pleasant."

63

"You're saying if I shower, I stand a chance?"

She hated women who giggled, but she giggled at Coop's flirting all the same. "I'm taking you to my office."

"Now we're talking. We're going to role-play. I'm the big bad boss, and you're my hot secretary."

"*If* we were to role-play, I get to be the big bad boss, and you're my administrative assistant. But we aren't doing that either."

"I dub thee Spoiler of Fun."

She ducked her head and hid her grin.

Once they were in her office, she pushed him toward the desk. "Have a seat."

"Ah, so this is more of a stripper-gram kind of thing." His wicked grin lit up the room, but more importantly, it lit a fire inside her.

Shoving aside any thoughts of sex with Coop, she set a laptop in front of him.

"Or is it porn? I love how open-minded you are, sweetheart."

"Get your mind out of the gutter, Coop. Now watch."

She played the tapes she'd illegally obtained from White Laboratories where Morty had been imprisoned as a test subject. His treatment by the after-hours crew was horrific.

"I get that it was bad but—"

Summer placed a finger over his lips. Her eyes were drawn to the gesture, and she desperately wanted to caress the fullness beneath her fingertips.

When he nipped her, she gasped and pulled away. Heat rose across her chest and spread to her hairline. "Sorry." She cleared her throat. "Watch this."

The current recordings were of Morty adjusting to life at her sanctuary. She'd spliced together clips to document the changes in his behavior, leaving nothing out.

Initially, the chimpanzee had been aggressive, and while it couldn't be seen, magic had been used to calm him. Less and less, the need for such tactics arose. Today was the first time she'd needed to freeze the chimp in nearly three months.

"I see him getting violent in these recordings, Summer."

"No, Coop. You see him posturing. At the lab, he was violent, attempting to attack and maim. In the early days here, it wasn't much different. But now, he stands up, beats his chest and swings a weapon, but he never gets close enough to strike."

She rewound the recording and played it again. "Look, it's like he's laughing when he's called on it. Immediately he puts his weapon down and reaches for reassurance that he's loved. He's no different than an abused kid readjusting to life without the abuse."

"Except chimps are twice as strong."

"He's a good boy, Coop. I don't know how to convince you he doesn't mean to harm anyone."

"Look, other than to argue my point, there's nothing I can do until he injures someone. But I intend to keep a close watch on him."

"I work with him every day. You can see by the tapes how far he's come. I'm not naive. I know it will be constant care." She sighed and shut the laptop. "I'd like to show you something else if you have time."

Together they moved to the secondary section of the attic where a habitat had been made for Morty. Inside, they found him painting, a red beret perched on the side of his head in a decidedly French fashion.

"He loves painting. And he's quite good, wouldn't you say?" she laughed.

Morty's head came around and the love for Summer was obvious. His happy expression quickly shifted to suspicion and anger. The paintbrush was thrown to the floor and hands moved in a rapid communication.

Summer knelt in front of the squatting ape and signed swiftly in return. "No, Morty. He's not here to take you away." She shook her head and signed again to the question the ape put to her. "No. You are staying with me. Forever."

Morty shuffled closer to Summer and peered around her shoulder at Coop. The suspicion was still present, but the simmering anger was gone.

"Would you like to meet Coop, sweet boy?"

With a nod of his head, Morty clasped Summer's outstretched hand. Together they ambled to where Coop stood.

"Introduce yourself, Morty. I can translate."

The little ape presented as the perfect gentleman, even going so far as to bow and hold out a hand.

"May I have the pleasure of introducing, Sir Mortimer Von Chimpanzee." She laughed when Morty drew back his lips in his version of a smile.

Coop surprised her when he gripped Morty's hand and shook it. "How do you do, Sir Mortimer. I'm Cooper Carlyle. My friends call me C.C. or Coop."

Her heart swelled.

Coop didn't need to show kindness to Morty. He could choose to stay aloof and disapproving. Yet here he was exhibiting a softer side.

And didn't that make her all gooey inside?

8

"*C*oop coming by again today?"

Summer glanced up from where she stood washing her breakfast dishes.

Spring had a wicked knowing look.

"I don't know. I'm not his secretary."

The second the words left her mouth, a fiery blush burned her cheeks.

"Oh, he is!"

"No, I… it was just something he said the first day he was here."

"Don't leave us hanging," Winnie said over the rim of her mug.

"You're worse than two nosy old hens," Summer scolded her laughing sisters.

"Things seem to be progressing between you," Winnie observed.

"I think you're reading things into the situation that aren't there." Goddess, she sounded like an uptight virgin at a rave.

Winnie's smirk didn't help.

"What?" Summer snapped as she dried her hands.

"Oh, I don't know. Coop is arguably one of the hottest men in town, and he's showed up for the last ten days to help you maintain the sanctuary. Yet here you are, acting as if you're oblivious to his interest in you. We all know darned well you're not."

Summer's eyes flew from Winnie to Spring and back. "Because he's not. Interested in me, that is."

And that was the kick in the pants, because since that first day, he hadn't attempted to kiss her again.

He'd arrived every morning by six o'clock, coffee in hand, ready to tackle whatever chores she had for him to do. By eight he was heading home to shower and start his workday.

Two hours. For two hours every morning she would surreptitiously watch him pick stalls, feed her growing horde of rescues, and haul hay. As he bent, lifted, or hauled, she'd admire the trim lines of his backside. If her eyes lingered overly long on his ass, who was to know?

"Earth to Summer."

She scowled and grabbed a muffin from the basket on the light stone countertop.

"She has it bad," Spring teased.

"Has what bad?" Cooper's voice startled all three women, but only Summer screamed and fumbled her muffin.

He laughed at her black look. "I knocked, but when no one answered, I let myself in. The coffeemaker at the house has given up the ghost." He raised his empty travel mug. "I was hoping to steal a cup."

Summer could feel his amused gaze as she scooped up the blueberry muffin from the floor. "Help yourself," she offered with a wave of her hand.

She hadn't thought through the logistics of him, her, and two others in the small kitchen.

As he inched by her, his hand hooked her hip. Full body contact ensued, his front to her back.

A strangled cry escaped her.

"Sorry," he murmured in her ear. "Close quarters."

Not that close, but she didn't intend to complain if he took advantage. "Mmhmm. No worries."

Maybe when he was ready to exit, she could turn around and have him rub her front.

Poised to throw the muffin in the garbage, Summer let out an odd little chirp when Coop grabbed her hand.

"What are you doing? That's a perfectly good muffin," he said.

"It hit the floor."

"Haven't you heard of the five second rule?"

"Okay, that's just gross, and it was more like twenty seconds."

A delighted grin flashed, as if her response entertained him, and he leaned in to take a bite of the muffin.

"Something is wrong with you," Summer charged.

"'Scuse us, lovebirds, but you're blocking the entrance," Spring said and gave Coop's back a light shove.

Instead of moving out into the hall to allow her sister to pass, he stepped in closer to Summer. Once again, full contact ensued.

Exactly what you wished for, the little voice in her head crowed.

This close, she smelled the subtle scent of his body wash and whatever laundry soap he used. Citrus with a hint of fresh spring along with something more, some elusive scent she couldn't place, hijacked her senses. Nose to his chest, she closed her eyes and sniffed. She nearly groaned her pleasure.

Whatever pheromones he had going on, he should bottle. He'd make a killing.

The quiet in the room registered.

Her cheeks burned as she wondered how long they'd been standing alone.

"I think you can back up now." She didn't dare shove him away. If she touched him, she might not let go.

"I could. But I don't necessarily want to." His husky voice turned her on as nothing had before.

Stomach muscles clenched, and the tops of her thighs tingled. "I have to get to the barn, and you'll be late for work."

"Today's my day off."

The entire time he was in the kitchen, she'd avoided his gaze, certain he'd understood the embarrassing comment when he'd first entered was due mainly because of her feelings for him. Inch by inch, she raised her eyes from where she'd focused on his chest.

Morning stubble and lids at half-mast gave him a sexy, just-rolled-out-of-bed look.

Her finger itched to tousle his dark-blond hair to complete the picture her mind's eye had created.

"If you keep looking at me that way, we won't get to the barn at all," he told her.

She snapped out of the sexual haze she was caught in and edged from between him and the counter. "The rescue will always come first."

His brows met, and his eyes narrowed. Had he picked up on what she was trying to say? It was important he understood.

"I'll always put the welfare of those animals above everything else, Coop."

Slowly, he nodded, the frown never leaving his face. "Let me grab my coffee, and I'll meet you out there."

Without a backward glance, she escaped. The entire walk to the barn she berated herself for dropping her guard. For as much as he seemed to have changed, she couldn't be positive Cooper's motives were pure. She couldn't be sure of his motives at all.

What did he want? Was it to sleep with her? Was it to ease her plight and help with the labor? Or was it more sinister? He could be looking for a weakness. That fit with his personality much more than his sudden change of heart.

She hated herself for doubting him, but how could she not? He went from despising and avoiding her to kissing her and spending every morning helping. It didn't add up.

Tonight, she'd see if her sisters could assist her. Perhaps they could scry and discover his true intentions. Certainly, it wouldn't be to just spy on him. Although, she wouldn't be opposed to seeing him in the shower the way Winnie had Zane back in high school.

Yeah, she definitely needed to perfect Granny Thorne's cloaking spell.

COOP REACHED FOR HIS WALLET TO PAY FOR HIS GROCERIES. HE PATTED his back pocket. First the left, then the right. Nothing. Shoving aside the panicky feeling, he checked the basket to see if maybe he'd thrown it in with his phone and keys. Nothing.

Angel, the young cashier, masticated her gum with the bored impatience only a teenager managed to perfect.

"I could've sworn I had it," he hedged, doing a recheck of his pockets as if the wallet would mysteriously be back in place.

With a roll of her eyes, Angel popped her gum.

Someone coughed in the long line that had formed behind him.

Sweat beaded his brow. For God's sake, this was ridiculous. He was a grown man, the sheriff of this town, and he was the one feeling criminal.

Coop cleared his throat, apologized to his fellow grocery shoppers, and told Angel he needed to run to his cruiser.

A shrug was her answer, as if she didn't care one way or another. She probably didn't.

The detailed check of his cruiser turned up nothing.

As he jogged back to the store, he mentally ran through the day's events. The only place he'd been was Summer's this morning for his standard stall-cleaning duties.

"Yeah, I'm sorry. I seemed to have misplaced my wallet. Can we put this stuff to the side, and I'll be back for it?" he asked.

"I've got this."

Coop turned to see Keaton grinning behind him. Relief flooded him. "Thanks, man. I don't know what could've happened to my wallet. I must've dropped it at Summer's."

"Summer Thorne?" A female voice questioned.

He faced a tiny, hunched-back, lavender-haired woman who stood third in line. Damned fine hearing for the elderly.

"Uh, yeah."

Amusement lit the woman's rheumy purple eyes—oddly, the same light color as her dyed hair. "If she still has old Sampson, that's probably where your wallet is."

"Who's old Sampson?"

"Beatrice Wilson's cat."

"Beatrice Wilson? Wasn't she the one arrested for stealing thousands of dollars in jewelry and wallets?" Keaton asked, not bothering to keep the laughter from his face. "Are you saying Summer Thorne took in the kleptomaniac cats after Beatrice went to jail?"

"That's what I'm saying, Mayor." She grinned and her false teeth shifted forward. With a short, gnarled finger, she shoved them back in place, chomped down twice, and said, "Old Beatrice trained close to eighty-five cats to steal from her neighbors. She made off with over ten thousand in goods. Damn fool woman's mistake was hoarding the spoils instead of getting rid of the evidence."

The purple hair needed to be under surveillance. She was way too wily and had a criminal bend to her thinking.

"You watch that Summer Thorne and her Weird Season Sisters, Sheriff. They're up to no good. Bad business goes on up at that Thorne place," the woman warned.

Others in line nodded their heads in agreement.

His heart dropped into his stomach.

Perhaps the Thornes leaving town would be for the best. The Leiper's Fork citizens didn't hold them in the highest esteem.

Angrily, he scooped up his bags. "Just pay for the damned groceries, Keaton, and let's go."

As they strode to the cruiser, Keaton asked, "What has you so upset, C.C.? I suspect I know, but humor me."

"Where do these people get off?" Coop swept his arm to encompass the store. "She takes in all their castoffs, and yet they treat her like she's beneath them. Like a damned outsider or leper. What the fuck?"

Heads turned in their direction.

"Not here, C.C."

"If not here, then where, Keaton? Huh?"

Gawkers moved closer. The sheriff and the mayor in a heated discussion at the local grocery store parking lot was newsworthy stuff.

Coop's expression turned feral. "Move along or I'll arrest your ass," he barked at a particularly bold pedestrian. When the man paled and scurried off to find his truck, Coop grunted his irritation.

"Cooper."

Keaton rarely called him by his full name, only when he had a point to make.

"What?" Coop snapped.

"If the people of this town are suspicious of the Thornes, maybe they have good reason."

The seriousness and warning in his brother's tone couldn't be ignored.

"What do you know?"

Keaton opened his mouth to answer, but no words came out. With a frown, he tried again. After a third attempt, he shook his head. "Never mind. But you'd do well to stay away from Summer and her sisters."

Coop watched as Keaton stalked away. The jerky movements as he climbed into his vehicle spoke of agitation. What did Keaton have to be upset about? Was his irritation leftover from Autumn? Did it taint how he saw all the sisters? Wasn't his brother the one who tried to get Coop to take it easy on Summer?

As Coop swung open the door to his cruiser, he noticed the purple-haired woman standing ten feet away. Her gleeful expression sparked a frisson of unease.

Whatever she and Keaton knew, Coop intended to discover.

9

*C*oop knocked on the massive mahogany and iron door of Thorne Manor. He'd been standing on their porch for about five minutes with no response.

A side glance showed Summer's old white Dodge van in the drive. Winnie's sporty Altima was parked in front of the truck. Only Spring's florist van was missing, but that wasn't unusual this time of day since she was probably out making deliveries.

Perhaps Summer and Winnie were helping.

Once again, he knocked, this time harder than the last. No answer.

"Summer?" he called.

A twist of the handle proved the door unlocked.

"Summer?"

The sound of his voice echoed around the foyer.

He shouldn't be here, intruding on their private space. However, Coop couldn't get Keaton's anxious expression out of his head. His brother had been trying hard to tell him something important, or at least important to him.

The image of the lavender-haired older woman with the knowing expression also bothered him. It was as if he'd played into her hands by coming here. But what was her ultimate goal?

As he passed through the foyer, a black square on the entry table caught his attention. *His wallet.*

A boom, followed by a loud thump shook the house. The crystals in the overhead chandelier tinkled together, and plaster dust from the ceiling floated down around him.

"Summer!" Coop took the stairs two at a time. "Summer!"

She appeared at the top of the second landing, flushed and out of breath, stopping him in his tracks.

"Coop!" She cast her gaze over her shoulder and a look of guilt flitted across her face. "I… uh, what are you doing here?"

She had another man here with her.

The deep-seated suspicion socked him right in the nads. He found it difficult to catch his breath, and it wasn't from running up the stairs. Perhaps this sense of betrayal he felt was what she'd experienced the night he kissed Rosie.

"What's going on, Summer? Who's here?" he demanded although he had no right.

She must've thought so too because she frowned and reared back as if surprised by his harshness.

"Only me and Winnie."

"Why do you look…?" What? Excited? Aroused? Like she'd been exerting herself in ways he wished she'd exert herself with him? "Uh, flushed. Why do you look flushed?"

She laughed and waved a hand. "Winnie and I were moving furniture around. What are you doing here? Did you find your wallet?"

His wallet. The reason he'd come back today. "Yes, on the entry table."

"You must've dropped it in the barn. I found one of the cats playing with it."

She's lying.

He didn't know how he knew, he just did. Perhaps it was the years interrogating criminals, but he'd developed an instinct for when he was being lied to—as he was now.

"One of Beatrice Wilson's trained criminal cats?" he asked tightly.

She remained quiet, but the guilt clouding her features told him all he needed to know.

"If I got a warrant, will I find the wallets of other visitors, Summer?"

The happy light left her eyes, and she slowly shook her head. Her disappointment obvious. "Feel free to come back with your warrant, Sheriff. Until that time, get out of my house."

She pivoted on the landing to head back the way she'd come, clearly a dismissal.

Coop panicked at the idea of her walking away and made a grab for her.

Summer avoided his touch and fisted her hand.

And like the incident with Morty in the barn, he was frozen in place.

The satisfied half-smile she sported had the hair on the back of his neck standing at attention. He struggled against the invisible hold. He strained and surged forward, not gaining an inch.

Then she opened her fist and spread her fingers wide.

It was as if a large hand shoved him, and he slammed into the wall behind him.

A small wood-framed picture tumbled to the floor.

Summer gasped and horrified tears filled her eyes. "Papa's Monet! It's ruined."

Ignoring the throbbing of his head and spine, Coop surged forward to comfort.

Summer turned feral. "Don't you touch me. Do you know what you've done? What you've made *me* do?"

Due to the ringing in his head, he couldn't be positive, but he'd have sworn she muttered words like *goddess* and *shall harm none*. What any of her mumbling meant was anyone's guess.

The unfairness of her accusation stuck in his craw. "How is any of this my fault?" he demanded.

"You came here and made me believe you'd changed. That you were open-minded and fair. But you're no different than any other self-right-eous asshat in this damned town." She sneezed.

A scurrying sounded overhead, and she waved her arm. "I'm fine," she said to someone outside his view.

He craned his neck to see who she'd spoken to.

Summer side-stepped and blocked his view. "I think it's best you leave and not come back unless it's official business, Sheriff."

Coop studied her closed face. What he was looking for, God only knew. Perhaps a softening, an indication she didn't want him to go.

For once, her eyes were no longer the sparkling blue he remembered. Instead they appeared to be a darker hue. It had to be a trick of the light. No one's eyes could change color. But the dull eyes had his stomach in knots.

"There's still the matter of the cats, Summer."

"There's always the matter of some animal or another, isn't there?" She closed her eyes and shook her head. "I've retrained and found homes for all but ten. Once those are free of their larcenous ways, I'll find forever homes for them as well. Nothing sinister is going on here, Coop. But then I don't expect you to believe me."

In this, he did. "I'm sorry."

"Yeah, well. If you'll excuse me, I have work to do."

"I can hel—"

His offer was cut short.

"I don't want your help. If I had my way, I'd never have to see you ever again, *Sheriff.*"

AFTER COOP DROVE AWAY, SUMMER DROPPED TO THE BOTTOM PORCH step.

How had she ever thought she could develop a relationship with him?

He'd forever be suspicious of her and her family.

Everyone always was.

They were the Weird Season Sisters. The town shunned them unless they wanted something specific; Winnie's lotions, Spring's prize flowers, or Summer to re-home an unwanted pet.

Autumn had been the smart one. She'd seen this cursed little town for what it was and gotten the hell out.

But Summer, always the optimist, believed in the general goodness of people, despite what she'd witnessed in her twenty-eight years. Little by little, her optimism was disappearing. With each incident, each ugly scene perpetuated by some vindictive person, her world view became a little smaller. A little more clouded by others' ugly behavior.

She absently rubbed the spot over her heart.

Cooper's mistrust stung the worst. He'd arrived looking for a fight today.

She could tell in the way he demanded to know who else was in the house, then again when he'd practically accused her of housing the cats so they could steal visitors' wallets.

Oh, she could've told the truth, but mentioning that she and Winnie had attempted to teleport an antique vanity to where Autumn now lived in Maine would surely have freaked Coop right the fuck out.

"What has you troubled, dear?"

The tiny lavender-haired woman appearing on the porch swing almost had Summer wetting her pants. Not many people snuck up on her, but GiGi Gillespie tended to be sneakier than most.

"You really should warn people, you know," Summer snapped. "It isn't polite to spy."

The elderly woman smiled, revealing a set of oversized dentures.

As she looked on, Summer noticed they shifted about in her mouth. "A dab or two of Fixodent wouldn't be remiss if you are going to use that disguise, Aunt G."

In a showy move, GiGi stood, swirled her hands, and morphed back into the tall, supple blonde she normally appeared to be.

"The sheriff left in a state, didn't he?"

"I don't suppose you'd know anything about that, would you?"

"I might have dropped the information bomb that your cats once belonged to Beatrice."

"Why would you do that?" Summer asked, inexplicably hurt.

GiGi patted the cushioned seat next to her, and when Summer joined her, the other woman clasped her hand in her own smooth, elegant hand.

"It's the order of things, dear heart."

"What order?"

"All things will be revealed in time, Summer Thorne."

Her aunt turned Summer's palm skyward and traced the line running from the base of her middle finger to the outside edge of her pinky. An arc of purple light trailed across the line she'd traced. "You'll only love the one, child. He needs to be worthy of you."

"Why does he always make me feel like *I'm* the unworthy one?" Summer whispered tiredly and rested her head on her aunt's shoulder.

"Because he's a man, and men are dumb creatures."

Summer snorted. "You ain't lyin', Aunt G."

"Come. Let's fix your father's painting then eat some of that delicious apple pie I made for you."

"Is the pie payment for your meddling?"

"Perhaps." It was the closest her aunt would come to admitting she'd caused trouble.

"You know I adore you, right? Even with your never-ending need to interfere with my life."

Summer's statement was rewarded with a hug. "I adore you too, dear girl. In fact, you're my favorite of all your sisters. But if you tell the others, I'll know."

"Of course, you'll know. You spy on us constantly."

"Well, I did promise your mother I'd look out for you all."

"In case you can't tell, Aunt G, we're adults now. And the occasional visit to see if we are okay is a lot different than hovering above your mirror, scrying twenty-four-seven."

Aunt GiGi giggled like a girl of fifteen. "How is an old woman supposed to live vicariously through all of you if you take away my only means of spying?"

"Ah, so you admit it!"

"I admit nothing." The beautiful troublemaker smiled and winked. "But that kiss you shared with your young man in the barn near set fire to my altar."

The heat of embarrassment near set fire to Summer's skin.

"Come on, dear. The pie is getting cold. We'll eat a slice first then tackle the painting."

Like an obedient toddler, Summer wrapped her hand into the outstretched one before her and followed the mischief-maker into the kitchen. "I hope you brought two. I'm a stress eater, Aunt G."

*E*leven days passed. Coop should know, each one was endless.

Funny how he used to go out of his way to avoid Summer whenever possible. Yet now that he didn't see her every morning, he'd experienced the sensation of being set adrift. A ship that had lost its mooring.

Coop found himself waking the same time every morning, lying in bed and ruminating on the fight with Summer. If he thought a standard apology would suffice, he'd have given one.

However, Summer's disillusioned expression had spoken volumes.

Whatever flirtation they'd started, he murdered in the moment he'd accused her of using Beatrice's cats for her own gains.

He was an idiot. No doubt about it.

The one thing he circled around to time and again was freezing on the landing. Maybe he needed to get a physical. Perhaps the doctor could tell him why, when he experienced a moment of panic, he seized up. If that happened in the line of duty, he was screwed with a capital S.

His door flew open, and a child-size tornado entered the room. "Uncle Coop! Uncle Coop!"

"You can turn it down three notches and I'll still hear you, midget. I'm not deaf... yet."

"Why do old people think they're funny?" she asked.

"I don't know. When I find an old person, I'll ask them," he retorted playfully.

"Dad wanted to know if you'd drive me over to Miss Spring's house. Yesterday, she said I could help pick the flowers for Ryan's sister's wedding arrangements."

Coop stilled. "Why can't he take you?"

Keaton peeked his head in the door to answer for his daughter, "Mayoral duties."

"You've been listening all along?"

Keaton grinned around his cup of coffee then took a sip.

"Can you? I want to pet Eddie," Chloe begged and tugged on his arm.

"Seriously, it's not a good idea for me to go to the Thorne estate, midget."

Chloe's dark head tilted to the side to study him. "Is that because you accused Miss Summer of stealing your wallet?"

Coop bit the inside of his cheek to keep swear words at bay. He shot a speaking look at Keaton. One that promised retribution. "I didn't accuse Summer of stealing. I…" But he had. He'd threatened a warrant for goodness' sake. He sighed and sat up, careful to keep the bedding covering his essentials. "I'll tell you what. You go call Miss Spring and ask her if it's all right if you come assist her in the garden today. Let them know I'll be the one bringing you by. If it's still okay, I'll take you."

"Okay, Uncle Coop." She ran off to do his bidding.

"Mayoral duties? On a Saturday? That's the best you could come up with?" Coop asked dryly.

Keaton shrugged.

"Weren't you the one trying to warn me off Summer eleven days ago?"

"Eleven? You know exactly how many days it's been since we discussed it?"

Coop grunted. Not only did he know the days, he knew down to the minute since he'd last seen Summer. He was a sap. Worse than a chick.

But he missed her. Missed her bubbling laughter. Missed the mock scolding when he'd teased her. Missed seeing the sweat bead on her brow and her wipe it away with her forearm during a hard morning of work. More than once, he'd fantasized about sweat on her body for an entirely different reason.

Yep, he was worse than a chick.

"Did you eat or drink anything while you were there?" Keaton asked, suspicion heavy in his voice.

"*Excuse* me?"

"You heard me. Did you eat or drink anything any of the women made?"

His brother was deranged. "Keat—"

"I'm not kidding, Cooper. Answer the damned question!"

The intensity in his brother's query made Coop stand up and take notice. "What's going on, Keaton?"

"I can't say," Keaton ground out. "I can't…" His brother's gaze sharpened as he spotted the notepad by the bed, and he smiled grimly. "But maybe I can write it."

Coop shrugged into a shirt and shorts as he waited for Keaton to write the explanation of his weird behavior.

Finally, after he'd read through what he'd written twice, Keaton handed Coop the notepad. "Here."

The paper was blank. Coop turned the empty page outward. "Uh, Keat? What's up, man?"

Keaton turned gray and stared at the paper in shock. Mouth compressed, he shook his head and stalked toward the hall. Before disappearing, he snarled, "You may want to ask Summer when you see her today." Taking a deep breath in, he exhaled. "I might not be able to reveal the truth, but there isn't any reason *she* can't explain what she is."

With one last tortured look, Keaton left.

His brother's vehemence held him immobile. This was unlike the paralysis at Summer's. No, this was more of a shock. Coop shook his head and stared down at the pad of paper in his hand. Indentations in the paper caught his attention.

He almost yelled for Keaton to return but decided to try a trick he'd learned somewhere along the way in his career. Probably a late-night episode of CSI or Monk.

A quick search of the desk drawer by the window turned up a pencil. Holding the tip perpendicular to the paper, he softly rubbed the lead across the indentations. It provided a negative image and made the words plain.

Cooper's eyes bulged when he read what Keaton had written.

The Thorne sisters are witches.
Real, honest-to-God witches.
Be careful, C.C. *Please.*

WAS THIS KEATON'S IDEA OF A JOKE?

Coop found Keaton on the pool deck, overlooking the back forty. "Keaton!" He held up the notepad. "What the hell is this?"

The bleakness dropped from Keaton's face, replaced by a dawning sense of wonder. "You brilliant bastard!"

"Are you for real right now? Because I don't find this funny."

"I'm completely serious. Autumn confessed back when we were dating. She showed me what she could do. It was terrifying." Keaton's eyes widened. "It's gone. You broke her spell! I can speak about it." He threw back his head and laughed with wonder. With a fist skyward, he shouted, "Yes!"

The very real fear that his brother had taken a dive off the deep end grabbed Coop and refused to let go. "Uh, Keat. You know there's no such thing as witches, right?"

Solemn again, Keaton snorted and shook his head. "I know how all this sounds. I'm not crazy, C.C. I swear I'm not."

After studying Keaton for a minute, he said, "Get in the car. Knox can watch Chloe. We're going to get to the bottom of this."

A kernel of suspicion popped in his mind. If Keaton was telling the truth, if witches did indeed exist, could that explain why he'd been locked in place? Remembering back, Summer had made an odd gesture with her fist, as if... *Sonofabitch! She'd slammed him into the wall without ever touching him!*

"You're not lying," he whispered hoarsely.

"No, C.C. I'm not lying, and this isn't a joke."

"Why?" Coop swallowed audibly. "Why would you allow Chloe around them to pick flowers?"

"Because Spring seems to be the normal one."

"Seems to be or is?" he demanded.

Keaton didn't have any answers.

But Coop damned well intended to get a few—from the witches themselves. "Are you coming?"

"Wouldn't miss it. I've got your back."

———

SUMMER EYED THE RANGE CLOCK. SEVEN FORTY-FIVE. SHE'D OVERSLEPT for the second time in her life since opening her sanctuary.

Last night had been a particularly fun one.

She, along with her two sisters and Aunt GiGi, had teleported to visit Autumn in Maine.

There had been wine, chocolate, and lots of laughter. So much so, Summer couldn't recall returning home after the fact.

Spring bound into the room, her usually sunny self. "Good morning, sister."

Summer grabbed her skull between her palms and pressed. "Not so loud. Please," she croaked.

"You didn't take any of Aunt GiGi's elixir when we got home, did you?"

"I forgot." She refused to say aloud that the elixir tastes like liquid dirt and was avoided at all costs.

"Mmm, yeah, well now you have to deal with the consequences of the wine *and* the teleport. Poor thing."

If her sister had been in the least bit condescending or mocking, Summer would've tried her hand at turning her into a toad. As it was, she settled for a bleary-eyed glare.

"Want me to…" Spring wiggled her fingers in the direction of the barn.

"Goddess, yes! Think it would be okay just this once?"

"Twice," Winnie inserted as she breezed into the room. "This would be the second time. But it's to benefit the animals, so I say go for it."

Summer sighed her gratitude and dropped her head to the wooden table. "I love you both so much."

The sound of a vehicle tearing down the gravel drive brought her head back up. She winced at the sudden movement. "Who could that be at this hour?"

"It's Cooper and Keaton," Winnie said from where she leaned over the sink to peer out the front window. "I wonder if everything's okay?"

Summer groaned. "Can someone check the monitor and make sure Eddie is in his pen? I need another minute before fishing him out of their pool if he's escaped."

Two car doors slammed.

"Summer Thorne! Get out here!" Cooper shouted.

"I don't think you have another minute," muttered Spring.

Summer popped up and raced to the window.

Cooper stood posed with his hands on his hips, infuriated as she'd never seen him. What the hell did he have to be mad about?

Beside him, Keaton wore a look of unease. His eyes darted about, as if he expected to be attacked from all sides.

"They look like they're prepared for a shootout at the O.K. Corral," Spring giggled.

Summer turned on her sister in stunned amazement. "What is it about six-feet of furious male that you find amusing, Spring?"

"What can they really do?"

Summer's jaw dropped. Why hadn't she thought of that?

What *could* they really do? When faced with the power of three witches, at most, the men could bluster and yell. Coop and Keaton couldn't physically hurt them. It would only take one thought to stop the men in their tracks if it came to that.

"Okay, let's go."

"Summer?"

She pivoted around in the entry at Winnie's call. "What?"

"You might want to put on a bra and pants. Unless you hope to distract Coop with the t-shirt and undies outfit."

Summer ducked and scrambled to cover herself as if the men were standing in front of her half-naked form.

Both sisters laughed at the ridiculousness of her gesture.

Flipping them the bird, she raised her hands and swirled them about. The 1970s hot pink pants were an eyesore and clashed abominably with her yellow top, but hungover witches unable to control their powers couldn't be picky.

Her sisters' laughter trailed her out the door.

"What the hell are you wearing?" Cooper asked, aghast.

A quick look down reaffirmed she was completely covered. "Is that why you stopped by, Sheriff? To criticize my early morning wardrobe choice?"

Steely eyes mere slits, he stormed forward.

And damned if liquid heat didn't pool between her thighs.

The angry alpha male mantle suited Coop. Made him every woman's wet dream come to life. Muscles bulging, color high, hair mussed, passionate. So very passionate.

Oh, the angry sex they could have.

Summer nearly melted into a pool of desire on the spot. Her breathing kicked up in speed and she licked her lips.

"C.C.," Keaton warned. "Be careful. She's planning something."

All three sisters gawked at Keaton in confusion.

Planning something? What the hell was she planning other than to beg Coop to drag her up to the hayloft and have his wicked way with her?

Her confusion ratcheted up when Coop stepped protectively in front of his brother and placed a hand on the grip of his weapon.

Obviously, she'd missed something, but her pounding head refused to allow her to piece the puzzle together. "What's going on, Coop?" she asked as she took a step forward. As one, the men stepped back.

They're afraid of us!

Summer hadn't realized she spoke her thoughts aloud until Coop's chin came up and red crept along his neck.

But in the end, he didn't lower his hand from his weapon. "Keaton informed me of some disturbing facts this morning. I'm here to get to the bottom of it."

"What might those facts be, Cooper?" she asked in a quiet, controlled tone which seemed to surprise everyone, herself included.

His cheeks took on the red hue of his neck. "He said you were witches. Real, honest-to-God spell-casting witches."

She maintained eye contact, although it was an effort. "That's correct."

If she'd have let Morty hit him with the bat, he couldn't have looked more stunned. His hand spasmed on the grip of his gun.

With a silent prayer of *"please let the safety be on"* to the Goddess, Summer stepped forward again.

"You're not going to deny it?" he asked, incredulous.

She shrugged. "Why? It's true."

"Summer," Winnie warned as Summer took another step.

"In the barn, then again on the stairs, was that you?" Coop demanded.

He appeared two seconds away from losing his breakfast.

"Yes," she admitted with another step.

"*Jesus.*" The sickly expression worsened. "Don't come any closer, Summer," he warned and unclipped the leather strap holding the weapon in the holster.

Was it wrong to wish he'd pull the trigger and end her misery? Here she was, in love with a man who now despised her, feared her, and saw her as some kind of monster. "Are you going to shoot me, Coop?" she asked softly.

Autumn materialized in front of her. Cooper had his gun drawn and aimed before any of the women could think to freeze his actions.

Surprisingly, the quickest to react was Keaton, who shoved Coop's arm skyward just as he pulled the trigger.

Summer fell to her knees, sick at what might've happened had Keaton not acted to prevent a tragedy.

"Morty, no!"

Her head whipped around at Spring's alarmed cry.

Morty, enraged and feral, charged straight for Cooper.

From deep within, a power Summer didn't know she possessed or had been too scared to tap took over. Her insides seemed to shift alignment, and her cells lit, burning within. She flung up her glowing hands. *"Stop!"*

Time itself froze.

No one moved. Not her sisters, each locked in a horrified stupor; not Morty, who was frozen mid-leap; not Coop who had redirected his gun to point at Morty's chest; and not Keaton who, oddly enough, was staring at Autumn as if he feared for her safety.

Only Summer could move. And she did, directly in the path of Coop's gun, to stop Morty's attack.

Time caught up with a snap and a fizzle.

A gun's report echoed.

Summer felt the impact from front and back.

"*S*ummer! Oh, Goddess no!" one of the Thorne sisters screamed.

Coop rushed to Summer, where she lay on her side and clung to the chimp. Her fisted hand started to loosen.

Morty twitched against the restraint. In about two seconds, one pissed off ape was going to be given free rein of his emotions.

"Keaton, the tranq gun! Now!" He pressed his hand to the wound in Summer's back. "Hang in there, sweetheart. We're going to get you help. Winnie, call nine-one-one."

Summer frowned and blinked at him, dazed. Her mouth worked but no words would come.

"I've got Morty, sister. You can let go," Autumn said as tears streamed down her ashen cheeks.

Let go? What the fuck? "Hell, no she can't let go! She's not going anywhere." Why would they encourage her to go into the light? Could witches even go into the light? Or were they destined for a hotter climate when they passed on? He couldn't reconcile what he'd been taught about religion in SmallTown, USA right at that moment.

"She can let go of Morty, Coop," Spring clarified as she laid one hand on Summer's furrowed brow and curled the other into a fist.

Autumn scooped up the chimp and held him as if he were a small babe.

Cooper intended to see that fucking thing put down the first chance he got.

Anguished sapphire-blue eyes pleaded with him. "Please don't shoot my Morty, Coop. Please," Summer whispered. She arched her back as if the pain were just then registering.

"Morty will be kept safe, sister. Concentrate on me. On my fingertips on your brow," crooned Spring.

Cooper glanced up from Summer's wound to bark orders. "Get me a blanket, and some towels. Do you have a first aid kit?" When he noticed none of the sisters moving, he lost his shit. "*Move!* She'll go into shock and every second counts here! Why are you all just standing around?"

Winnie laid a hand on his shoulder. "You need to leave, Coop. We have this."

"I'm not going anywhere. She... it's my fault," he croaked out.

"Coop, I need you to listen." Spring's voice was grave. "We can't help her if you won't let her go. Right now, we can only pause her body's reaction. I need you to release her for us to heal her."

What the hell was Spring saying? The blood loss alone could kill Summer. Time was of the essence, and they treated this with all the importance of a damned paper cut.

"Cooper, they have it." His brother gave him a shake and nodded to the light show taking place beside him.

The elegantly clad blonde woman appeared like Cinderella's Fairy Godmother right before his eyes. The only thing missing was the Bibbidi-Bobbidi-Boo song and a pumpkin, but the long wand clutched in her fist wasn't a result of his active imagination.

She nudged him with the pointy end. "Step aside, Sheriff. 'Every second counts here.'"

Strong arms came around him and jerked him away from Summer.

A wretched cry arose, and Coop realized belatedly the sound had come from his own throat in protest to the movement.

"She needs a doctor!" he shouted.

"Coop, this is our Aunt GiGi. She's skilled in healing."

"Healing? As in she can remove a bullet, stop the blood flow, and prevent sepsis?" he argued as he struggled against Keaton's strong embrace.

A purple light arced from her wand to Summer's wound and effectively silenced him.

He was dreaming. It was the only reasonable explanation for such a nightmarish incident as the one he currently found himself embroiled in. He was dreaming, and Summer was not lying on the ground suffering a gunshot wound he was responsible for inflicting. When he woke up, he'd head straight to her house and verify she was fine.

Except none of this felt like a dream. The metallic smell of blood filled his nostrils even as it dried on his dangling hands. The air crackled with magic and his own anxious energy.

The Thorne sisters gathered around their aunt, each chanting in a language foreign to him.

As he stared, Summer's body rose three feet off the ground, her back arched as if she were suspended by invisible cables. Her mouth opened as if to scream her agony, but no sound emerged.

Coop surged forward only to be caught by Keaton and held tight.

Christ, this was insane. All these years, right under his nose, these women had been performing rituals, casting God only knew what type of spells.

Perhaps Keaton wasn't wrong to believe in love spells. How else could he explain his own unnatural desire for Summer? It bordered on obsession.

Yet, hadn't she had years to work her wiles on him? To bind him to her with some magic? If she'd wanted to do so, she would've done it in high school when she'd made herself his shadow.

Doubts crept in and reminded him that he'd been intent on shutting her down. Maybe that's when she had the idea to cast a spell.

This was messed up. All of it.

How could he sit here wondering about being bewitched by Summer when he should be wondering if she was going to lose her life because of his actions?

He should've known better than to approach her in such a heightened state of emotion. But as he replayed the shooting over in his head, he couldn't have predicted she'd throw herself in front of a bullet for the ape. He should've because it was exactly the type of thing she'd do; put herself in danger to save an animal.

She'd been too far away to be in any real peril. Yet, there she lay—er, *levitated*—injured.

Coop glanced over at a subdued Morty.

The chimp sat, arms wrapped tightly around his own torso as he rocked to and fro. The animal never removed its gaze from Summer.

If Coop didn't know any better, he'd assume the little terror regretted his part in this tragedy.

As if he sensed Coop's regard, Morty turned his soulful eyes on him. The chimp signed something Coop didn't understand. Never more so in that moment had Morty appeared like a lost child.

"Please don't shoot my Morty, Coop."

Damn it all to hell.

Coop squatted and opened his arms.

Morty didn't pause. He ambled over to Coop and lifted his arms for comfort.

"Your mama's going to be okay, buddy. Mama's going to be okay."

If Coop repeated it often enough, it might be so.

*S*ummer opened her eyes and winced at the bright light streaming through her bedroom window. Her dry mouth felt stuffed with cotton.

"Welcome back."

The husky baritone sounded like Coop, but she'd be damned if she could recall ever inviting him up to her room. The last thing she remembered was Autumn's party in Maine. Had she returned home and summoned Coop for a booty call? After all this time, it pissed her off to think doing the deed with him was unmemorable.

Her eyes closed as she struggled to recall. She hadn't realized how much time had passed until she felt chubby fingers sifting through her hair. *Morty.*

"Are you grooming Mama, sweet boy?" she managed to croak out the question.

Coop perched on the edge of her bed and ran a hand over Morty's back. "He's been worried about you."

"Why? What happened?"

In the process of sitting up, the sheet fell to her waist.

Coop's indrawn breath alerted her to the fact she was naked.

Aghast, she jerked up the covers. What the hell?

A deep frown drew his brows low over his questioning steel-blue gaze. "You don't remember?"

"Did we play hide the salami?"

Horrified amusement had him sputtering a laugh.

Heat started in her chest and spread to her cheeks in an instant.

Okay, they hadn't bumped nasties.

"Um, where are my sisters? Did they just let you in my room to creep on me while I'm sleeping?"

He scrubbed a hand across his lower face. A clear indication he attempted to hide his grin.

Summer had seen that move at least two-hundred times since she'd known him.

"Spring is in the garden. Winnie mentioned internet orders to fill. And Autumn took over your barn chores with help from Keaton."

She clutched the sheet tighter and her eyes flew about the room, looking for some clue as to the date. "How… how long was I out, and why?"

"A week." He cleared his throat. "Because I shot you."

The sheet fell from her cold, unfeeling fingers. Disbelief and a sense of shock rolled about in her brain. All ability to comprehend the situation lost. "A week? Shot me? Like with a gun?"

Without gawking at her exposed tatas, Coop settled a gentle hand on her shoulder and eased her back. He managed to cover her, while keeping his eyes focused on hers.

"A robe?" Coop asked.

"Behind the door."

He retrieved the article of clothing in question and kept his head averted while he held out her fuzzy, gray robe with the hot pink hearts.

"You seem to have a secret love of all things hot pink," he said, with a nod to the pillows on her window seat.

Summer slipped into her cover-up and tied the knot at her waist. "It appears so. Coop, can I ask you to get me a glass of water? I'd do it myself, but I'm—"

"I'll be right back."

After he left, she rushed to her bathroom to relieve her bladder and freshen up. A glance in the mirror showed she looked damn fine for a woman who'd slept seven days straight.

A week! She still couldn't wrap her brain around it.

What had happened? Cooper said he shot her. Why was she drawing a blank? Was a wiped memory the result of healing magic? Having never been on the receiving end, she didn't know about side effects.

The mystery of Cooper Carlyle in her bedroom also remained to be solved.

She came out of the bathroom to find Coop playing a game of hide and seek with Morty in the covers.

Her heart melted.

The two of them playing Morty's favorite game spoke of a familiarity. Coop must've taken care of her beloved chimp while she was asleep.

"I thought the two of you only tolerated each other up to now."

Coop shot her a half-smile. "Morty and I reached an understanding. Haven't we, son?"

Her chimp's head nodded up and down in an emphatic gesture as if he understood and one-hundred percent agreed with Coop.

Coop rose and brought her the glass of water. "How are you feeling?" Coop asked after a quiet study of her.

"Fine."

"No lingering discomfort?"

"Please, can you just put me out of my misery already and tell me what happened?"

"The short version? Keaton and I showed up last week. Emotions ran high and Morty, being the staunch defender of all things Summer Thorne, rushed me."

She gasped and reached for him.

Coop stared down at their joined hands. His became clammy under hers, and he pulled them back to rub down the legs of his jeans. His withdrawal disturbed her, but she found it difficult to focus on the reason.

"Coop?"

He cleared his throat and crossed to the window. "I shot you."

A memory stirred. Brief glimpses only, but enough for her to start arranging pieces of the puzzle. "You were going to shoot Morty. I was in the way, I think."

"No!"

The harsh word jerked her head up.

"No, Summer, you weren't 'in the way'. You froze everything around you and put yourself directly in the path of my discharging weapon," he gruffly informed her.

The steely gaze—more gray than blue in his irritation—pinned her in place.

He knew she was a witch!

As if he read her mind, he said, "Yes. I know what you are."

And he hated it. No need to say it, his feelings crystalized in his cold eyes.

As if a trap door had been opened in her mind, memories slammed her. The report of the gun. The terror for Morty. The agony of the bullet ripping through flesh and muscle. The additional agony of Aunt GiGi's magical surgery.

Bile filled the back of her throat, and she rushed for the bathroom. Dry heaves bucked her frame where she bent over the toilet. With nothing but a sip of water in her belly, the spasms were especially painful.

Exhausted, she sat back against the pale pink bathroom wall. The running water caught her attention. Summer met Coop's contemplative gaze in the mirror above the sink.

"Have you ever cast any type of spell on me?"

Goddess, she was tired of his constant distrust. "Would you believe me if I said I haven't?"

"Maybe."

She dropped her head back with a light thud. "I haven't. Magic— real magic—can't be manipulated for personal gain."

"Personal gain?" He squatted before her and wiped her face with the damp cloth in his hand. "A desire spell is personal gain?"

A desire spell? What the hell was a desire spell?

His eyes dipped to her mouth and blazed a trail to her gaping robe.

Ah, a *desire* spell. She snorted. "I'm afraid there's no such thing as a desire spell, Sheriff. If you're feeling froggy, it's all on you."

His gaze snapped to her steady stare.

She held up three fingers and quirked a brow. "Scout's honor."

"Cut the crap. You weren't a Girl Scout."

"I was a Brownie in second grade. It counts. Once a scout, always a scout," she lied.

He tossed the rag in her face and stood, ignoring her sputtered outrage.

"Get dressed. I'll meet you downstairs. I want details."

"Of my days serving in the Brownie Brigade?"

His bark of genuine laughter pleased her in a warped, self-torturous sort of way. She didn't have long to bask in the sensation before he turned serious and left her alone in the room.

Yeah, so he felt desire. Big deal. He was still fearful. She sensed it in the air around him, in the wary light at the back of his eyes.

Tears threatened, and she pressed the heel of her palms to her closed lids. Crying would do no good. It changed nothing. Besides, she'd shed enough tears over Coop back in high school. She refused to cry any more. Not for him. Not for herself.

Inhaling a deep, shaky breath, she slowly regained her feet. First and foremost, she needed to brush the fuzzy feeling from her mouth.

When she'd stalled long enough, she made her way downstairs.

Coop was in the kitchen, cutting up a banana for Morty.

"This is a change from the man who wanted to put him down."

Her words were a mistake.

His expression closed off as he set the knife next to the sink and wiped his hands. Reaching behind him, he gripped the edge of the long porcelain sink and cleared his throat.

"I can't apologize enough for the shooting, Summer." His attention was focused on the floor, as if he didn't dare look into her eyes. Inch by inch, his gaze lifted to where Morty sat happily consuming the contents of his fruit bowl. "I was wrong."

"Thank you."

Surprised, he straightened.

She laughed at the dumbfounded expression. "Did you think I would yell or call you a horrible person?"

"Yes."

Her humor died. "Yeah, well, I won't. You did what you thought was right at the time."

"At the expense of your life." Self-disgust; he was wallowing in it.

Summer didn't know how to ease his emotional trauma. "Coop, look at me. Please."

His impenetrable mask was in place.

She'd seen it enough times to know the front he'd put up was intended to keep people at a distance. Keep *her* at a distance. Heartache mingled with regret and self-loathing. After all this time, her need for his affection bordered on pitiful.

"I don't blame you for what happened, and I'm perfectly fine. No one died. Nothing and no one was injured beyond repair."

She stepped forward.

He shifted away.

She inhaled sharply. When would she get it through her thick skull he didn't want or need anything from her?

"Summer—" he began.

She held up a hand palm out. The immediate loss of his tan clued her in to his aversion to her magic. Just as quickly, she dropped her arm. "I suppose this is the perfect lead-in to the next topic. Witchcraft. What do you want to know?"

Long moments ticked by as he topped off his cup of coffee and stared out the window over the sink.

She'd given up hope he intended to speak when he finally asked, "Have you ever used your magic against me?"

Her stomach dropped somewhere around her kneecaps. "I thought we clarified that the day you showed up. Yes."

He nodded as if he'd expected as much. "How many times?"

"Against you personally? Only the two times. In your presence, I can't recall. We, my sisters and I, levitated Eddie from the pool on occasion. And the goat incident... there might have been some magic involved there."

"Might've been or was?" His tone was hard and demanded truth.

"Was."

"I'm sure I know, but what did you do to me?"

"In the barn, I didn't want to take the chance Morty would hurt you. I suspended movement for you both."

"That's once. What was the second time?"

"On the stairs."

"You threw me into the wall."

"Not on purpose, Coop. I needed to stop you, but you were struggling against the hold." She sighed and shook her head. "I'm an embarrassment to the Thorne line. My powers are wonky at the best of times."

"You threw me into a wall, Summer!" he charged, slamming his mug on the counter. "Your face was full of smugness that day. You did it on purpose."

"No!" she shouted. She stepped toward him, and again, he backed up. "I didn't, Coop. I swear. I was holding you, you struggled, and I couldn't maintain the magic. You flying backward was a result of how hard you were fighting the pull." His disbelieving look broke her heart. "If I was smug, it was because, for once, it seemed I could control the magic."

"I want you gone," he ground out.

Her heart pounded so loudly in her ears, she thought she'd misheard. "Pardon?"

"*I want you gone*. You. Your sanctuary. Your family. I want you out of my town."

The dry heaves threatened to return. She bit the inside of her cheek and concentrated on breathing. In and out. In and out. Deep breaths.

He skirted the table and stopped in the doorway. "Summer."

She didn't face him. Couldn't.

"You're a danger to this community. You have one month to be packed up and out of here," he decreed. "If you're not, I'll find something to charge you all with. *All* of you. Understood?"

How she managed to nod was beyond her.

"I mean it."

The desire to physically strike took root inside her. She tamped down the urge before she whirled around. Just because she wouldn't physically hurt him, didn't mean she couldn't wound with her words as he was doing to her.

"You're a coward, Cooper. You act all noble, as if you're looking out for the people of this town, when in all actuality you're a scared little boy, afraid the big bad witches will turn your exterior into a warty toad to match your interior," she ranted. "Fuck. You!"

She sneezed. Out of every open portal, mice of every color and size, scurried into the room. Roughly fifty rodents lined the space between her and Coop like a battalion of soldiers marching into war.

His fear was palpable, and she reveled in it.

"One month, Summer. And tell your sister to remove whatever curse she saddled my brother with."

"She didn't, you jackass!" She sneezed harder. Her rodent army squeaked and took a collective step forward.

Coop backed away.

"They were in love. Or at least she was. Your brother's too stupid to understand that. Seems all the Carlyle men are dim witted."

Rage darkened his face. "One. Month."

"Yeah, yeah, yeah. I heard you the first time, you posturing warthog. Get the *hell* out of my house," she snarled. *Achoo!*

The mice surged forward. Coop ran for the door as if the hounds of hell were on his heels.

Summer's wicked laughter carried out the open window and echoed in the breeze. Sure, she'd given the sound a little boost to freak him the fuck out. She had to take her pleasure where she could.

As he tore from the drive, she hung her head and fought the moisture building behind her lids. She would *not* cry. Not over that POS. Not again.

13

Chapter Thirteen has been omitted for obvious reasons. Consider this intermission. Feel free to take a bathroom break or get a cup of coffee. Your story will resume momentarily. This book is an all-nighter.

14

"*I*'m not 'fraid of her," Coop slurred from where he sat sprawled in his recliner.

Keaton snorted and took a pull of his beer.

"I'm not!" Coop tried to sit up and tilted to the left. "I'm. Not!"

"Keep telling yourself that, C.C."

"Doeshn't matter. Doeshn't matter no more." He stared morosely into his whisky.

"Don't use a double negative in a sentence. You sound like an idiot," Keaton corrected.

"Shu'up. Think you're so shmar...shmar...smart. Summer said you're shtupid."

Keaton straightened and glared. "She said *I'm* stupid? Are you sure she wasn't talking about you?"

"N-nope. Ssshe shaid you." Coop cast Keaton what he hoped was a superior grin then frowned. "Who'sh shitting next to you?"

Keaton spit out the beer he started to consume. "Shitting? No one is shitting next to me, dumbass."

"Sh-sh-..." Coop geared up to try again. "*Sitting* nest to you."

"Dude, you are so wasted," his brother laughed. "No one is sitting *next* to me either."

"Shu'up."

The brothers drank in silence.

"She shaid Autumn lovesh you."

"Doubtful." Keaton stood. "I don't want to talk about Autumn. Ever."

Coop nodded because words became too difficult to form.

After his brother left, his thoughts turned to Summer. If he'd have thought about it beforehand, he'd have realized she was a passion-packed pleasure palace in a pint-sized package.

He'd only kissed Summer twice, and yet somehow he knew he'd remember the feel of her mouth on his for the remainder of his days. The softness of her full, rosy lips already haunted his dreams. After this morning, he could add the visual of her incredible, creamy breasts.

He groaned and pressed his fists to his eyes. God, he needed to get laid.

Dating in the town where you worked was akin to shitting where you ate. You didn't do it. Yet, prior to finding out the Witches of East-wick lived next door, Coop was fine with the idea of dating Summer. But he had to stop fantasizing about that porn-worthy mouth and breasts that could make a grown man weep. No good would come of it.

She'd sworn she hadn't placed any type of spell on him, and he believed her. But it didn't lessen the fact that she'd used magic to control him. *That*, he couldn't forgive.

A little voice inside taunted, *"But she forgave you for shooting her."*

She also forgave him for being an ass to her in high school.

"Let's face it, you are an ass," Little Voice said.

"Shu'up!" he shouted. "Just shut the hell up!"

"Coop?"

Squinting through bleary eyes, he registered Knox leaning against the door frame to the man cave.

The sonofabitch probably still wanted Summer. Wouldn't care if she was a witch or not.

"Summer doesn't deserve name calling, Coop. I don't know what the two of you fought about but calling her a witch is beneath you."

The coldness in Knox's tone was unmistakable.

103

"You want her? She'ssh yoursh." Coop attempted a bow and waved his hand magnanimously, almost tumbling face first from his seat.

"Generous. But she isn't yours to give."

"She damn well ish mine!" he argued.

A mocking grin spread across the other man's face. "Ah, there's the Cooper we all know and love. The guy who hates to share. No one will dare touch your toy. Not if they know what's good for them," Knox snarked.

"Whadaya talking about?"

"You honestly don't remember, do you?"

The room continued to rotate back and forth long after he stopped shaking his head.

"You think this thing with Summer is all one sided, but it isn't. You forgot your part in her crush, don't you?" Knox sneered and shook his head. "Whenever another guy showed any interest, you made sure to give her just enough attention to keep her on the hook. But you never reeled that fish in, did you? You left her dangling… until the prom incident."

Coop remained silent and tried to focus on one of the two Knox figures standing before him.

"That poor kid Tommy Tomlinson would've given his left nut to date her." Knox said.

"He was jush-just a kid my dad hired part time to help in the barn."

"The end of summer your junior year, Uncle Phillip decided to throw us all a pool party for all the hard work we'd done. The Thornes were there, and Tommy had finally worked up the nerve to talk to Summer. Remember." Knox made the word "remember" sound like more of a command than a question.

Coop's drunken haze mysteriously vanished, and memories flooded back.

Summer had been sitting on the edge of the pool, laughing at something Tommy had said. Her laughter had been unrestrained and beckoned Coop forward. A true siren's song.

He'd never seen her so carefree before. Across the expanse of the pool, he'd caught her eye, blew her a kiss, and winked. Then he cannonballed into the pool, drenching the proffered cake Tommy had brought her. When the other kid left to get her another piece, Coop hauled himself from the pool and into Tommy's spot.

All he knew was that he'd wanted to hear that laughter again.

"You remember now," Knox said with grim satisfaction.

Yes, he remembered. "The kid never stood a chance," Coop retorted, all surly attitude.

"You made sure of it," Knox countered. "And let's not forget Henry Wallis. We were all at the Juke Box restaurant, and he mentioned to you that he planned to ask her to prom."

"He wasn't serious," Coop protested. "He was fucking with me."

"No, Coop. He was completely serious. He liked her and saw you treated her like an afterthought. But you mocked him so badly, he lied to save face. Said he was only asking her as a joke." Knox uncrossed his arms and strode forward. "That's the same night you had the bright idea to destroy any affection she had for you. Did you know the ride she caught home from prom was from Henry?"

He hadn't. Coop had tried to block the incident from his mind because he'd been ashamed of his behavior.

"When you went off to college, they dated for a while."

His snarl echoed in the cavernous basement room. "You're a liar."

"Nope. He was her first real boyfriend," Knox taunted.

In his mind's eye, Coop could picture Henry and Summer together. His lean, lithe body and her curvy frame complimented each other. They would've held hands and laughed while sharing cheese fries or some other thing young people loved so much. Henry would've teased the color into her cheeks, and she would've had the special glow that she got when a man flirted with her.

Those large sky-blue eyes would widen and shimmer with... *love.*

He was going to be sick. Coop staggered to the bathroom and splashed water on his clammy skin.

"Did you even know you've been in love with her all this time?" Knox asked gently from the doorway.

"No."

"You poor bastard." This time there was no real heat in his cousin's words.

Coop almost detected sympathy. And suddenly, he was sober as a judge. "It doesn't matter. She's leaving."

"Ask her to stay."

"It's not that simple, Knox. I'm the one who ordered her and her sisters to get the hell out of town or I'd arrest them on some trumped-up excuse."

"I guess you'd better figure out how to undo your fuck up." Knox slapped him on the back. Hard. Only his other hand on Coop's shoulder stopped him from flying into the mirror.

"Dude, you nearly knocked me into next week."

"Call it payback," Knox laughed. "For the record, Tommy and Henry weren't the only two who were crushing on Summer."

"You'd better not be referring to yourself."

Knox's amused laugh bounced around the small bathroom. "You're such an oblivious idiot, Coop. It might be endearing if it wasn't so frustrating."

"Why does everyone keep calling me an idiot?" he muttered.

"If the shoe fits, cuz. If the shoe fits."

"ARE WE DOING ROCK, PAPER, SCISSORS TO SEE WHICH OF US RUNS TO Harkins' Hardware for more boxes?" Summer asked.

"What's wrong with the Pack'N'Ship?" Autumn asked as she took care to encase their mother's good dishes in bubble wrap.

"I already called. They're out."

"They're a shipping store! How can they be out of supplies?"

Summer shrugged. "Rosie McDonough is the manager. That might have something to do with it."

"Say no more. I swear that woman sleeps her way into managerial positions in this town. She's had enough of them."

"It isn't Christian to judge your neighbors," Summer scolded but secretly agreed.

Autumn snorted. "Last time I checked, we fell under the category of pagans."

"Oh, yeah. Judge away."

"Did you really cast a spell that blacked out her teeth and added horns to Cooper in all their yearbook pictures that year?"

Summer grinned at the memory. "No. That was courtesy of Spring."

"No! Innocent little Spring? Butter wouldn't melt in our sister's mouth."

After a fit of laughter, the sisters wiped tears from their eyes.

"No amount of threatening phone calls from Rosie's mother could get the school to reprint them," Autumn added through her giggles.

"Ah, good times," Summer quipped as she returned to sorting through the pots and pans. "I want Mom's cast iron pan, but I feel it belongs to this house."

"They do seem to go hand-in-hand, don't they?"

With a sigh, Summer returned the pan to the cabinet.

"You know you aren't required to leave, right?"

She shrugged. "Cooper will make life miserable for all of us. It's better I go."

"I believe his dictate was that the whole lot of us clear out," Autumn reminded her.

"Yeah, but he meant me. He can't expect Spring and Winnie to close down their businesses."

"What about yours?" Autumn was working herself into a fine rage. "You're the large animal veterinarian to half the farmers in this county, and you run the local rescue. It's no small feat to pack up and relocate."

"To him, I'm a nuisance and a danger." And wasn't that a dagger to the old heart? Summer shook her head. "Never, in my whole life, have I done anything to hurt anyone. Half the time, I don't charge for my services. But the truth is, I'll never get any respect. Not from these people." She bit her lip and blinked back the tears of self-pity. "I'm that crazy Summer Thorne who collects exotic animals."

"It's so unfair," Autumn grumbled. "If it wasn't against the laws of magic, I'd—"

When her sister halted her threat, Summer pulled her head out of the lower cabinet. "You'd what—oh."

Cooper took up the entire kitchen doorway. Dark circles rimmed his eyes, making them, in contrast, a brighter, more vivid blue-gray. Even signs of restless nights looked fabulous on him.

Summer wanted to hate him. Wanted to stamp her foot and repeat Autumn's words because it really *was* so unfair.

"I still have two more weeks, Sheriff," Summer said, careful to keep her voice emotionless and her expression as neutral as she could manage.

"I need your help."

Whatever she expected, that wasn't it. As a result, she stayed in the half-crouched position, mouth hanging open.

"One of my mares. I can't reach Parsons."

Since she was the only other large animal veterinarian in the area, of course he'd come to her if Dr. Parsons was unavailable. She shoved down the resentful side of her emotions. "Gotcha. I'll follow you over."

Autumn stepped forward to block her exit. "No!"

For the second time in as many minutes, Summer was speechless.

Her sister not so much. "Screw you, Coop. You can't come in here, after ordering Summer to leave town like an old, drunk sheriff in a spaghetti western, then expect her to come running whenever you crook your little finger."

Autumn's loyalty was heartwarming—and hilarious.

It also helped infuse steel into Summer's spine. "It's okay. I'm not doing it for him, Tums. I'm doing it for the mare." They shared a hug. "Thank you for defending me," Summer whispered in her ear. "I love you."

"Me, too."

Summer giggled. "An old, drunk sheriff in a spaghetti western?"

"It was all I could think to come up with." Autumn cast Coop the stink eye. "Do you need me to come with you?"

"Not unless you want to."

"In that case, I'll stay and finish packing."

"Thanks, it's appreciated."

Coop cleared his throat. "You don't have to—"

Summer cut him off, not caring what he had to say. "Let's go see about your mare."

He followed her to the van. "Summer, I'm trying to tell you—"

Again, she didn't let him finish. She climbed behind the wheel and shut the door in his face. He wouldn't have another chance to wheedle his way into her good graces. She was done feeding off his meager emotional handouts.

As she drove the short distance to his estate, she gave herself a stern lecture on the necessity of remaining strong. She loved him. She always had and probably always would. That was the Thorne curse. But she didn't need to like it—or him. And she certainly refused to pine for a man who didn't appreciate her or her gifts. Summer Thorne was made of sterner stuff.

By the time she'd reached his barn, her resolve was firmly in place.

One look at the staggering mare, and she guessed the problem.

"How long has she been like this?" she asked Knox, who tried to lend support to the horse.

"We found her this way about twenty minutes ago. She was fine this morning."

Summer grabbed the lead and guided the horse to a prone position.

"We thought it might be colic or founder. We wanted to keep her on her feet." Coop inserted.

"I understand. But it's neither."

A check of her ears, mouth and nose turned up clean. Summer finished the general exam.

"What's bothering you?"

"I—"

For the third time, she cut Coop off. "I'm not talking to you. I'm talking to the mare. Can you please be quiet so she can answer?"

Both men stood, mouths agape.

"You literally talk to the..."

She glared at Coop.

"I'm going to be quiet now."

"Thank the Goddess," she muttered.

"What's bothering you, pretty lady?" As the mare provided feedback in the only way horses could—images and a soft blow of air—Summer gently pushed aside the forelock and laid her palm flat on the horse's head just above her eyes. "Mmhmm. Okay. We're going to get you fixed up. You'll be right as rain, darling girl. Stay where you are and don't move."

Summer rose and faced the men. "She's got a condition called Vestibular. I don't see anything with the visual inspection, so I suspect it's neurological and not brought on by an ear infection. We can run a blood panel, but I'm ninety-nine percent positive."

Knox frowned, but Coop understood the underlying reason she could confirm the diagnosis.

"Will she need to be put down?" Coop asked.

Knox answered for her. "No. We aren't putting Macy down."

"She won't need to be," Summer affirmed. "Vestibular affects the balance. There is a good chance of her falling and injuring herself if we don't create a counter balance."

"How do we do that?" Coop asked.

"You aren't going to like it, Sheriff." Was she evil to take delight in the suspicion that crossed his face? *Probably.* "I want to put a cone on her head."

"A cone? What kind of cone? Like what dogs wear to keep them from licking a wound?"

"Nope. I need you to run to the hardware store and see if Old Man Harkins has a street construction cone."

Knox laughed even as Cooper swore.

"You've got to be kidding me, Summer! I can't have my prized mare walking around with an orange construction cone on her head."

Summer went toe-to-toe with him. "What's the matter, Coop? Worried about appearances? That mare deserves a chance. Until the vestibular goes away, or she gets used to the new normal of a head tilt, she needs help."

"Do I need to worry about the rest of my stock?"

"I would keep her quarantined. It's possible this is virus related. There's no way to tell." She walked into the wash area and soaped up her hands. "Make sure you keep her buckets scrubbed and water fresh. Always wash your hands before and after you have had contact with her. Four weeks should do it."

"A cone?" Coop asked again in disbelief.

"Do I need to write it down for you?" she asked innocently.

His brows dropped to a dangerous level. "I think I've got it."

"Good. Would you like me to check any of the other stock while I'm here?"

Knox pushed off the stall wall he'd been resting his booted foot against. "This was the only emergency."

"Okay. When Coop returns with the cone, you will need to slice off the base and utilize the top two-thirds of the cone. You'll need to modify a halter or bridal to attach it to her forehead and add about an inch of soft material or foam underneath to prevent sores. Since her tilt is to the right, the weight needs to be on the left between her ears for the counter balance."

Knox grasped the concept right away. "We're going to make her a lopsided unicorn."

"Exactly." Summer grinned up into his gorgeous face. "You always were the intelligent one of the group, Knox."

"I'm standing right here," Coop growled.

"I know," she replied without bothering to glance in his direction.

Knox laughed and hugged her. "You're adorable, Summer Thorne. Thanks for your help."

"If I get hugs like that in payment, I'll always be on-call for you, Knox."

"That's going to be hard to do since you're leaving town," Coop snapped.

Her warm bubble burst. Leave it to the fun police to cast a dark cloud over the day.

"Right. I'll be back in the morning to check on her. I have a few other patients to check today. I'll need to wrap up some things before I go, but I can make the time to come back later if I'm needed."

"Summer, I didn't mean—"

"Parsons can follow up with your mare if you have a problem with me."

"Will you stop cutting me off?" Coop yelled.

"No, because I don't give a *shit* what you have to say." She sneezed. Within two seconds, squeaking drifted to their ears. A glance up at the rafters showed she'd attracted what few mice dared live on the Carlyle estate. "Don't go near the traps or eat anything suspicious, guys. You stand a better chance in the woods behind the house."

"You are Dr. Doolittle," Coop breathed.

Without a backward glance, she left the two men staring, mouths agape.

15

*A*fter Summer had finished her appointments for the day, she pulled into her driveway to find Coop's cruiser.

He leaned against the driver's door, arms crossed, scuffing the dirt with his toe. The image of an impatient boy.

Why couldn't he leave her alone? It wasn't as if she kept seeking *him* out. With a sigh, she turned off the ignition and climbed from the vehicle. She didn't want this confrontation, but better to get it over with.

"Is your mare okay?"

Coop grimaced. "Knox is working on what he is calling the unicorn contraption. But, yeah, I think she is."

"Good." Deciding she was a coward who didn't want to fight after all, Summer turned to go.

"Can we talk? Without you interrupting me?"

"I need a shower and a cup of tea," she hedged.

"Is that a no?" he persisted.

Knowing he wasn't going to stop until she gave in, she said, "Fine. Go ahead. But can I at least sit down? It's been a long day."

She dropped to the porch step.

Coop sat uncomfortably close.

To maintain the distance her sanity required, she scooted away. "What's up, Sheriff?"

"Coop. My name is Coop."

"I think, after all this time, I know your name," she said dryly.

"Then use it."

"Another order, *Sheriff*?" Goddess, she was sick of this constant back and forth. She held up a hand and noted he cringed. "Whatever. You know what? I'm tired, and honestly, I don't need your crap right now. Say what you have to say and go."

"I came to apologize."

Okay, she didn't see that coming. "Fine. Apology accepted. Have a nice life." She stood.

He rose to his feet. "Summer, please. I need you to hear me."

"I've never *not* heard you, Coop." She swallowed and blinked back the unexpected tears. For nearly eleven years, she hadn't cried once. Now the waterworks threatened at every turn. "From the day I first saw you, I thought, *he's the one*. I hung on your every word." She swallowed and shook her head. "There wasn't a day that went by that I didn't wonder why you couldn't see me as something more than an annoyance."

She stepped off the porch and stared out over the land that had been in their family for over two centuries. "The one time you did, obviously you were out to make me a laughing stock."

"It wasn't like that," he said gruffly, coming to stand beside her.

"Yeah, Coop. It was." She faced him. "But I don't hold grudges. Life is too short for most people. And, what's the point? A grudge lets another person take up space inside your head, fills you with anger, self-doubt. No, thanks."

He remained quiet and studied her set face.

She shrugged and said, "Mostly, I thought we were past all of that. Then the Morty incident happened." She shook her head and graced him with a bittersweet half-smile. "I knew you came by here to see what you could discover to shut me down. To force me to get rid of Eddie and Morty."

"If you did, why let me stay and help around here?"

Because he was curious and not confrontational, she answered. "I'd hoped if you got to know them, you'd understand what I was trying to do." She waved her hand to encompass the land around them. "We don't own this. No human truly owns anything. We are the custodians of the earth. Piss-poor ones at that. But my sisters and I decided a long time ago, we would do our part."

She pointed to the greenhouse. "Spring grows rare herbs and replants them in their natural habitat when it hasn't been completely destroyed."

She nodded toward an outbuilding. "Winnie's lotions and potions heal the sick and elderly."

She faced her barn. "I do what I can for unwanted and abused animals."

His face held a contemplative frown. "And Autumn?"

"When she isn't maintaining the family bank balance and safe-keeping our secrets, she's an environmental activist. Her and Aunt GiGi run a foundation to clean up the oceans."

"I had no idea."

"No, you wouldn't have. You never bothered to see us as anything more than the Weird Season Sisters like the rest of this town."

He didn't try to deny it. For that, she was grateful. Platitudes angered her.

Coop cleared his throat. "I came to tell you that you don't have to leave."

Genuine amusement struck, and she laughed. "I never had to, Coop. I could've easily had one of my sisters wipe your memories." She enjoyed the moment her words registered and his face turned ashen. Ah, it was the little things. "But I'm leaving for me. I need a fresh start."

"Why?"

Because I'm tired of being invisible to the man I love.

She bent down and picked up Saul where he'd come to rest at her feet. She snuggled him against her cheek and absorbed the comfort from her familiar, exactly as he intended. With a kiss to the top of his adorable head, she released him.

"What difference does it make?" she asked after she rose.

"Why, Summer?"

"The next time Morty or Eddie escapes, and they will, because I don't have an armed guard to prevent my mischievous friends from unlocking gates, you'll be back. You'll swear they are dangerous and do everything in your power to have them removed from my care." She closed her eyes to gather herself before she met his troubled gaze. "Because you see me as an incompetent handler."

"I won't, and I don't."

"You do."

"I don't," he argued. He stepped forward and tilted up her chin. "I just think sometimes it's a lot more than you can handle."

His gentle touch created havoc to her senses and clouded her mind. She jerked away to regain a semblance of reason. "I'll see about hiring help at my next location."

"Don't go, Summer. This town needs you, whether they realize it or not."

COOP, HEART HEAVY, WANTED TO ADD HE NEEDED HER TOO. IF HE DID, she'd most likely laugh in his face. He'd done nothing to earn the love she had so freely offered. Now it was gone, he'd give anything to have it back. Regret was a bitch. All he could do was stare down into her impassive face, helpless and frustrated because of it.

"You really should make up your mind, Sheriff. The hot and cold routine gets old." Autumn's voice cut across the lawn to where Coop and Summer were locked in place by some strange cosmic pull. The snark was enough to snap him out of whatever odd enchantment had surrounded the two of them.

Relief flooded Summer's face, and she hurried toward her sister.

Good to know she also experienced the sensation and he wasn't alone.

"Summer cleared things up for me. I realize now, although you have the power to be, you're no threat to my family or the people here."

Autumn's laughter contained a hard edge. "Really? I think there are members of your immediate family who feel differently. Now, run along, Sheriff. It's a full moon tonight. Time for us witches to dance naked and collect newt for our cauldron."

He narrowed his eyes, not caring for the dismissal.

Summer bit her lip to curb her own amusement. But seeing the twinkle return her eyes to a brighter blue, even for a minute, made all the difference and eased the ache in his chest.

The second half of Autumn's comment sunk in. Dance naked under the moon? Did they really do that? Perhaps it was worth investigating, and not for legal reasons, but because *hello*, four gorgeous women naked in the moonlight!

The image of Summer's creamy breasts rose up to taunt him.

Instead of ordering her to leave the morning she woke from the gunshot wound, he should've accepted the sleepy invitation in her soft eyes.

"I have one more thing to do before I go," he heard himself say.

Both women stared in confusion as he stormed the porch and stopped in front of Summer. Coop cupped her face in his palms and lowered his head. "I want to clarify, there will be no more cold."

His lips swooped down to claim her parted mouth. His tongue plunged into the warm depth, and her enthusiastic response was instantaneous. One of them moaned, and the other's moan followed shortly thereafter.

After a minute, or ten, Coop drew back. "I hope you decide to stay, Summer Thorne. I have about fifteen years of stupidity to make up for."

A slow, steady clapping ricocheted around them. "'Bout damned time, Sheriff," Autumn said. "'Bout damned time."

He paused and glanced around. "No mice."

"It only happens when our reverse Disney Princess here swears."

"Reverse Disney Princess?"

Summer rolled her eyes and stomped away, leaving him and Autumn on the porch. Coop curbed the desire to follow, scoop Summer up, and head for the bedroom. *Too soon.*

"Yes, Snow White and Cinderella sing to attract the wildlife. Summer swears and can't carry a tune."

For the first time in what seemed like forever, Cooper laughed. Once he started, he couldn't stop. He sat on the porch step, and Autumn joined him. The two of them sat in a sort of unspoken truce.

"Don't pursue her if you aren't serious about your intentions, Coop. She doesn't need her heart broken a third time."

Third? "Was she in love with Henry then?"

"Henry?"

"Knox told me they were an item."

"Pfft. Summer was never in love with Henry. The Thornes only ever have one true soulmate each."

Summer's words echoed about his head. *"From the day I first saw you, I thought, he's the one."*

Coop held his breath and slowly turned his head to meet the challenge in Autumn's amber gaze. "Only one?"

"You aren't as dumb as you look, Sheriff."

"Thanks for that little vote of confidence," he muttered.

"You have your work cut out for you, Coop," she said in all seriousness. "None of us are going to make it easy for you this time around."

"Nothing worthwhile ever came easy, Autumn." He stood and dusted off the seat of his pants. "And I've always loved a challenge."

"Just make sure you're going after her for the right reasons. She's not a challenge to be won."

"I promise. I'm in it for the right reasons this time around."

16

*S*tating intent and carrying through on that intent were two different animals.

Cooper found it difficult to get Summer to give him the time of day. Not dissimilar to their high school days after prom. If he showed up to help her with the barn work, she claimed a prior appointment and vamoosed. When he tried to hire her as the official veterinarian for the Carlyle barn, she turned him down flat. She insisted she was leaving town and easing her caseload.

Meanwhile, he continually maintained that he wanted her to stay. Nothing he'd done to sabotage her efforts to leave worked. Even with the help of her sisters and mischievous Aunt GiGi, Coop's grand ideas died a painful death.

Today was one such incident.

Autumn informed him that Summer had placed a deposit and scheduled a closing on a property in North Carolina.

Coop swore long and hard, not caring if he singed the hair of the people around him with his fiery temper. "What do you mean? I thought you got the realtor to agree to say the property was under contract to another buyer?"

"I tried. The back-stabbing wench decided she wanted the commission more. There isn't a lot of business in the area where she lives."

Coop paced his office, his agitation directly at odds with Autumn's calmness.

"Okay, let me think."

"Not your strong suit, Sheriff."

"I don't need your attitude right now, Autumn."

She grinned and waved a hand. "Carry on."

The fission of unease when one of the sisters waved a hand was something that would take a long while to overcome.

"Sorry. I forgot. No sudden hand movements," she laughed.

"I'm glad this is funny to you. The woman I love is determined to skip town."

Her expression softened to amused affection. "Skip town? You make it sound so nefarious."

He rolled his eyes and resumed pacing. "How much is this realtor's commission supposed to be?"

"You intend to pay her off?"

"If I have to."

Autumn straightened from her slouched position. "Just how wealthy is your family, Coop?"

"My parents are on an extended tour of Europe. What does that tell you?"

"Fucking A. I want to talk to your investment broker."

"That would be Keaton. Should I set up a meeting?"

She deflated back into the visitor chair. "You sure know how to ruin a witch's day."

He cast a wary glance through the office window overlooking the deputy pit. "Shhh, not so loud."

"They can't hear us. Sound protection spell."

"I…" Yeah, he had no words.

Autumn studied her nails before buffing them on her shirt. "I still think you need to storm the castle, sweep Summer into your arms, and screw her brains out."

Once again, she stole his speech. Why had he never thought to use the sex option? Because Summer would turn him into a slug, that's why. He said as much to her sister.

"Nah. She isn't that powerful."

"I beg to differ. Don't you remember what she did the day she was sh—?" His throat seized. He'd almost killed her. The memory of her lying there as her blood stained the ground made him ill all over again.

Autumn was at his side in an instant. "Breathe, Coop. It's going to be okay." She hugged him. "We witches are harder to kill than all that."

"Isn't this cozy?" Keaton ground out.

His brother stood inside the doorway, arms crossed, and a stormy expression in place of his normally happy-go-lucky countenance. Next to him stood Summer, white lipped, trying hard to appear unaffected.

"It's not how it appears," Coop directed to Summer.

"I don't care. You and Autumn are consenting adults." She dragged Keaton into the room and closed the door. "I'm not here about you anyway."

"You're not? Then—"

"Reps from White Labs are in the front lobby. They have a court order to get Morty back."

"What?" Coop was stunned. He'd assumed Morty was obtained legally.

"Yes, and they are attempting to wrangle a deputy to head out to their place and serve the writ right now," Keaton added.

A sneaking suspicion started to form. "Autumn, would you and Keaton give me a second with Summer, please?"

"There's nothing you can't say in front of her. She knows everything," Summer said.

"Everything." Coop sighed heavily and sought his brother's gaze. "Stall them, please."

After Keaton left, Coop turned to face the sisters. "Start talking. Don't leave anything out."

"Aunt GiGi was the one who brought Morty to me. I assumed it was some activist cause to stop lab testing on animals." Summer shrugged. "I wasn't going to turn him away. He was just a baby."

"You didn't bother to question GiGi about *how* she'd obtained a chimpanzee? The legality never occurred to you?"

"I didn't care. It wasn't right, Coop," she argued, stepping forward. "You saw those tapes. What I didn't show you was the pictures of a hairless baby chimp with sores on his body." Tears filled her eyes. "Please, Coop. He can't be sent back."

Her tears gutted him.

"Fuck!" What was he supposed to do? He couldn't break the law, even for Summer.

But perhaps he could bend it. He only need think of a solution.

"I don't see what the problem is."

Both of them turned to Autumn.

"A cloaking spell will do the trick. They can search the house until the cows come home. They won't find him."

Summer blinked, and Coop had to wonder why she came to him when another solution was readily available.

"Okay, you two get home and do your, well, whatever it is you do. I'll find a few emergencies to occupy my deputies."

Summer gazed up at him with shining eyes. "Thank you, Coop."

His heart melted. "Go. Keep my little buddy safe."

He was wrong. He could definitely break the law for one of her smiles.

"Oh, just kiss and get it over with," Autumn said impatiently.

"No," he said.

Summer's smile dimmed.

Coop rubbed his thumb lightly over her full pink lips. "The next time I kiss you, I don't intend to stop."

"Well, fuck me, that was romantic," Autumn muttered.

The light was back in Summer's eyes and that was all he cared about. "Go, hide Morty."

THE SISTERS DECIDED TO FORGO THE DRIVE AND CHOSE THE FASTER method of Autumn's teleport. Thank the Goddess for Autumn's clear head, because once Coop touched her, Summer's mind turned to mush. She cursed herself for being a fool. Why was it, that every time he graced her with that sexy, sensual look, she forgot she was angry with him?

They arrived at their estate on a run.

"Spring! Winnie!" Summer called as she headed upstairs. "Sisters!"

Both women came from the attic followed by their Aunt GiGi.

Summer didn't have time to wonder about the why of the other witches gathering in the attic. "We need a foolproof cloaking spell. White Lab reps are at the Sheriff's office with a court order for Morty."

Aunt GiGi shook her fist. "Those dirty bastards! They want a fight? I'll give them a fight."

"Yeah, okay, but can we focus here, Aunt G? The chimp *you* stole is now in danger. Somehow they found out that we have him."

"Will Coop help?" Spring asked over her shoulder as she led the way to their grimoire.

Summer shook her head. "He's not going to lead them here, if that's what you're asking, but there isn't much more he can do. The law is the law."

Autumn snorted. "Yeah, like he wouldn't break it for you. That man would burn that lab to the ground if you asked him to."

"You're delusional if you think so, sister," Summer said coolly. "We're talking about the same man who intended to shoot Morty and who threatened to arrest us all if we didn't leave town."

"He was scared, Summer," Winnie said as she wrapped an arm around Summer's shoulders. "Cut him a break."

Because she wasn't able to recover from another betrayal, Summer shrugged off her touch and said, "No. Now let's get busy, please."

Her family sighed in unison. Had the whole mess not been serious, she'd probably have laughed at their forlorn expressions.

But hope was a dangerous thing to cling to. For years, Summer had held on to the hope that Cooper Carlyle would wake up and see what was right in front of him. Time and again, she'd dealt with the humiliation of being the star of a one-sided love story. The humiliation of neighbors whispering behind their hands, and, in the early years, his girlfriends lording over her in their triumph. She'd held her head high through it all, treating the animals of these same two-faced toad stools and all the while smiling politely.

And that was all *after* the intentional setup during high school. Because despite it all, she'd believed that deep down, he was a good guy. The optimist in her was certain he'd come around.

Now he had, and it was too little, too late.

Summer was optimism-ed out. She'd save any positive outlooks for her Sanctuary and leave love to everyone else on the planet. Obviously, she wasn't the best judge of character.

As far as this situation with Morty, well, Coop owed her this much. If he could help keep her beloved little ape from the hands of those evil lab owners, she'd call it even and be content to move on.

She wasn't an ugly troll, she'd find someone to ease the lonely nights on occasion. Nothing permanent. No. She didn't dare allow anyone a glimpse behind the curtain. Their little witchy oz needed to be kept under wraps.

When she was ready to leave Leiper's Fork, she had one last request for her sibling and aunt. She wanted both her memory of Coop and his of her wiped clean. A fresh start for each of them. He didn't suffer the Thorne curse of loving only once. She had no doubt he'd find another to share his life.

But the memory scrub could wait until the current crisis was taken care of first.

Aunt GiGi gathered the necessary oils, herbs, and the Thorne athamé then lit candles to cast the circle. Meanwhile, the four sisters purified and centered themselves for the upcoming spell.

As one, the sisters stood and joined hands with GiGi. The power of generations of Thorne witches shot through them. Magic pulsed in the surrounding air. Four of the family's familiars occupied the four corners of the room and kept guard.

They drew on the main elements; water, air, earth, fire, and metal, then started to chant.

The sound of vehicles on the graveled drive traveled to the attic just as GiGi closed the circle. They all shared a confident look and headed downstairs. The time for confrontation was at hand. The five women lined up on the porch, ready to take on the horned one himself if it came to that. Morty was to be protected at all costs.

Coop cautiously exited his vehicle.

Summer met his uneasy gaze across the distance. She understood his watchfulness. The last time he arrived to the Thorne women lining the porch, things had gone to hell in a hand basket.

Dismissing him, she focused on the smarmy motherfucker next to the man in the White Laboratories lab coat. The suit was dressed all in black with a red power tie. His blond slicked-back hair sported at least three ounces of hair product. But it was his superior expression that set Summer's teeth on edge.

"May we help you?" Her voice couldn't be any colder, and the average person would've received frostbite.

But Summer recognized the tall man in front who strode toward the porch, and he was anything but average. He was a warlock. An extremely powerful warlock.

"Shit." She sneezed, and her army of mice arrived.

"I can see by the arrival of your... backup, we are going to dispense with the fake formalities and get to it," the warlock said.

"You're not welcome here, Alastair Thorne."

Coop jerked to a stop and gaped. Slowly, he shifted shocked eyes to Summer.

She felt the pull of his glorious blue-gray gaze. However, she didn't dare take hers from the dangerous man before her.

"That is no way to greet your family, my dear."

"We should forget and forgive, is that it?" Autumn asked with a sneer.

Alastair straightened his already perfect tie and tugged on his shirt cuffs. "I see GiGi has filled your head with stories again. My little sister always did have a flair for drama."

"You killed our mother, you piece of shit!" Summer yelled. Her sneeze followed.

Another wave of mice arrived.

His lids dropped to shield his expression, and his sapphire-blue eyes shifted to the rodents lined up in front of him. "If you care about them, I suggest you have your army disperse, Summer dear."

"Don't you threaten my niece, you black-hearted knave!" GiGi snarled.

"You may be powerful, Alastair, but are you more powerful than the five of us combined?" Spring asked. Her tone remained neutral as if she discussed the weather.

The air rippled around them, a shifting of space and time.

"He's not more powerful than I am," a deep baritone inserted.

All heads turned to the auburn-haired man who'd appeared behind the women.

"Daddy," Summer breathed. "Welcome home."

"Hello, brother." Alastair sneered. "I'm surprised you could pull yourself away from your little *antiques* long enough to bother with anyone else."

"I'm always aware of what's happening with my girls, brother. I made the mistake of leaving my wife unprotected with you on the loose. I won't make the same mistake with my children."

Alastair's cold stare traveled witch to witch. He paused overlong on Summer before he returned his attention to Preston Thorne. "It doesn't matter. I'm here in a legal capacity. It seems our sister has stolen something from my company, and I've come to retrieve it."

"You have a warrant to search my home?" Preston asked.

"I have a court order for the chimpanzee," Alastair's lab tech inserted, stepping forward and waving a piece of paper.

The paper went up in flames and caused the man holding it to emit a bloodcurdling scream. The high-pitched sound made everyone wince, Alastair and Preston included. The technician jumped about, stomping on the burning paper.

"What a sissy," Summer laughed as she fisted her hand and splashed him with water.

"Need a little ice for that burn?" Winter fisted her hand to blast the man with freezing wind.

Preston moved forward, squeezed Summer's shoulder, then continued down the steps. "I think he's had enough. Take your minions and get off my property, Alastair. If you ever return, I'll set the coven on your evil ass. I'm sure GiGi would love to lead the charge."

"I want that ape, Preston."

Their father cocked his head. "What ape? I don't recall any such animal in Summer's rescue." He didn't look away from Alastair when he asked, "Ladies? Have you seen any apes?"

"Nope," they chorused as one.

Alastair's irritated gaze shot to Summer's smug face, flicked to sweep Coop from head to toe, and returned to Summer. "There are other ways for me to go about this, Summer. Are you sure you want this fight?"

Her heart stopped.

Cooper must've believed her uncle meant to harm her because he scowled and stepped toward Alastair.

Alastair and Summer raised their hands simultaneously; Alastair to strike, and Summer to protect.

A bolt of light shot from her uncle's palm headed directly for the center of Coop's chest.

Ringing started in her ears, and the ground shook. A surge of raw power radiated from her core to her extremities. As she had the day she'd been shot, Summer froze time without trying.

Only her father remained unaffected and shifted to stand protectively in front of Coop.

"Daddy, no!"

He winked and waved his hand to restore time with a snap.

The red arc of electricity was absorbed into Preston's massive chest with a grunt. "That all you have, brother?"

He slammed his hands together, and a resounding boom echoed around the property. Shingles on the roof lifted in a wave, and all the occupants in the yard were thrown off their feet.

Alastair disappeared in the blink of an eye.

"Where did you send that low-life brother of ours?" GiGi asked Preston.

"Antarctica."

"Without a coat?" Autumn grinned as she helped GiGi to her feet. "Is it too much to hope that he'll freeze to death?"

Preston chuckled and hugged Autumn. "Sorry, my sweet. It was just a scare tactic. I suspect he'll be home by dinner." He hugged each of his other three daughters in turn.

"I thought you were going to be killed," Summer croaked from the comfort of her father's arms.

"No need to worry about me, my sunshine. I saw his intent and prepared ahead of time."

"Don't ever do that again, Dad," she scolded.

Preston raised a brow. "You mean as you did to protect the chimp that none of us have seen?" He tilted her chin up. "If you ever put yourself in front of a bullet again, there will be hell to pay. Understood?"

"I won't make promises I can't keep."

"You're stubborn—just like your mother." Grief briefly clouded Preston's eyes. "Come, I need a shot of whisky. Oh, and GiGi, do you mind?" He waved his hand at the lab employees.

GiGi was the master at altering memories.

"Excuse me, but what the fuck just happened?" Coop asked, shaken and looking like he was ready to lose his cookies.

"Old Uncle Alastair intended to kill you. My father saved your life," Summer bluntly informed him, leaving out her part. "You may want to thank him."

"He'll have plenty of time to thank me when we have our sit-down," Preston informed her. "Cooper and I need to get a few things straight."

"It's not necessary, Dad. We're not—"

Her protest fell on deaf ears.

"Oh, but it is," Preston stated. His hard tone ended the discussion.

17

"*S*it down, son." Preston pointed to a burgundy upholstered seat across from a massive antique desk. "Shall I pour you a dram?"

"No, sir. I'm still on duty."

The older man paused and cast a sardonic glance over his shoulder then proceeded to pour two drinks anyway.

The question was only a formality. Coop was expected to drink.

"You may want to call Lil and let her know you're taking the rest of the day off, son."

"No disrespect, Mr. Thorne, but I'll make my own decisions, thank you."

Preston set the crystal tumbler before Coop, taking care to center it directly on a marble coaster. "This is a nineteen-thirty-seven bottle of Glenfiddich, boy. There were only sixty-one bottles in existence, and this pour is from one of them. *Drink.*"

When he put it like that, Coop felt churlish refusing and admittedly a little fearful after witnessing the man's power.

"Now tell me. What are your intentions toward my daughter?"

Coop, in the process of sipping his whisky, inhaled. The sensation was liquid fire to his lungs, throat, and nostrils. Somewhere, the question floated about his brain, *Why would he wait until I was sipping an eighty-plus-year-old whisky?*

Preston waited patiently on the edge of his desk, one leg swinging casually to and fro, arms rested on his thigh as he leaned forward.

As intimidation went, the man was a pro.

"I have no intentions," Coop managed after a minute.

One dark auburn brow shot up. Christ, the man was terrifying.

"Uh, that is to say, I don't not have intentions." What the hell does that even mean? *I don't not have intentions.* Idiot!

Amber eyes narrowed on him, and Coop wiped his forearm across his sweaty brow.

"I... look, I like Summer. But we've only ever kissed twice—"

"Three times."

Coop frowned. When the hell had he kissed her a third time? He certainly would've remembered. The other two times damned near blew his socks off.

"Shall I clarify?"

"Please do."

"The Fourth of July celebration in town. You were five and she was four. She'd just dropped her ice cream on the ground. She was crying, heartbroken that she'd lost her treat. You hugged and kissed her, begged her not to cry. Then proceeded to give her your cone."

Coop grinned at the memory. He'd forgotten until Preston recounted the incident. "That was Summer? I thought your family didn't move here until the girls were in high school?"

Preston ignored the questions to say, "All she talked about from that moment was Cooper and her intent to marry you."

"I had no idea."

"Quite clearly, what had been an impressionable moment for her, had been promptly forgotten by you." Preston swirled his drink and stared into its golden depths. "Then you set her up for heartbreak with your prom stunt."

"I was a kid, Mr. Thorne. A stupid kid."

"Granted. But what about more recently, Cooper? You drew on one daughter and shot the other."

All pretext of civility was gone. Standing before him was an enraged father. *And a powerful magical one at that.*

Coop eased to his feet.

"Sit *down*, boy," the older man boomed.

Coop sat.

"You started helping Summer in her sanctuary under false pretenses. Yes or no?"

"Yes."

"You shot at her beloved pet. Yes or no?"

"He was dang—uh, yes," Coop answered upon viewing Preston's expression darken further.

"You shot my daughter instead. Yes or no?"

"Yes, and I... there are no words to express how sorry I am."

"So sorry that you threatened my family with arrest if they didn't leave town? Yes or no?"

Closing his eyes, Coop exhaled, "Yes."

"Today, you brought a dangerous warlock to my home. Yes or no?"

"I'm going to stop you right there. I'm the sheriff, and he had a court order." Coop swallowed hard and shored up his spine. "I tried to give Summer and Autumn as much time as I could so they could hide Morty before I brought the lab reps out here."

"The fact remains, you brought him here, and had I not returned, he might've hurt my family."

"I had no idea he was a warlock."

"No. You didn't. And you have no idea what it takes to be a mate to a witch." Preston swallowed his whisky in one fell swoop as if it were no more than water. "We're done here. Don't come back. You aren't deserving of my daughter."

Coop surged to his feet. "She's a grown woman and doesn't need you to make her decisions for her, Mr. Thorne."

Preston cocked his head and lifted his hand.

The wince was involuntary—a sort of post-traumatic stress—but Coop recovered his nerve and stood his ground.

A flame flared to life in the older man's palm. Round and round he swirled it, never taking his eyes from Coop.

Was Summer's father going to smite him on the spot?

"You were saying?" Preston asked.

He was? Oh, *right*. "I stand by what I said. Summer can make her own decisions."

Preston clapped his hands together and extinguished the flame.

Coop couldn't help but wince again. This man had him jumpy as fuck.

"Son, your nerves won't be able to handle the strain. Get out now while you still can."

Didn't that sound ominous?

The door opened behind him, and the back of his neck tingled. A sensation Coop associated with GiGi Thorne-Gillespie.

"Preston, stop torturing the poor boy. He's had enough."

"Who's torturing him?" Preston poured a second whisky for himself and another for his sister. "I'm seeing what he's made of." The older man sent him a penetrating look. "I'm not impressed."

"As if you would be with any man courting your daughter."

Humor lit the amber eyes, and Coop could see Autumn in the man's roguish expression. "Especially not men who go around shooting their future wife."

"Wife? I don't—"

An elbow caught him in the ribs—hard. "Don't say something that's going to get you dead, boy," GiGi hissed. "My brother isn't as forgiving as some."

Preston's cold stare had Coop's insides in knots.

"Run along now," GiGi added more kindly.

Deciding discretion was the better part of valor, Coop took her suggestion and ran with it.

Outside the study door, he paused for a deep breath. A sound on the stairs caught his attention. Four female faces peeked through the banister at him, and the image of what these women must've been like as little girls flitted about his brain.

His eyes sought out Summer. Yes, he remembered the little girl who'd lost her ice cream. He'd forgotten for a while, but she'd declared her love for him on the spot. Oddly enough, his heart had been claimed that day, too. He just hadn't known it at the time.

"How's Morty?"

"Safe." She graced him with a soft smile. "Thanks for trying to protect us earlier. While you're no match for Alastair, the effort was appreciated."

Coop glanced over his shoulder at the closed study door. "Yeah, I'm starting to believe I'm no match for anyone in this family."

"Oh, I don't know, Sheriff," Autumn laughed. "Could be you're a match for one."

Ignoring her sisters, Coop extended a hand to Summer. "Can we talk?"

She rose, ignored his proffered hand, and walked past him out the front door.

As they strolled through the animal barn, he struggled for the words to make things right. They wouldn't come.

"You told me once, you didn't carry a grudge."

"I don't."

"What is your insistence on moving, if not a grudge?"

"It's me getting on with my life, Coop. I thought I made that clear."

"I don't want you to go," he declared achingly. "I don't know what I feel for you, Summer. I only know that a world without you in it is duller and holds less interest for me."

"You've discovered this in two months time? You've had the entirety of our lives to see me. Now I'm over you, and you decide you want me?"

Anger laced her voice, and her blue eyes took on a darker hue.

"Some people are slower than others. Ask any of my family—or yours—and they'll tell you I'm an idiot."

Her lips quirked, and she dropped her eyes, but not before he saw the amusement there.

"Don't go. If nothing else, it's not safe. Alastair proved that today. If he catches you alone and unaware..." Coop shuddered internally at the thought. "I can't stand the thought of you not safe and happy somewhere in the world, Summer Thorne."

SONOFABITCH, THE MAN WAS SMOOTH. WITH A FEW SENTENCES, HE crumbled her walls.

Summer was hard pressed to not fling herself into his arms. She maintained her cool, but only by a thread.

"What happens if I stay?"

"We can see where this thing leads."

"This thing?"

"Yeah, this…" His hand cupped her face as he lowered his head to brush his nose gently against hers. "… thing."

When his mouth captured hers, the kiss was like none they'd shared before. Fire and something remarkably like love burned between them this time. The tenderness he exhibited weakened her knees.

As if sensing her imminent collapse, Coop's strong arm wrapped around her waist and hauled her closer. The hand cupping her face shifted to her nape and held her steady while his tongue plundered the warm depths of her mouth.

Her hands crept to cup his ass through his jeans. She told herself she had to hold on in order to not slump at his feet. But in reality, his curvy ass made her mouth water. Nothing was finer than a man who filled out his jeans.

A moan filled the air around them, then another, and another.

Needing to feel the smooth expanse of his skin, her fingers tugged his shirt free of his pants and burrowed underneath. She caressed the tight muscles along his lower spine and inched up, tracing the solid V of his back.

He shifted to do a little exploring of his own. His long fingers traced the curve beneath her breast then lifted her bra to cup her more fully. As he toyed with her already sensitive nipple, it pebbled and elicited a deeper moan.

His lips left hers, and the two of them dragged in much-needed oxygen. "God, I want you so much."

She wanted him too. And her thought was, *why not?* Why not experience what countless others had from him? Why not be able to look back with no regrets when the time came to leave?

"Hold on tight," she whispered, confident in her decision and ability to teleport them the short distance to the hayloft. They landed in a heap with a soft thud.

His reaction wasn't what she expected. Instead of being ecstatic about potentially getting laid, his response was more unfavorable.

"Good Christ, Summer! *What the fuck?*" He crab crawled back from her.

"I thought you wanted to—"

"What? Fly through space in the blink of an eye? Great way to kill a hard on, babe."

Cold seeped through her veins. She'd done it again; shown trust and been rejected for her openness. The need to get away weighed heavy on her. She didn't know exactly where to go, but it couldn't be anywhere he was.

"Look, I—"

She didn't give him time to come up with another excuse to rebuff her. With a wave of her hands, she went the first place she visualized.

The white, sandy beach softened Summer's landing.

She shot a quick glance around. No one saw her. Excellent. Now, if she could figure out where the hell she'd teleported to, she'd be doing well. Not that it mattered. She intended to hang out for a few days. Soon enough, she'd have to go back, but she could enjoy a small reprieve.

In a little while, she'd send a message to her family and let them know she was all right. But for now, she needed this time to herself. A place where no one knew who she was or what she could do. A place where people didn't judge her because her name was Thorne. A place without Coop, who humiliated her at every turn.

Another study of the landscape to make sure she was alone, and then she waved her hands. A pale pink bikini took the place of her jeans and t-shirt. A snap of her fingers provided the rest of her beach essentials: sunglasses, blanket, towel, sunscreen, and an umbrella drink.

She sat back and closed her eyes. Yep. She was going to enjoy her first vacation in two years.

A dark shadow fell across her, and she held back her curse. Even the sun decided to toy with her.

Opening her eyes, she gasped.

"Hello, child."

18

"Summer!" His voice rang out in the empty hayloft. Where the devil had she gone?

He climbed down the ladder and checked every crook and crevice of the barn. "Summer, if you're here, let's discuss this," he called.

Nothing.

Coop really didn't want to return to the house. What could he say? "Uh, hey, did Summer pop back in here because I crushed her feelings *again*?"

When he'd stalled as long as he could, he knocked on the enormous mahogany door.

"Coop? I thought you were with Summer," Spring acted surprised to see him.

"We might've had an argument. One second we were… uh, talking, and the next she was gone. Can you check to see if maybe she… popped into her room?"

"Sure, come in."

He waited while Spring jogged up the stairs and returned.

"She's not here."

"Not here, or not here to me?" he asked, voice grim.

"No, I'd tell you if she didn't want to see you. She's honestly not here." Worry coated her words and ignited Coop's own nervousness.

"Is there anywhere you can think she might've gone? A special place she likes to visit?"

"She takes comfort in her animals. If she's not in the barn..."

"Morty?" he suggested.

"We can check."

He appreciated that she included him in the search.

They found Morty, a safari hat perched on his head, happily painting a jungle landscape. Backing from the room, they exchanged an anxious look.

"Where could she be, Spring?"

"I don't know. But come on, we can scry."

"I don't know what that means."

"There are two ways to go about searching. One is to gaze into a bowl of liquid or mirror. The other is to take something of hers, a necklace or ring, and hold it over a map in hopes of discovering a location. It works like a water divining rod. It will go right to the spot."

"Why aren't you working for the FBI and searching for fugitives?"

She giggled as only Spring could. "Come on, let's find my sister."

When they stepped through the door of an older, cramped section of the house, Spring waved a hand.

The vision before him pulsed and changed from one of dusty old boxes to a large open room. There wasn't a speck of dust to be found, and a large table at the center of the room was already lit with a dozen or more candles.

"Holy shit."

"It takes getting used to, I'm sure."

"Am I the only human to have seen what goes on here?"

Censure filled her green eyes. "We're human too, Coop."

"I didn't mean it the way it sounded."

"Tell us exactly what you *did* mean, Sheriff," Autumn snapped from behind him.

"I *meant* non-magical human," he stressed.

The anger didn't leave Autumn. "You should watch your words,

Coop. According to Saul, you've upset our sister again." She held up the chattering squirrel.

Getting used to witches was one thing. Getting used to witches communicating with animals was another and harder to wrap his brain around.

"She surprised me with her powers again. Y'all were born into this. For someone who has only known magic exists for maybe a month, it's still disconcerting at times."

His words provided Autumn with something to think about. He could tell she'd not viewed it from his perspective before.

"Perhaps if you'd have given Keaton more time to come to grips with it all…" he started to suggest.

"I don't talk about Keaton. Ever."

Her comment startled a short laugh from him. "Funny you should say that. He said the exact same thing about you. I think you two need to hash it out," Coop suggested.

"I think you need to get your own house in order," she retorted and presented her back. "Sister, let's scry for Summer."

"Can a mortal—"

Both sisters snorted their laughter.

"I'm really putting my foot in this, aren't I? Should we go with the Harry Potter description of muggle?" he joked.

"How about we call you dead if something has happened to my daughter?" Preston's voice countered.

Saul was handed off to Coop while the sisters prepared. During the entire time the women set up the altar to scry, the squirrel read him the riot act and scolded in furry rodent speak.

"I get it, Saul. I fucked up," he muttered. "Give it a rest."

The chattering became more emphatic.

"Yeah, I'll make it up to her. I swear."

The squirrel grunted his discontent but soon fell quiet as everyone leaned forward to see what the mirror held.

At first glance, Summer appeared relaxed on the beach, daiquiri in hand.

Coop was perturbed by her casual disregard for everyone's worry.

He'd almost turned away in anger, when he noted the shadow cast upon her body. "What's that?"

"More like *who*," growled Preston. "Get me a location, now!"

Autumn grabbed a map while Spring ran for Summer's room to find a piece of jewelry to use.

The rage simmering below Preston's coolly controlled exterior terrified Coop. He could literally feel the pulsing heat coming off the other man. While he didn't want to be here, Coop certainly didn't want to be Alastair when Preston showed up to retrieve his daughter.

"I'm surprised you'd leave the safety of the nest, Summer. It's not like you're the courageous one," Alastair said as he stood over her reclining body.

"Do you mind? You're blocking out my sun." If she appeared bored and unaffected, perhaps he'd leave off the cat and mouse game.

His deep chuckle almost sounded affectionate. "Do you mind if I join you?"

"Do I have a choice?"

"Not really."

She sighed and sat up. "Then by all means, Uncle. Sit."

Before his bottom hit the sand, a chair appeared beneath him.

Summer toyed with the idea of shifting it so he fell on his ass.

"You're smart not to give in to the urge," he told her.

"Was I that obvious?"

Again, he chuckled. "You and the boyfriend have a fight?"

"It's creepy that you watch us. Does it get your rocks off?"

Alastair tilted his head and studied her. "You *did* have a fight. It's the only reason you'd run away."

"We aren't in a relationship. You're mistaken if you think striking out at him will hurt me." She shrugged and took a casual sip of her drink.

"Never play poker, Summer Thorne. You don't have the face for it."

Dammit.

"What do you want, Uncle Alastair? I'd really like to get back to enjoying my vacation."

He leaned forward as if to impart a secret. The sun glistened off the sheen of his hair product. With the slicked-back blond hair and tan complexion, he reminded her of a movie actor of old 80s movies. Good-looking, but outdated.

"What if I told you I could give you what you want most in the world?" he offered.

"What if I told you to get bent?"

Anger flared to life in his eyes and turned his dark-blue eyes the color of a stormy sky. "Don't believe I can't hurt you, child. I don't want to, but I will." He sat back and fidgeted with his perfect red tie.

"Isn't the suit hot for...?" She glanced around. She *still* had no idea where she was.

"Mexico."

"Really? Huh. I would've thought I ended up in the Florida Keys," she mused aloud.

"Your training is sorely lacking, dear heart. Regardless, I can hand you a spell to bind the Carlyle boy to you for eternity. Would you like that?"

"If your smile wasn't smarmy, you might come across as genuine, Uncle. As it is... meh."

His brows clashed together, and his lips tightened to a thin white line. He took several deep breaths in what Summer assumed was an effort to control his temper.

To hide her shaky hand, she set her drink in the sand and leaned back on her flattened palms. "Besides, everyone knows there's no such thing as a love spell," she scoffed.

"Who said anything about love? I said binding spell."

He acted as if the offering was a special gift, but everyone knew magic done for your own personal gain came with a price.

"If he doesn't love me, I don't want him."

A smile, similar to that creepy fucking Cheshire Cat from Alice in Wonderland, bloomed across his face.

"Ah, dear Summer, thank you for confirming what I suspected."

Her stomach dropped into the sand. "And what is that?"

"You're in love with him."

She felt the blood leave her face, but she tried to bluff anyway. "That's a big nope. I suppose with age comes poor deductive reasoning."

"I'm offering you the moon and stars, child."

Yeah, but what did he want in return?

"I want the ape."

"Why?"

"You know, no one has bothered to ask that question until now," he laughed.

"I figure he must be pretty essential to some scheme you have planned. What's his purpose, Uncle?"

"He amuses me. I like to watch him paint."

Her gaze sharpened on his face. If one looked close enough, his tell was apparent just as hers had been. "I suppose I'm not the only one who shouldn't play poker."

"Look, I don't have much time. I expect Preston here momentarily. Trade me the monkey, and I'll spare the Sheriff."

"No." Denying his request was the hardest thing she'd ever had to do.

Alastair hadn't been prepared for her negative response. "No? What is one animal's life over true love?" he sneered.

"Because I don't have true love. The joke's on you. As for the animal, he's suffered enough abuse at your laboratory. I won't return him."

Lightning flashed across the sky, and the immediate crack of thunder shook the very ground she sat on.

Instead of making her fearful, his rage had the opposite effect.

Summer gathered her calm around her like a blanket and drew from her element the power she needed. Never taking her eyes from him, she imagined the wave forming.

The water's reversal caught his attention. The ocean receded at an alarming rate. "Don't! You'll kill us both!" he shouted.

"But then you can't hurt Morty or Coop."

"You're crazy!"

His panic fed her power.

"Summer, I don't want to hurt you, but I will," he warned, raising his hand, palm out and faced in her direction. "Stop the wave."

"Take a deep breath, Uncle. We wouldn't want you to drown."

"You foolish girl!"

Alastair, in a move that surprised her, lunged forward and wrapped his arms around her as the tidal wave crashed upon them.

The force of the ocean battered the bubble he'd created to encompass them.

"Pull it back!" he shouted over the roar of the sea. "Do it now, Summer!"

"I can't!" she yelled in return.

"Goddess, we're doomed. I can't hold it. I'm sorry, child."

Just as the bubble buckled under the pressure, the water rushed away, as if it were a blanket being torn back.

"Summer!"

The shout sounded as if it came from far away.

"I saved your life, Summer. I could've teleported, but I didn't. Remember that."

In a blink, Alastair was gone, and her father stood in his place.

"Dear Goddess, what were you thinking?" His large hands alternated between clutching her to him and shaking her. "Why would you ever take on someone like him alone? You foolish girl!"

She pulled back from his warm embrace. "I'm an adult. I knew what I was doing."

Her haughty proclamation was ruined by the chatter of her teeth.

"Then you have a damned death wish!" he thundered. "Is that it? You want to die because of that pathetic excuse for a man you claim to love?"

Her own anger built and warmed her. "I get that you're upset, Dad. But let me clarify a few things." She held up her index finger. "One, Coop is not a pathetic excuse for a man. He has a kind heart, and he champions the people of Leiper's Fork. He also would do anything to protect those he loves."

When Preston opened his mouth to argue, she held up her middle finger alongside the first. "Second, I don't have a death wish. I was trying to protect my family. If that costs me my life, then I consider it well spent."

"You—"

"I'm not finished," she snapped. "From this moment forward, you'll cease trying to intimidate Coop. Don't think we weren't listening at the keyhole while you threatened him with the fireball."

Her father smirked. "I know. I expected you to charge in any second. What kept you?"

Her answering smirk blossomed. "Winnie and Spring held me back."

He turned serious. "I won't stop intimidating him. He needs to earn your love."

"Aww, Dad. Please, give it a rest. Coop is never going to love me."

"He'd be a fool not to," he said gruffly as he pulled her into another embrace.

"Yeah, well, we won't argue that. But I'm not going to waste my time pining away. The Goddess has a plan for me. By Her grace, I intend to see it through."

"You're so much like your mother," he whispered achingly sweet.

"Everyone keeps saying that."

In that moment, she felt the kinship of love lost. But while she never truly held Coop's affections, her father and mother had a love to envy.

"Is that why you stay away from home?"

"When I'm on location, I have full hours of forgetfulness. I can get lost in my work and research. And for a brief time, I can pretend I'm not missing half of my soul."

She swallowed back the emotion clogging her throat. That's what her sanctuary and medical practice allowed her.

"But it's not because of you, my sunshine. I'd never stay away because of you. I need you to know that."

"I do, Daddy."

"Let's go home."

"Are we really in Mexico?"

He laughed. "Didn't think you had that kind of power, huh?"

"I pictured Key West."

Preston threw back his head and laughed.

For once, she wasn't ashamed of her wonky powers and laughed along with him.

19

*C*oop didn't have time to process what he'd seen before Preston returned with Summer in tow.

"What are you doing here?" she asked as if surprised he'd hung around.

Words refused to come. He had to touch her. Had to make sure she was alive and well. With great care, he cupped her face. The pads of his thumbs traced her sun-tinged cheekbones.

This small woman had taken on the big baddie, attempted a strike that would've taken her own life in order to protect him and Morty, and verbally defended Coop against her terrifying father.

"You're killing me, Summer Thorne," he said huskily. "Every time I turn around, you are throwing yourself in the path of danger to protect someone. Can you not do that anymore? Please?"

"I can't promise anything," she told him. Her seriousness was endearing.

He bit back an amused smile. "You're wrong, you know."

She frowned her question.

"I do love you."

"You don't need to say—"

Coop cut her off by gently settling his lips on hers. A butterfly kiss. "I love you, Summer."

"No, you're just—"

He kissed her again, harder. "I. Love. You."

Tears flooded her eyes.

A pang of fear struck. "Am I too late?"

She stared, seemingly unable to decide.

A sniffle from somewhere behind him reminded Coop they weren't alone. "Can we talk somewhere private?"

"That's mean spirited, Sheriff. This is better than the Hallmark channel," Autumn inserted.

Coop hung his head and sighed. Her family was killing this for him. "Maybe you can teleport us out of here," he suggested, hoping she'd take it as an olive branch.

Preston laughed. "Not a good idea, Carlyle. She thought she went to Florida."

A fiery blush stained Summer's skin. "He's right."

"I don't care as long as I'm there with you." Coop brushed back her wild mane of hair.

"Coop developed game," Autumn crowed.

"Or duct tape. I'd be happy if you could conjure duct tape to shut—"

Summer's hand flew up to cover his mouth. "She's more skilled than I am. You might not want to go there."

"And she's got a worse temper, too," Spring added cheerfully.

Running footsteps alerted them to company. Winnie skidded to a halt just inside the room and used the doorframe to halt her forward movement. "What did I miss?"

"I'll leave you all to fill her in," Summer said as she walked toward the exit. "I need to check on Morty."

"The house is protected, sunshine. Not even Alastair can break the wards we put in place," Preston assured her.

Coop drew to a stop in front of the other man. "I'm assuming a ward is a spell to keep evil out?" When he received confirmation, Coop asked, "Does that include muggles?"

"What the hell is a muggle?" Preston demanded.

Spring giggled. "It's his way of saying non-witches, Dad."

"You're referencing Harry Potter?" Summer asked incredulously.

Coop grabbed her hand and squeezed, but otherwise ignored her question.

Her father nodded. "Yes. It includes non-witches."

"How does your house determine intent? I mean, I've walked in twice with no one around."

"You obviously never intended the occupants of the house any harm," the older man said. "We don't lock the door. If you can open it and walk in, the wards have judged you safe."

"Does this only apply to the house? What about the barn and the rest of the out buildings?" Coop asked.

Preston seemed surprised by the question. "I hadn't thought to protect the out buildings. The Thorne grimoire is here."

Good grief there was a lot to learn. "What is a grimoire?"

"Spellbook," Summer supplied as she continued to try to pull her hand away.

Coop nodded and addressed Preston again. "I think it would be a good idea to protect the entire property from now on, don't you?"

"Indeed."

Coop tightened his fingers around Summer's. "Do you need Summer for this?"

Her father's face softened infinitesimally as he focused on his daughter. "We always need her. She's vital to our family. But in this, her other sisters can help me."

"Thank you, Mr. Thorne."

Surprised, Preston asked, "For what?"

"For saving me from Alastair's attack. In all the excitement, I failed to thank you properly."

"You can thank me by not hurting my daughter again."

"That's the plan."

The two men shared a moment of understanding.

Coop faced Summer and brought their joined hands to his lips. "Ready?"

If questioned, he'd have to admit she looked as if she were going to the gallows. It didn't bode well for his cause.

"Morty's welfare first, then we talk."

Her expression eased into a soft smile. "Morty first."

When they entered the attic loft Morty called home, he appeared happy as he picked banana slices from the food bowl in front of him.

"Hey, buddy," Coop called in low tones.

Morty signed, and whatever he'd said had Summer placing her hand over her mouth.

"What did he say?"

"He said, 'I love you'."

"Of course he loves you, you're his Mama."

"No, Coop. He meant you."

Aww, hell. Didn't that just gut a fella? He discovered the need to clear his throat.

"I love you too, Morty."

The chimp put his arms up and puckered his lips. It was the first real affectionate gesture he'd shown Coop other than grooming his hair during the week Summer had been recovering.

Coop bent and offered his face.

Morty leaned in and... blew a raspberry on his cheek. Lips drawn back to reveal his version of a grin, Morty hooted.

Summer's unrestrained giggles joined Morty's raucous laughter.

Coop picked banana pieces off his face and out of his hair.

"You both set me up for that one, didn't you?"

"Yep," she laughed. "Sir Mortimer loves a good prank."

"Were you toying with my affections, buddy?"

Morty nodded vigorously and blew him a kiss.

"Come on, you little beast. Show me what you've painted today."

Chubby fingers gripped his and dragged him toward the canvas.

As he studied the landscape, Coop's curiosity got the better of him. "How does he know what to paint? I'm assuming he was never in the wild, yet he paints this jungle scene like he's been there."

Summer joined him, her brows dipped into a thoughtful frown. "You know, I never thought about it at length. I assumed he'd seen a picture or memorized a scene from the television."

He leaned closer to examine the surprisingly detailed painting. "What's this? Is that a shovel?"

"It is!" she exclaimed. "Why would he paint a shovel in the middle of the jungle?"

"You think this is why old Uncle Al wants him? For his talent?"

"No. My uncle is only ever after anything that will help him amass power. It's why I don't understand his reason for wanting Morty…"

Her face took on a contemplative expression, and she rushed to the covered canvases at the back of the room. With a care for the paintings, she ripped off the sheet. "Help me bring them over by the light."

Even Morty got into the act. Soon, four more canvases were lined up along the wall in front of the window.

The images were of pyramids, a jungle, a beach which looked remarkably like the one Summer teleported to, and a snow-capped mountain. Each scene had a shovel resting against a tree.

"Are these all his paintings?" Coop asked, glancing around the attic.

"Yes. He paints constantly. We erase the canvases and give them back to him."

"So we have no idea if he's created any scenes other than these."

Summer shrugged and shook her head. "Most days one of us praises his work, wipes the canvas, and replenishes his paint supply. I feel like an idiot for not seeing this before now."

"I think we may know why your uncle wants him. Did White Labs always have him in their custody?"

"I don't know. Aunt GiGi might."

"I wonder if she knew Morty was painting treasure maps." Coop whipped out his smartphone and took photos from various angles of each painting. "Let's find a way to keep hidden what we have here. In the meantime, don't tell anyone. Not even your sisters."

"Coop, we don't hide anything in our family."

He shot a nervous glance around the room and covered the paintings.

"What are you doing?" she asked, helping him straighten the sheet.

"When your sisters scried for you, we witnessed your conversation with Alastair on the beach. I don't want what we discuss overheard. I got the impression if you possess the ability, you can spy on anyone with only a mirror."

"Yes. Most witches wouldn't because we all know we wouldn't like to have *our* privacy invaded."

"Right, but what if Morty is painting these scenes, these treasure maps of sorts, and Alastair is spying and documenting each scene?"

Comprehension dawned. "He can't. The wards prevent it. If the paintings were outside the house, then maybe he could."

"Okay. I feel marginally better, but let's not take chances okay?"

"I agree."

Their gazes collided, and Coop knew the time was upon them to discuss their relationship.

She knew it, too.

He extended his hand and waited while she made up her mind.

For every second Summer delayed, Coop died a thousand deaths. But he deserved her distrust. Time and time again, he'd crushed her hopes when she offered her love. Sometimes on purpose, and sometimes accidentally.

Right now she had the power to crush his.

Her rapid breathing indicated her uncertainty, and Coop hated himself for his part in building on her insecurities.

"I won't hurt you again, sweetheart. Not on purpose."

SUMMER, FROZEN WITH INDECISION, CONTEMPLATED THE HAND REACHING for her. If she gave in, if she trusted him again and he betrayed her, a part of her soul would shrivel and die.

But what was the alternative? A long, lonely life without Coop.

He'd been her obsession for the better part of a quarter of a century.

To him, her crush started in high school.

For her, love started the day he handed her his cone when they were small children.

She'd seen his inner light and wanted part of that beautiful glow for her own.

Nothing had changed. She still wanted him. She always would. But it didn't mean theirs was a healthy relationship. And what did it say if she continued to forgive him at every turn?

Alastair said she wasn't the courageous one, but he was wrong. It took strength and determination to continually hold her head high when everyone mocked her.

She peeked at Coop and bit her lip.

The intensity in his eyes was shaded by worry.

If she refused him now, a nail would be added to the coffin of their relationship.

He knew it.

She knew it.

And yet she didn't have it in her to place her hand in his.

Bleakness settled like shutters over his blue eyes.

Coop dropped his hand.

"I'm sorry, Coop. I can't."

"I understand. I do." His gaze fell to the floor. "I'll, um, I'll send Knox to help out around here until we determine Alastair's plan."

"You don't need to do that."

"I'd feel better if there was another man around in addition to your dad."

"We can take care of ourselves."

He closed his eyes and sighed heavily. "Summer, please," he pleaded softly. "Humor me on this one. At least until this situation with your uncle is resolved."

"Okay."

"Thank you."

Coop squatted in front of Morty. "You take care of Mama, buddy."

Morty's forlorn expression caused an ache in her heart.

When Coop straightened, he caught her eye and graced her with a bittersweet smile. "Well, that's it then. Catch ya on the flip side, Summer Thorne."

Words left unsaid floated in the air around them.

"If you change your mind, you know where to find me."

"Goodbye, Cooper." The finality in her tone couldn't be ignored.

Summer stared at the doorway long after he'd left. Her shaky legs were unable to hold her, and she dropped to the wooden floor. In an attempt to offer comfort, Morty curled up in her lap, and Saul snuggled against her neck.

She had her boys. She'd be all right. Or so she kept telling herself. A large part of her wanted to sob her grief. But she'd sworn to herself after the last time she wouldn't give in to tears. Wouldn't give in to the crippling emotions lost love provided. The wretched feeling would pass —eventually.

Only a little more wallowing, then she'd get off this floor and finish packing for her move.

Shadows darkened the attic, and still she sat.

That's where Autumn found her.

Her sister sat next to her. "Hey."

"Hey." Her return greeting came out dry and scratchy.

"Coop left?"

Summer nodded, still staring at the empty doorway, unable to look away.

Perhaps a small part of her never expected Coop to meekly leave. He wasn't the type. The Cooper Carlyles of the world took what they wanted, didn't they?

"Want to talk about it?"

She shook her head.

"I've been where you are, sister." Autumn stroked Summer's hair back from her face. "It's as if someone has taken a dull blade and carved your heart from your chest."

"I sent him away," Summer whispered.

"You didn't believe he told the truth about his feelings for you?"

"We were never meant to be. I pushed and pushed, wanting more than he was willing to give. At every turn, he shoved me away. Now *he* wants *me*. Or at least that's what he says."

"Why can't you accept that he does?"

"Because earlier today he rejected me," Summer confessed on a ragged exhale.

Autumn removed a sleepy Morty from Summer's arms and placed him in his bed. Her sister then tugged Summer to her feet and ducked to meet her eyes. "The man who watched you in the mirror was a man in love, sister. He was half-crazed when he saw Alastair approach you on that beach."

Summer focused on Autumn's earnestness. The truth of her words couldn't be ignored.

"You weren't there and couldn't see, but I did. It was as if you throat punched him when you said you didn't have true love. But in the next instant, you were going toe to toe with Alastair. You were willing to trade your life to save Coop and Morty. Then he knew." Autumn smiled, and it softened her standard cynical expression. "He paced a hole in the floor waiting for your return."

"Something inside me is broken, Tums." Summer shook her head slowly. "He stood right here and promised not to hurt me again. I couldn't close the distance to take his hand. Couldn't believe him."

"Was a small part of you tempted to accept Alastair's offer of a binding spell?"

"No. I could never do that to Coop. Or to Morty."

"Then you have your answer, sister."

"I don't understand."

Autumn snorted and shook her head at Summer's obtuseness. "You were willing to die for him. What love is truer than that?" She threw up her hands. "If Keaton had offered me even half of what Coop is offering you, I'd have grabbed it with both hands."

"I'm sorry, Tums."

"Don't be. I was a hormonal kid with stupid dreams. But you? What you have with Coop is real. You'd be a fool to throw it away."

"I'm afraid I already did." The tears started then. All the self-pity she didn't know she'd stockpiled poured out of Summer.

"Then stop being a whiny bitch and go after him." Autumn softened her words with a grin and a hug.

*C*oop took a pull of his beer and stared at the darkening panorama. One by one, small twinkling stars dotted the inky sky. The night was exceptionally warm, and he sat in his swimming trunks as he waited for the evening air to dry them from his earlier dip.

Headlights sped down the road toward him. He ignored the vehicle as it turned into the drive. It wasn't Summer's van, and he couldn't care less who might be visiting.

A car door slammed, and heels clicked along the cement path leading to the overlarge front porch.

"Coop?"

Rosie McDonough. The absolute last person on earth he cared to see.

"Rosie. What's up?"

"I haven't seen much of you in town lately. The third Friday of the month you can almost always be found at the Hitching Post."

Yeah, it was in no way creepy that she knew his schedule.

"What do you want, Rosie?"

She moved closer and ran her hand along his bare shin, inching it up to caress his knee. "A woman has needs, Coop."

Angry at the female population in general, he dropped his feet and surged upright. "And you came out here thinking that I'd what? Bend you over the porch railing and scratch your itch?"

A spark of true interest flared to life in her eyes—much different from the act she'd put on a moment ago. She sidled closer and tip-toed her fingers up his chest. She paused to circle the nipple and then laid her hand flat over his heart. "That works for me."

Well, it damned well didn't work for him. Rosie was beautiful and perfect like a high-quality, faceted diamond. Designed to sparkle and reflect brilliance, yet just as cold and hard.

"Go home, Rosie."

"Don't be that way, Sheriff."

"I'm not in the mood."

Her over-confident smile should've warned him of her intent, but the beers had dulled his brain.

In a flash, she'd draped herself against him, crushed her augmented double D's against his chest, and sought his mouth with her own.

His hands found her hips, but his intent to shove her back came too late.

A creaking of the wood and gasp alerted him to another presence, the one he'd been hoping for all evening. *Summer.*

He yanked back as if burned.

Christ, he couldn't catch a break where she was concerned.

Coop dragged Rosie's arms from where they were hooked behind his neck. "Summer, it's not what it looks like."

"Let me tell you what it looks like to me. Then you can tell me if what I'm seeing is correct," Summer suggested.

Where her calm came from was anyone's guess, because if the situation were reversed, he would be pounding any man found kissing her right into the ground at this point.

"When I walked up, Rosie had her tongue tickling your tonsils. You weren't doing much to shove her away. Now, you are standing there with her lipgloss highlighting your mouth, trying to find a way to justify the fact I caught you in a lip-lock. How am I doing so far?"

"Give it up, C.C. She's found out about us," Rosie purred as she ran an arm up his bare chest.

He felt as ill as Summer looked. "I swear, it's not what you think."

Moisture was building in her pain-filled blue eyes. She nodded and turned to go. He suspected it was because she didn't want to shame herself by crying in front of Rosie.

Emotion caused his voice to crack. "Summer, please."

He was behind her in an instant. Placing his hands on her waist, he spun her back to face him. "She came on to me seconds before you walked up. I didn't have time to react."

"This is a replay of eleven years ago, Coop. You don't have to keep setting me up this way. I'm a big girl. I can take it when someone isn't interested."

"See, C.C.? She understands," Rosie said. Smugness coated her words like a blanket.

"I swear, it wasn't a set up."

"Whatever you do is your business. I'm just embarrassed to find you making out on the porch," Summer informed him.

"Oh, honey, you need to develop a better poker face. Yours says you're lying," Rosie laughed.

ONE WART. IF SUMMER COULD JUST CONJURE ONE UGLY-ASS WART ON the forehead of that rotten little tart, she would never ask her witch ancestors for another thing. She squinted and concentrated her hardest. *Was that a bump forming?*

Because Summer was drained, she let it go. Her magic was wonky at the best of times. If she pushed when exhaustion had set in, the spell was likely to backfire, and she'd cover herself with boils.

"We're done here, Rosie," Coop snapped.

"Oh, no, Sheriff. We are *far* from done," she countered with a husky laugh. "However, if you want to convince poor pathetic Summer, I suppose I don't mind playing along."

Enough was enough. Rosie's snide comments snapped the last wire holding Summer's temper in place. "Tell the truth, dammit!"

She sneezed.

The chatter of rodents could be heard as they scurried down along the wooden planks of the porch.

She closed her eyes and groaned. This was why she never swore.

When she did, she was inundated with mice. Every. Single. Time. Autumn was right, Summer was the witchy Pied Piper of Leiper's Fork.

Cooper and Rosie, as if automatons, started reciting the facts of their kiss in unison. Their voices were emotionless as they relayed the details of how Coop had been sitting and drinking his beer when Rosie arrived uninvited, came onto him, then kissed him after he rejected her.

Summer didn't even have time to register the success of her magic before Cooper recovered his will and lost his shit. "What the hell was *that*? How…? Who…? Why…?"

"You forgot where and when," Summer couldn't resist adding. She should've if the redness of his face was any indication. Causing Coop a stroke wasn't on her agenda for today.

Rosie, white-faced and on the verge of hysteria, backed away from Summer and her army of rodents. "You're evil!"

"I'm not the one throwing myself at all the men in Leiper's Fork or blowing my way into management positions." Summer would've used the word fucking, but she didn't need to add to her collection of mice.

Rosie's skin turned an alarming shade of purple. In all seriousness, someone was probably going to have a stroke before the night was out. If anyone had to, Summer hoped it would be Rosie. Taking delight in watching her drool out of the side of her mouth for the remainder of her days would be mean but entertaining all the same.

Soundlessly, Autumn appeared behind Summer's nemesis and put a finger to her lips. With her other hand, she swirled a pattern around the area of Rosie's head while silently mouthing a spell. Then she winked and disappeared as silently as she'd arrived. *Her sister was a ninja.*

While Rosie remained in a blank state, Summer shooed her mice away and faced a gobsmacked Cooper. "Sit down and prop your feet up."

To her surprise, he sat without an argument, and Summer plunked down in his lap and wiped the hated garish lipgloss from his mouth. A second before snapping her fingers, she said, "Play along."

The trance left, and Rosie stared. "I didn't see you when I walked up." She spun around to check behind her and returned her confused gaze to view Summer's smug expression. "Since when are you and Coop an item?" she demanded.

Coop surprised them all when he answered, "Always, and we always will be."

His arm tightened around her, and Rosie was forgotten.

Summer wanted so badly to kiss him in that moment. But she refused to give in to the urge. What if she ended up with Rosie cooties? Coop was going to need to wash his mouth out with disinfectant or something.

Without tearing his eyes from Summer's, Coop addressed Rosie, "Was there an emergency or something you needed?"

"Can I talk to you in private, Coop?" Rosie asked, her most seductive pose in place.

"Is it official business? Because if it isn't, the answer is a standing no. If it is, then you need to go through proper channels, Rosie."

Summer's heart swelled to bursting.

Coop was laying down the ground rules and assuring her he meant to keep them.

"No more game playing," he said in a low, sweet tone. "I love you, Summer Thorne."

Rosie gasped. "You and Summer? You can't be serious?" The sexy, throaty invitation was gone and in its place was the voice of a shrew.

"Quite serious," Coop returned, expression and voice hard, the no-nonsense Sheriff through and through. "Have a good night, Rosie. And in the future, you're not welcome on Carlyle property. The sheriff's department is open twenty-four-seven if you need assistance."

She took a step forward in her fury. The cloying scent of her expensive perfume permeated the air. "No one rejects me, Cooper Carlyle."

Summer sighed and rose to her feet. "This is like a bad eighties movie. I should know because I binge watched a ton of them last weekend." Getting right up in Rosie's grill, she said, "Let me give it to you straight. The perky, mean-spirited high-school cheerleader always loses out to the spunky, little science nerd in the end. Guess who is who in this little scenario."

Rosie's lips curled back in a perfect imitation of an enraged Morty.

Leaning in, Summer whispered, "Careful, Rosie, your ugly is showing."

Coop rose to wrap a proprietary arm around Summer's waist. "If you don't mind, we'd like to get back to our evening."

"Always so politically correct," Summer murmured after Rosie had walked away.

"Question."

She peered up into his austere face. Her stomach dropped with a clunk. "Sure."

"Do I have to worry about your sister popping in to erase my memory?"

"Is this a serious question?"

"You bet your life it is."

Summer shrugged. "I can't control Autumn, Coop, and I wouldn't want to. However, I will make her promise not to wipe your memory."

"Ever. She can't do it ever," he stated firmly.

"Done."

"I have another question."

"Shoot."

He grimaced. "Yeah, we aren't going to use that word."

"Gotcha. I think we need a pen and paper for this list of rules forming."

"No rules, sweetheart. Well, except for the memory erase thing. That terrifies me." He wove his fingers into her hair and lowered his head as if to kiss her.

Summer pulled back.

"Does this mean you aren't here for us?" he asked.

"Oh, no. I am. But I'm not kissing you until you wash the Rosie cooties from your mouth."

"Will beer work?"

"Bleach would be better, but I suppose the alcohol is good enough."

He laughed and released her. "After I brush my teeth and gargle, I'm going to kiss the hell out of you, Summer Thorne."

"And I'm going to let you, Cooper Carlyle."

He toyed with a lock of her hair. "I accept you for who and what you are. But can we keep magic out of the bedroom?"

"We can try, but if you want me to talk dirty, we might have a rodent audience."

He gave a laugh and a light tug of her hair. "I'm okay with that as long as they don't hold up signs judging my performance."

"I'll be the only one judging your performance."

The heat in his eyes told her she had nothing to worry about in the sex department. Coop would in all likelihood rank tens across the board.

"Coop, before we, you know—"

"Have sex?"

"Yeah, um, can we talk?"

"We can take this as slow as you need to."

"No, it's not that. I just need you to understand a few things before you're in too deep."

"I'm already in too deep, Summer. The realization hit me when you were on the beach and the tsunami struck."

"You know I caused that wave, right?"

"I do. And as waves go, it was pretty fucking impressive. Or it would've been had it not been about to kill you." He shook his head and exhaled. "I'm grateful your father could get to you in time."

Because there wasn't an easy way to say it, she blurted, "Our children will be witches."

His slack-jawed expression had her biting her lip.

Coop had no words. Twice he opened his mouth to speak, and twice he shut it, unable to vocalize his discombobulated thoughts.

Kids. *Jesus!* Was she already to the marriage stage in her mind?

Because in *his* mind, he'd never gotten beyond doing wild, wicked things to Summer's hot, curvy body.

"Say something."

Her anxiety caused her voice to break. Once again, his reaction was freaking her out. Without needing to ask, he knew rejection was her worst fear.

"I don't know what to say," he confessed. "I hadn't gotten that far. Hell, we've only kissed three times, Summer. I hadn't thought about the future, or marriage and babies."

Her musical laughter rang out and surprised him yet again.

"I wasn't expecting you to drop to your knee and propose, Coop.

But if you're that guy who wants a home, hearth, and 2.5 kids, you should know before we go further that any child of mine, by the Goddess's grace, will have powers."

If he'd thought about it before now, he'd have come to that conclusion. But he hadn't, and he didn't know how he felt about having little witches or warlocks running around. "Will they have the power to erase my memories?"

"This is a serious issue for you, isn't it?" she laughed.

"It kind of is."

"We'll cast a mind protection spell for you."

The twinkle in her eye belied her words.

He crossed his arms and raised a brow. "There's no such thing, is there?"

Her straight white teeth captured the corner of her lower lip, and she shook her head.

"Great. Just great. Every time one of our kids decides to sneak out, they just need to wave their hands around my head and wiggle their nose."

"I'll teach you to scry. You'll always be a step ahead of them."

*S*ummer felt conspicuous as she perched on the edge of the living room sofa.

Keaton wandered into the room. "C.C. asked me to entertain you for a bit while he takes a shower. He said something about a scorching shower to disinfect Rosie cooties, whatever that meant."

She bit back her smile.

"I don't pretend to know what's going on with you two, Summer. But I do know I don't want to see his heart crushed. He should have free will in all things."

Coop's brother was worried. His downturned mouth and solemn eyes told a story all their own.

"Keaton, we cannot control someone's will," she said gently. "Whatever you felt for my sister when you were dating was real."

"We're not talking about Autumn."

"I think we are. You're under a misguided belief that we can cast spells willy-nilly. To a degree, witches can. But you should know, there are laws in the magical world just as there are laws in the non-magical world." She frowned and tried to explain. "There is no such thing as a love spell, desire spell, or any type of will-altering spell to make you attracted to someone you wouldn't normally be attracted to."

He burrowed his hands into the hair on either side of his temples. "You're wrong."

"I'm not."

"Then why was I so consumed? My every waking thought was Autumn. Hell, my every dream was of her." His scathing tone hinted at bitterness.

"That was all you, Keaton. But even if a spell like that existed, a twenty-two-year-old young woman doesn't have the experience or power to cast it. Not without help from a more experienced witch." She shrugged. "Aunt GiGi was our mentor. She'd never condone something like that even if it were possible."

He paled. "If she didn't…"

Summer waited him out. Keaton needed to wrap his head around his mistake.

"If she didn't, then I'm a complete ass."

She inched forward and placed her hand on his. "No. You were young and scared. But you should know, she loved you."

"Past tense," he said softly. He wasn't asking a question but stating what he believed to be fact.

Summer didn't have an answer. "I don't know her feelings now. She won't talk about you. Or she wouldn't until the day you showed up about your truck."

"What did she say?"

"I'm not going to betray a confidence. But you owe her an apology for your ugliness that day."

His stubborn expression returned. "She torched my truck."

"And you broke her heart by sleeping with another woman. I'd say you're even."

"Not even close. For almost ten years, she bound me." He stood to pace. "You preach free will, but she made it so I couldn't reveal what you were. Not in speech, not in writing. I felt like I was losing my damned mind." White-hot rage made his voice hoarse.

Summer realized Keaton wouldn't get over his anger anytime soon, and her heart pinged for her sister. Autumn's battle, if she chose to fight for Keaton, would be all uphill. But her stubbornness matched his. The probability of these two strong-willed individuals setting aside their differences was slim to none.

"She thought she was protecting her family. You know how she was; young, impulsive, fierce," Summer tried to explain.

He shook his head. "I don't want to discuss her. The remote is on the table. You can entertain yourself. C.C. should be done soon." He glared down at her. "Don't you dare hurt him. Don't even *think* about using magic on him. *Ever.* I'll tear your family apart."

"Keaton!" Coop snapped out his brother's name as warning. "Whatever your issue is with Autumn, that's between the two of you. But Summer doesn't deserve your hatefulness."

The two brothers, alike in size and looks, squared off.

"You can't see it, but I can," Keaton sneered. "She has you wrapped around her finger ready to fight your own brother for a taste of her magic pussy."

Summer gasped at his crudeness.

"The only reason I'm not throat punching you right now is because you're my brother and I love you. But talk about her like that again, and I won't hold back." The ice in Coop's tone chilled Summer to her core.

"Guys, please don't fight." She inserted herself between them, her back pressed to Coop. "Keaton, I swear on my life, and the lives of my sisters, Coop will always have free will in our relationship for as long as it lasts." She placed a hand on Keaton's arm. "If you believe nothing else, believe me when I say that I don't want anyone that doesn't want me. I'd like to think I have more pride than that."

"Pride? Really?" he scoffed. "This whole town knows you've been in love with him since the second you set eyes on him." He didn't soften his stance. "I'm sorry, Summer, but I don't believe you. I don't believe you wouldn't do anything within your power to have him."

Her own anger took hold. "Then why wouldn't I have done it years ago?"

Coop's arms enfolded her from behind. "Sweetheart, you don't have to justify anything to him. He's determined to be a bitter fucktard. You can't change that."

Keaton laughed humorlessly. "Oh, that's rich coming from you. You sat here not two weeks ago, drunk off your ass, telling everyone to shut up when they tried to talk to you. All because of a little lover's spat between you two."

"Yeah, well it didn't take me ten years to wake the hell up," Coop retorted.

Keaton scrunched his nose and squinted his eyes. "Didn't it, though?"

"I'm going to go," Summer said. "Coop, when things have settled down on both sides, we can talk."

"Both sides? What's that supposed to mean? Your family thinks you're too good for my brother?" Keaton demanded in an abrupt about-face.

"No. There are other factors in play, Keaton. I'm done defending my family to you," she snapped.

Coop's arms tightened. "You aren't going anywhere, Summer." To his brother he said, "Keaton, don't you have a kid to tuck in for the night or horses to check?"

Keaton threw up his hands in surrender. "Fine. Don't say I didn't warn you."

CLASHING WITH HIS BROTHER DIDN'T SIT WELL. BUT COOP WOULD BE damned if Keaton would dictate his relationship. "I'm sorry."

"Don't apologize for someone else. You can't control their actions, Coop."

He cupped her face and met her eyes. "I need you to know, I don't believe anything he was spouting."

Her face morphed from upset to sanguine. "And I need you to know, I'll never use what limited power I have on you."

"Limited?" he snorted. "I think you underestimate yourself, sweetheart. The things I've seen you do don't appear to be a novice witch."

"Oh, and do you know many witches?" she challenged.

"There's only one witch I want to know." Coop bent his head and brushed his lips lightly against hers, a test of the waters.

Her response was all he could've hoped for and more. Her arms came around him, and she rose on her toes to press closer.

He pulled back and quirked a brow. "No lingering Rosie cooties?"

"Not that I can tell. You taste like pure Coop based on the few kisses we've shared."

"Excellent. Let's make out."

Her giggle warmed his heart.

"I'd sweep you up and carry you, but my room is upstairs, and I'm not as young as I used to be."

Summer squinted her glorious eyes. "Are you saying I'm fat, Cooper Carlyle?"

"Hell, no! You're a wet dream with those curves." To emphasize his point, he cupped her full breasts and sighed. "I could feast on your beauty for days."

"That just scored you major Brownie points."

"Yeah, about that Brownie Brigade thing, can you still squeeze into the uniform? Because I have a thing for women in tight little skirts."

"Like this?" She waved her hands and created a sexy, adult version of a Girl Scout uniform.

The material barely covered her butt cheeks. Coop was in heaven.

"Fuck. Yes!" He ran a hand under her skirt to cup her ass. "I think I'm going to like this particular parlor trick of yours."

They raced up the stairs with Coop insisting on Summer going first in order to catch a glimpse beneath her miniskirt.

She laughingly held her hands behind her all the way to the top.

"Second door on the left," he instructed as she hesitated.

"Now that we're upstairs, and there's no chance of breaking your back, I think you should carry me," she teased.

The sparkle in her eye sang to his heart. If he wasn't eager to taste every inch of her, he would've stayed in this moment forever.

"Whatever the lady wants," he murmured against her lips. But instead of the grand sweeping gesture she expected, he scooped her up in a fireman's hold and tossed her over his shoulder.

Her squeal almost brought the walls down around them.

With a chuckle, he swatted her ass. Not hard enough to hurt, just enough to get her attention. "Quiet, woman! You'll wake the house."

"You are so going to get it when I get loose," Summer threatened.

"That's what I'm hoping," he quipped.

After entering his room, he quietly shut and locked the door before shifting Summer in his arms to gaze into her beautiful flushed face. "Have I told you how happy I am you decided to give me another chance?"

"After you left today, I didn't know how to react. I only knew that I didn't want to move from that spot. That if I did, it would make the whole thing real. It would mean you were gone from my life for good."

He remained silent to give her the opportunity to formulate the words.

"Autumn told me that if Keaton had offered her even half the love you'd laid on the line, she'd have grabbed it with both hands. I think it was her way of calling me an idiot for letting you leave."

"You're the smart one in this duo, sweetheart. Sometimes your capacity for love and forgiveness scares me."

"Why?"

Coop crossed to the bed and sat on the edge, cradling her in his lap. He took his time answering

"Because I don't deserve you," he finally said. "You're too good for me. I knew that eleven years ago, and I know it now. Maybe that's why I tried to hurt you back then. Maybe it was my way of saving you from me."

"You're a much better person than you know." She stroked her fingertips over his furrowed brow and down his cheek until she reached his lips. The light caress shot straight to his groin by way of his heart.

"You see the good in me. Like I said, it scares the hell out of me."

"I see you for who you are, Coop. Flaws and all. None of it matters."

He kissed her.

There was no way he couldn't when she said something that profound. The kiss was beautiful in its simplicity. Lips on lips in a gentle touch to convey all the words a man didn't know how to say aloud.

She drew back, and their eyes connected in a perfect moment of understanding.

Within seconds, mischief altered her expression, and she shifted to straddle him. "I believe we were about to get busy before you became all serious on me."

His hands gripped the smooth skin of her upper thighs and his fingers toyed with the hemline of the skirt. Coop opened his mouth to speak, but the not-so-subtle shift of her pelvis against his dick chased any thoughts out of his head.

He sucked in a sharp breath. "Oh, babe."

She laughed and nipped his lip.

In a spiral roll that would do an alligator proud, he pinned her beneath him. "You have too many clothes on," he growled.

As he reached for the zipper of her skirt, the material dissolved into thin air.

"I think I'm going to like magic in the bedroom," he laughed. "Can we make the shirt go the same route?"

Her shirt disappeared, leaving her in a matching bra and panty set.

"Oh, babe," he said again. "I don't think I've ever seen anything as beautiful as you are at this moment." And he hadn't. With the color high in her cheeks, her blond curls spread over his chocolate colored pillow-case, and her glorious chest heaving in her red lace underwear, Summer stole his breath away.

He buried his face in the valley of her breasts and sighed his plea-sure. The silky-smooth softness of her skin begged to be kissed, and Coop ran featherlight kisses up across the divide between the mounds. He scooped her breast from beneath the bra's cup and nuzzled the hard-ened nipple before circling his tongue around the tip.

A sultry moan escaped her lips and egged him on. He gently bit down then sucked her into his mouth. Her hands came up to cradle the back of his skull and press him closer. Coop became more aggressive in his ministrations.

"Oh, Coop," she gasped.

The sound of his name in that breathy little voice caused the blood to drain from his head straight to his cock. He'd never tire of hearing her pleasure-filled gasps.

Coop tasted his way down the slight curve of her stomach on his way to the promised land. With one finger, he dipped beneath the edge of her panties and glided along the wetness he found there. "So hot," he murmured. "So fucking hot."

She squirmed beneath his touch when he grazed his teeth along the satiny material covering. In his experience, it wouldn't take much to send her over the edge. He grinned against her mound and applied pressure with his tongue. In a move that made him blink, her panties dissolved into a red mist.

He lifted his head and met her desire-laden gaze.

"I thought I'd help you," she said saucily, one brow lifted in challenge.

"Impatient much?"

"You have no idea."

Coop swirled his fingers up and down along her slick opening, never taking his eyes from hers. When he inserted a finger, Summer's eyes rolled back.

"Again," she whispered.

He slid in another finger.

"Goddess!" she groaned. "Again."

Coop continued to finger her. Sometimes hard and fast. Sometimes gentle and slow. Stopping now and again to worship her with his tongue. He took an inordinate amount of time and leisurely explored every part of her below the waist.

With her fingers tangled in his hair, she urged him on—both with words, whimpers, and hip thrusts. His tongue toyed with her clit and she squealed when he bit down, bucking wildly against his mouth as the wave of release crashed upon her.

He didn't give her time to recover. Tightening his hold on her hips, he dove in for seconds. Tasting. Teasing. Tantalizing.

When she was on the verge of another orgasm, he stopped and rose to his knees.

"Please," Summer begged.

Her tongue swept across her parted lips. The glistening sight of her cherry lips made his cock jump and cum bead on its head.

"Please, Coop."

Along the way, she'd magically dispensed with his clothing, for which Coop was exceedingly grateful. He didn't want to break their contact any more than she did.

He gripped himself and worked the tip along her wet folds. "Tell me what you want."

"You. In me. *Now*."

As Coop went for the condoms in the top dresser drawer, Summer stopped the forward movement of his hand.

"No need."

His heart hammered in his chest. "For a condom?"

"Not unless you want to. Witches can't catch STDs."

"What about baby witches?"

"Already taken care of."

"Oh, sweetheart, you know how to make a man's dick stand up and salute you."

She giggled and wrapped her hand around his girth, giving him a light tug. "*Now*."

"You're a pushy little thing. I like it."

He sank into her warmth with a long, low groan. When she contracted around him, he hissed. "Fuck *me*, you feel so tight."

"Don't be gentle, Coop."

His wits deserted him.

"You heard me. Fuck me like you mean it," she growled.

He didn't have time to ponder why she didn't sneeze, but he was grateful for the lack of a rodent audience.

With one arm hooked around her knee, he lifted and parted her wider.

Thrust after thrust, he pounded into her as she voiced her encouragement with words like harder, faster, deeper.

Sweat beaded his brow as he fought to hold back his orgasm.

"Come for me, babe," he urged.

Summer dragged his mouth to her breast. "Suck me, Coop," she panted.

Christ, he wasn't going to make it. The tightening of his balls told him his time was near.

He cupped her and drew her pebbled bud into his mouth, sucking hard.

The resulting contraction of her vagina had him repeating the action, following up with a bite. Fingernails scratched a path down to his ass and she gripped him hard enough to bruise. She slammed her hips against his twice and cried out. The pulse of her womb sent him over the edge. He pumped until every last drop was milked from him then ground against her once more for good measure.

For two full minutes, he lay atop her, unable to move. His heart hammered in rhythm with hers. "I think I might be in the midst of a heart attack," he gasped.

She laughed and ran her fingers through his sweat-dampened hair. The gesture soothed and allowed his lungs to draw in much-needed oxygen.

Coop grinned. "You know, I wasn't expecting anything more than an incredible necking session. I honestly believe you've spoiled me for all other women."

"My job here is done," she managed through her own short panted breaths.

"Christ, I could die happy right now."

She giggled and rolled with him as he shifted their positions. One of her delicate hands trailed over his chest, tracing hearts on his bare skin. "Me, too."

"You've never said it, you know."

Summer raised her head to look into his face. "Said what?"

"That you love me."

Her eyes made a study of his face, lingered on his mouth, and then met his probing stare.

Coop held his breath in expectation of her response.

A half-smile tugged at her lips. "I thought it was understood. I've loved you since the moment you gave me your ice cream."

He released the pent-up air. "I think I've loved you since then too."

She scrunched her face and would've ducked her head, but he placed a finger under her chin.

"I mean it, Summer. I've never said those words to another woman who wasn't a family member. I wouldn't lie about something as important as this." He stretched to drop a light kiss on her lips. "Granted, I didn't realize that girl was you, or maybe somewhere deep inside I did, but you captured my heart that day and have held it ever since."

"You're a silver-tongued devil, do you know that?"

"I might've been told that a time or two," he agreed with a deep chuckle. "I have another question."

"What's that?"

"Do you and your sisters really dance naked in the moonlight?"

"Another fantasy, Coop?"

"Darlin', that's every man's fantasy. Four gorgeous women naked in nature? Hell, yes!"

Her happy laughter triggered his.

"What if I told you we did?" she teased.

"I'd ask if I could get a calendar of dates and times so I could watch."

"Okay."

He lifted his head from the pillow and gaped. "Seriously?"

"Seriously."

"You'd better not be messing with me, Summer Thorne. A man can only take so much teasing."

She laughed again and held up three fingers. "Scout's honor."

He laid his head back on the pillow and sighed happily. "I am so going to love being your boyfriend."

After a moment, he frowned. No woman would allow him to see her sisters naked. "Wait a sec. What's the catch?"

"The catch?" she murmured sleepily.

"Yeah, the catch. You'll give me the dates and times when you and your sisters dance naked under the moonlight. Location, too?"

"Location, too," she agreed. "It's in the clearing between our properties."

He rolled on top of her and settled between her legs. "I don't trust you."

"You are the most suspicious person I've ever met, Cooper Carlyle."

"The twinkle in your eye tells me you're having me on."

"You think you know me?"

"Oh, I *know* I know you, sweetheart. You come across as sweet and innocent, but underneath that hot-ass exterior beats the heart of a naughty girl."

"Hmm, maybe I need a spanking."

He lowered his head and tugged her nipple between his teeth. "That is definitely one option. The other is that I torture you until you tell me what I want to know."

"What kind of torture are we talking here?"

Coop blew on her wet bud. "What kind do you think?"

"Oh, fuc—"

He clapped a hand over her mouth. "No swearing. I don't know how you kept the mice away last time, but I don't want to risk it."

Her muffled laughter had him grinning in return. She licked his palm and arched a brow.

Coop tasted his way down her body and inserted a finger into her drenched core. "What's the catch, Summer?"

"I'll never tell."

He inserted a second finger and pumped her hard.

She moaned, and he withdrew.

"The catch."

"I'm not telling," she countered in a husky voice that shot straight to his groin.

He inserted his fingers again and ran his tongue the length of her stomach. "Tell me," he ordered as he pumped her.

"A cloaking spell," she gasped out.

He rose up. "I knew it! Turn over. You're getting a spanking for being a dirty rotten tease."

She grinned and rolled over on all fours. "Do your worst."

"Oh, sweetheart, you shouldn't tempt a man like that."

*S*ummer lifted her hand to levitate another bale of hay much to Morty's delight. The chimp hooted and clapped as if she were the best magician on the planet.

"You're easily amused, sweet boy."

He nodded his agreement, hooted again, and blew her a kiss.

"Do you want to help Mama with chores? You can feed today."

He leaped off the stack of hay and straight into her arms.

Summer grunted at the impact. "I think you're putting on weight. Should we tell Coop to cut back on the treats?"

The man in question walked up behind her, removed his work gloves, and stroked Morty's back. "I don't know what you're talking about."

"Mmhmm. If this keeps up, I'm going to have to levitate him just to hold him."

Coop tucked his head in the crook of her neck and kissed below her earlobe. Before he pulled away, he traced the delicate shell of her ear with his tongue.

"I'm off today. Want to sneak away and get busy in the hayloft?" he murmured.

Boy did she ever.

Morty puckered his lips and made kissing noises.

Coop laughed. "Exactly what I had in mind, buddy."

A droll, arrogant voice came from a darkened corner of the barn. "How domesticated the two of you have become."

Summer's heart kicked into overdrive.

"Coop, will you return Morty to the house?"

"No way I'm leaving you here with him, sweetheart."

"Please. I need to know you're both safe," she begged quietly.

"I'm not here to hurt anyone, child. I'm here to reason with you. To tell you a little tale and allow you to make up your own mind."

"Why should I believe anything you have to say?" she demanded angrily. "You killed my mother!"

In an instant, Alastair stood in front of her. His anger was palpable. "Did I? Did you actually *see* me kill your mother, Summer?"

His question took her aback. "N-no."

As quickly as it appeared, his irritation disappeared. Resignation and weariness replaced the other emotion. "I loved your mother, and she loved me. Did anyone ever tell you that part of the story?"

"You're lying." She hugged Morty tighter as her uncle reached out a hand.

Instead of stroking the chimp as she'd expected, he tugged a lock of her hair. "Did you ever wonder why you're the only one with my coloring?"

Her world shifted on its axis. "What?" she croaked.

"Ask Preston for the true story. Ask him where he really goes when he disappears for months at a time."

"Are you saying her mother is alive?" Coop demanded.

Alastair shrugged. "I'm saying I didn't kill her."

Eyes the exact color of her own stared back at her. Open, honest, and urging her to see the truth. "You're my father?" she asked hoarsely.

His expression softened infinitesimally. "A DNA test would verify it one-hundred percent, but according to your mother, yes."

"I can't believe this!"

Silence reigned as Alastair allowed her to process the impact of his words. The idea that she'd been lied to her entire life didn't sit well.

"Why did you never claim me?" she demanded.

"You think I didn't want to?" Sadness replaced all other emotion on his classically handsome features. "But your mother returned to Preston. She believed it would be better if you believed he was your real father." He frowned and stroked a finger down her cheek. "After she was gone... Tell me, Summer, how do you shatter a child's whole world? How do you pull a perfectly happy little girl away from the only family she's ever known?" He dropped his hand and a shutter fell over his pain-filled gaze. "You don't."

Tears blurred her vision, and she struggled with this new insight into Alastair.

"I don't believe you."

He smiled, not unkindly. "You do, because you know the truth when you hear it. A gift from me to you."

Coop pulled her back and confronted Alastair. "What kind of piece of shit threatens their own daughter?"

"I never threatened her, boy. Think back. I threatened *you*," Alastair said in silky tones.

Anticipating where the conversation would lead, she surged forward. "No!"

Alastair barely flicked a glance in her direction. His cold gazed locked onto Coop. "Mistreat her and you'll have me to deal with. Remember, I'm not as nice as my brother and sister."

"Don't you dare threaten him!" She inserted a shoulder between the two, careful to twist her body to keep the oddly subdued Morty out of Alastair's reach. She still didn't trust that her uncle—no, *father*—had pure motives for being in her barn. "How did you get past the wards?"

"I intend you no harm," he said simply. "I can see you want to argue the point. You're all fire, like Aurora. It threw me to discover you were a water element—*like me*."

A sound at the entrance to the barn caught their attention.

"Alastair, step away from my daughter." The seething rage in Preston Thorne's voice had them all taking a step back.

"*Your* daughter?" Alastair sneered.

Preston's face lost all color and his uneasy amber gaze sought Summer.

"Dad?" Her voice broke, and she cleared her throat. "Is it true?"

"Tell her the truth, brother. She deserves to know." Alastair gestured to Summer's trio of sisters entering the barn behind Preston. "They *all* deserve to know what really happened."

"I could kill you for this," Preston growled.

"It isn't as if you didn't try. Tell them who got caught in the cross-fire and why."

A keening wail rose up. Summer hadn't even been aware of making the sound until Coop caught her as her knees gave out.

Morty's hands gripped her neck and buried his forehead to her throat.

The three of them huddled against the stall wall.

"I think you've done enough damage for one day, Alastair," Coop told him frostily. "Take a hike."

Summer's tear-filled eyes raised to view her real father.

Regret stole across his features. "I'm sorry, child. Truly. When you're ready to talk, call out to me. I'll come."

She shook her head and swiped at the tears pouring down her cheeks. "I won't. I can't care for a man who would let his company experiment on animals."

He frowned his confusion. "Your ape was brought to my lab to heal him. GiGi took him before I could. I've never laid eyes on that animal before today."

That explained why Morty hadn't gone ape-shit over Alastair's appearance. Her chimp had never had contact and, as a result, hadn't made the association between the lab and Alastair.

"What about the recordings?" Coop asked, less hostile.

Summer had the sense he believed Alastair, just as she did.

Goddess, she was confused. Up was down and down was up. Nothing made sense and it seemed as if everyone she loved and trusted had lied to her.

"I don't know what you're talking about," Alastair said as he shook his head.

"We have videos of Morty being mistreated at your lab after hours. A tech used a cattle prod through the bars and denied him food." Strength returned to Summer's spine. In this, she wasn't mistaken.

Fury, dark and forbidding, shifted Alastair's eyes from sapphire-blue to black. "One of *my* lab techs?"

His quicksilver moods were alarming considering the power he wielded.

Her vocal cords decided discretion was the better part of valor and abandoned her. She merely nodded.

"I want to see those tapes."

Summer shot a nervous look at Coop, who nodded. "Okay."

"Meet me at Monica's Cafe in one hour. I'll be waiting in the back booth." Alastair disappeared before she could agree.

"Holy shit," Coop muttered. "That man lends a whole new meaning to the word terrifying."

She snorted her laughter through her tears. "He really does. I thought it was only me."

"My respect for you has increased tenfold. I don't think I could've faced him down alone like you did on that beach."

"But now we both know he never intended to harm me," she said quietly as she pinned Preston with a glare across the aisle. "But somehow, I think my *dad* knew all along."

"We need to talk," Preston declared.

Betrayal was a funny thing. Its effects altered perspective. Where she'd once viewed Alastair as an evil sonofabitch, she now viewed him as a victim, similar to herself. And where she once viewed Preston as a God among men, she now viewed him as a lying, spiteful bastard. While the truth probably resided somewhere in the middle, she wasn't magnanimous enough to utilize that logic.

"I have nothing to say to you right now," she snapped. "You lied to me. My whole fucking life—*achoo*— you lied to me!"

A hundred rodents of every species and size raced down the barn aisle. Her stunned sisters stood silently by and watched, helpless, as the drama unfolded.

Preston, unperturbed by the rodent infestation, snapped his fingers.

The aisle was clear except for humans and Morty.

Summer handed the chimp off to Coop before she faced Preston. "What did you do with the mice?"

"I relocated them to the woods by the clearing *where they belong*."

Saul sounded off from his location in the rafters. Because she knew what to expect, Summer caught him as he plummeted to the ground.

"That goes for your squirrels too, Summer. They either learn manners or they go."

She stepped to within a foot of Preston. "Don't even *think* about threatening Saul, *Dad*. You know damned well he's my familiar." She sneezed, and one tiny squeak was emitted from the stall behind her.

Preston, his eyes boring into Summer's, positioned his fingers to snap.

Autumn's hand closed over his. "Daddy." She only uttered the single word, but the censure in her tone was obvious.

He shrugged her off but lowered his hand. "Are you going to meet him?"

The betrayal in his eyes stung. Yet, he'd betrayed Summer first. "I am."

"Then I have nothing more to say to you. You have until the end of the week to have your animals relocated and be out of my home."

Her sisters gasped and cried his name in a chorus of "Daddy!"

"No, it's okay," Summer choked out as Spring's arms encircled her. "I'm a big girl. I can survive perfectly well on my own."

"Really?" Preston scoffed. "Because last I checked it was Thorne money footing the bill to feed your misfits."

"That's enough, Mr. Thorne," Coop snapped. "I get your feelings are a little bruised here, but Summer is the only one who has the right to be pissed. You lied to her."

"I don't need you to tell me how to handle my child, Cooper."

"But I'm not your child, am I?" she choked out. Moisture burned behind her lids, and she struggled to contain her grief.

"You're mine. Perhaps not biologically, but you're my sunshine. I raised you as my own," he told her. The gruffness in his voice, the tension along his shoulders, and the pain in his eyes spoke of his emotional investment.

Her throat worked convulsively.

"Why couldn't you trust us with the truth, Dad?" Winnie asked. "I can see maybe not when we were small kids, but we've all grown into successful adults with the ability to reason."

Preston closed his eyes and seemed to age a century in the seconds before he opened them to focus on Summer. "Stay or go, I can't stop you. But don't believe everything he says. What I did, I did for your well-being. I need you to understand that."

Summer nodded and folded her arms around her. "I'm going to show him the video of Morty's abuse. Other than that, I have no agenda. If he wants to tell me his side, I'll listen and try to withhold judgment—just as I'll listen to your side, Dad. It's all I'm willing to offer either of you right now."

He gave a single sharp nod and headed for the door. He paused without turning. "You don't have to move out. I hope you'll forgive my loss of temper." Without waiting for a response, he left.

As one, her sisters closed the gap and wrapped her in a sisterly hug, Thorne style.

"Are you really going to see Alastair by yourself?" Spring asked.

"No," Coop cut in. "I'm going with her."

The four women fought to hide their smiles and failed miserably.

"What's so funny?" he demanded.

Summer stretched up to place a soft kiss on his cheek. "You are by thinking you can protect me from one of the most powerful Warlocks in existence."

She nearly laughed at the green hue he'd acquired. "Most powerful?"

"One of the most powerful," she corrected with a pat on his arm.

"The other would be Preston?"

Autumn piped up. "That would be a big ten-four, Sheriff."

"Good Christ. I'll be lucky to survive this family."

23

*C*oop didn't like it. Not the emptiness of the restaurant that should be bustling this time of day. Not the vacant expressions on the faces of the staff. And certainly not the sinister aura surrounding Alastair where he sat in the back booth in his black suit and red tie. *Did the guy have another outfit?*

As they wove their way through the tables, he leaned in and lowered his voice. "Is it possible your new father is bipolar? Because, correct me if I'm wrong, but he is looking moody as fuck. It's a far cry from the touching reunion he was going for earlier today."

Summer snorted and rolled her eyes. "If he frightens you, you can wait outside, Coop."

He bowed up to his full height and threw his shoulders back. She might as well have told him to check his man card at the door.

Alastair, in a single swift elegant motion, stood and gestured to the seat opposite him. "I'm pleased you decided to come."

"Did we have a choice?" Coop said beneath his breath.

"You always have a choice in life, boy. You, knowing I can cook your brain with the snap of a finger, chose to escort Summer anyway. You're either extremely brave or extremely stupid. Perhaps a mixture of both."

His jaw clenched, and Coop had to talk himself down from an ugly retort. A verbal battle wouldn't solve anything. He shrugged and said, "I love her."

The older man cast him a winsome smile. "Perhaps smarter than I thought."

The wide grin cemented Alastair's relationship to Summer. His smile was her smile in male form.

Coop rubbed the tense spot on Summer's back. "Can we get this over with? I can't imagine mind control for the entire staff of Monica's is healthy."

Amusement lit Alastair's eyes, and the blue brightened by degrees.

Seeing the transition of color as it happened was creepy as hell. Irises weren't meant to do that.

Alastair turned all business in the blink of an eye. "I had my assistant go back through the video archives. Conveniently, any recordings of Morty's time with White Laboratory were missing. Would you know anything about that, child, or should I lay that at the doorstep of my meddling sister?"

"Both. She gave me a copy of the digital recording." Summer pulled out her laptop and played the keyed-up video.

Coop watched Alastair carefully as he viewed the screen. The subtle shifting of his jaw, the lowered brows, and the menace in his eyes let Coop know Alastair wasn't happy about the behavior of his employees.

"I've seen enough." Alastair closed the computer with a decisive click and picked up his cellphone from the table. "Please excuse me a moment. I need to make a phone call."

"I think you should know, if any of your staff turn up missing, I'm going to know it's you, Alastair." Where Coop got the balls to open his mouth, he had no idea.

Delighted laughter echoed around the empty diner. "I'm starting to like you, boy." A heavy hand settled on his shoulder and squeezed. "I also find it hilarious that you believe you'd be able to do anything should I decide to punish that lowlife by putting him to death."

Putting him to death? The antiquated term brought to mind Game of Thrones and punishments meted out to unfortunate characters on the show.

As Alastair walked away, Coop turned incredulous eyes to Summer. "Putting him to death?" he couldn't help repeating. "What the fuck?"

"He's messing with you, Coop."

"Is he? Because I'm pretty sure he's not."

"Well, he's right about one thing."

"What's that?"

She shrugged. "There's nothing you can do about it."

His brows clashed together. "You act as if warlocks murdering muggles is an everyday occurrence."

"Muggles?" she giggled. "I still can't believe you refer to yourself as a muggle."

He refused to acknowledge her comment and reached for a glass of water in front of him.

Summer stopped him with a hand on his arm. "I wouldn't drink that if I were you."

Keaton's warning from the day Coop found out Summer was a witch resurfaced. "Why?"

"You never know what potion the evil warlock might have put in the muggle's water." Deviltry sparkled in her eyes.

"You're a wicked little minx. Tonight I'll spank you again." He took a sip of the water and, for effect, clutched his throat.

"Not funny, Cooper Carlyle."

His own laughter rang out, and he leaned to touch his nose to hers. "Good to know you care."

"Pfft."

When Alastair returned, he wore a no-nonsense mask. "Now to the subject of returning my property."

Summer folded her arms across her chest and prepared for battle. "You're not getting Morty, daddy dearest. Give it up."

Her father's lips twitched. "After all these years, it's nice to hear you call me dad."

Both father and daughter wore matching looks of cold amusement.

"Whatever. You're not getting my sweet boy," she said.

Frustration fueled Alastair's exhalation. "You don't understand, child. I need him."

"Because of the paintings?" Coop asked.

Summer smacked a hand to his forehead. "I thought we were keeping that between us."

"Obviously, you know nothing about interrogation tactics," he retorted as he rubbed the spot over his brow. "It's an art."

"Speaking of art," Alastair's cultured tones opposed the blatant amusement dancing in his eyes. "What paintings?"

Summer opened her mouth to reply.

Coop anticipated her action and fastened his hand over her mouth. "Why don't you tell us? If I recall correctly, you mentioned you liked to watch him paint."

Summer licked his palm, and he jerked his hand away as if on fire. The action brought to mind the first time they made love. Heat scorched Coop's neck when Summer winked.

"Shall I book you a room?" Alastair sounded and looked decidedly less amused this time.

"No, thanks. I have a perfectly good hayloft," she replied.

Coop avoided Alastair's eyes and leaned close to murmur, "Uh, babe, he's your father whether you like it or not. And fathers tend to frown upon the idea of their daughters doing the deed. Let's not piss off the powerful warlock who can shrivel my man parts, okay?"

"I'll un-shrivel them," she returned and patted his leg.

Alastair's choked laughter was a good sign, right?

"Can we please focus here?" Coop begged. Yep, he'd definitely checked his man card at the door.

Father and daughter shared another amused glance.

Well, at least they were bonding, right?

Alastair picked up the lead. "I need Marty's memories."

"Morty," Coop and Summer corrected.

"Morty," Alastair acknowledged. "Believe it or not, I care about animals as much as you."

"Right. Is that why White Labs tests everything from mice to monkeys to puppies?" Summer scoffed.

"How much do you know about my business holdings?"

"Nothing. I didn't even know you owned the lab until the day you showed up in the driveway."

"My point exactly. I purchased the business two weeks before your beloved GiGi made off with all the animals." Alastair gave Coop's water a pointed look and raised his own water in salute before he turned his attention back to Summer. "It didn't concern me if she chose to free them. All animal testing had been discontinued the second I took over, and I knew they'd be safe wherever she re-homed them." With careful precision he placed his glass in the center of a paper napkin. "I didn't come for your pet until I realized he had valuable information I need. I was content to let you keep him. I still am as long as I can extract what I require."

"How do you plan to go about that?" she demanded.

A warm smile blossomed on the older man's face. "The same way you do, child. I'll ask him and allow him to show me the pictures of his mind."

"So I inherited that ability from you as well?"

"You did. While all the Thornes can understand animal speak, only a handful of us can actually see the images they provide." He indicated the hand she rested on the table. "May I?"

Summer held it out palm up.

Coop had no idea what the fuck was happening or why. But because she showed no fear, he reined in his own.

A red arc of light shot from the fingers Alastair trailed along her palm.

Coop attempted to interfere, but Summer placed her opposite hand on his chest.

"He's not hurting me, Coop. It's like an animal sniffing your hand. He's testing my magic."

"Well, it's fucking weird if you ask me," he muttered.

Again, Alastair's lips twitched. "I can check your level of magic next if you'd like."

"What magic? What the hell are you talking about?"

"Why the Carlyle witches, of course."

"Carlyle witches?" Coop and Summer echoed, mouths agape.

Completely out of character, Alastair snorted. And damned if he didn't sound just like Summer when she was scoffing at Coop.

"If I had to guess, your parents bound your powers."

"Okay, hold the boat. Are you saying Coop and Keaton are warlocks?"

"I am. Any born of that line have power."

"This is ridiculous," Coop exploded. "Now I *know* you are making shit up."

Summer grabbed his hand and shoved it toward Alastair.

The desire to snatch it back overwhelmed him and had him sweating bullets.

"May I?" Alastair asked.

Coop gave a curt nod.

Red arced from Alastair's fingertips. A tickling sensation started in his palm and, one by one, spread to his fingers. As it traveled the length of his arm, Cooper's nerves got the better of him, and he pulled back.

"Did you feel the surge, son?" Alastair asked.

"Yeah. What was that?"

"That, my warlock friend, was magic."

"You're not a muggle," Summer laughed.

Fuck a duck!

COOP LOOKED LIKE SUMMER HAD ASKED HIM TO EAT GREEN EGGS AND ham. His sickly expression didn't bode well for his state of mind.

She gripped his hand under the table and turned her attention to Alastair.

His watchful gaze noted everything and caused a shiver of appreciation for the master manipulator he must be.

"Calling you dad or father after all this time seems odd," she said.

His face hardened. "You still believe Preston is your father?"

"No." She sighed and shook her head. "No, I don't. But you have to understand, I've spent twenty years believing you to be the bad guy in this little family drama. While I am adult enough to realize not everything is one-sided, a small part of me knows you're not as innocent as you'd have me believe."

She shot a quick glance in Coop's direction. His coloring was returning to normal, but the troubled look still remained.

"I suppose I'll continue to call you Alastair until I get to know you better if that's all right."

Shockingly, Alastair cleared his throat as if his emotions got the better of him. "You… you want to get to know me better?"

Summer bit her lip and nodded.

"I'd like that," he admitted. "Very much."

"I have one condition. Well, more than one really."

Amusement twisted his lips. "Why does that not surprise me?"

She ignored his sarcasm. "One, you cannot threaten Coop. Not in look, not in deed, not ever. What happens—or doesn't—in my relationship is between him and I."

"No breaking him if he breaks your heart. Got it."

She pressed her lips together to hold back a laugh. Laughing during serious negotiations was a no-no.

"Two, you cannot hurt Morty."

Ice coated his words as he said, "I don't go around hurting innocent creatures, Summer. Despite what you may think of me."

"I don't think anything of you."

His blond brows shot skyward.

"Or, um, what I meant to say is that I'm trying to start this relationship with a clean slate." She leaned forward in her seat and took the large, ringed hand in hers.

Silently, she studied the scars on the back of his hand.

"If you have questions, ask."

Unable to meet his probing gaze, she shrugged. "I don't know if I'm ready for the answers."

His hand tightened over hers, but not to the point of pain. "When you are, I'll answer honestly."

"I get the feeling you're always honest. Brutally so."

"Look at me, child."

Unexpected tears flooded the eyes she lifted to his.

"When you know me better, you'll know whatever I've done, good or bad, has been for you or your mother."

She picked up his air of sadness and tightened her own fingers before she released him.

With a clearing of her throat, she continued. "Three, I intend to be there when you retrieve whatever information from Morty that you suspect he knows."

Alastair nodded his acceptance of her condition.

"Four, you have to train me and Coop in magic."

"Excuse me?" Coop, who'd remained silent and watchful, straightened in his seat.

His dark scowl had her rushing to explain. "If you truly have latent power, you need to uncover it and learn how to use it. And we all know how hit or miss mine is."

"I don't have power, Summer. This is some twisted joke on his part." Coop jerked his chin in Alastair's direction. "I'd know if my parents were witches."

"Would you?"

They both whipped their heads around to stare at Alastair.

"If a witch or warlock didn't want you to know what they were, believe me, you wouldn't know. The Thorne sisters have lived next door to you for your entire life, boy. You had no idea what they are."

"Not my entire life," Coop grumbled.

"Summer. Care to inform him of the truth?"

"What truth?" Coop demanded. "Summer?"

She winced. With a glare in Alastair's direction, she confessed, "We've always lived on our estate. We made up the story of moving to Leiper's Fork when we were teens."

"No way! You're our neighbor. I think we would've..." He shook his head when it sunk in. "A cloaking spell? For *years?*" When she nodded, he asked, "What was the purpose?"

Alastair answered for her. "When witches are young and testing their boundaries, they need to be kept away from the population at large. Only when they have learned not to share what they are and to curb the impulse to use magic in public, will they be allowed to join the non-magical community."

"But we met when we were children," Coop argued.

Summer shifted to face him. "We all wanted to see the fireworks and were relentless in pestering Dad—er, Preston. He and my mother bound our powers for the day. We were sworn to secrecy under the threat of severe punishment if we spoke a word about magic."

"Then what? You went back home, put up your invisible barriers and went about your life for the next nine years?"

"Essentially, yes."

"Your children will be treated the same way? Shut away from society?" he demanded.

The words "your children" hurt. It was as if he took himself out of the running for fathering her kids.

"Yes."

"Kids need social interaction, Summer. Look at you and your sisters. You're practically outsiders in this town." He shook his head and slapped the table. "You have no real friends. No..." He pinned her with a frustrated stare. "It's no wonder you clung to your crush. You've never had any real-life socialization."

Clung to her crush? As if she didn't love him?

"I've had plenty 'real-life socialization', Coop. I left and went to college, remember? Friends are tricky because I don't like lying. But I've had boyfriends and lovers."

His mouth tightened. "Are you saying it was okay to lie to boyfriends and... lovers?"

She looked to Alastair. "Care to help me out here?"

"I'm Switzerland in this conversation."

"Thanks a lot." Summer blew out a breath and faced an irate Coop. She searched for the right words, found herself at a loss, and decided to speak from the heart. "Coop, if you truly are a warlock, if your parents are descended from witches, you would have been raised the same way. I can only assume they felt as you do right now and decided to bind you and Keaton in order for you to have a normal childhood."

His brows slashed downward.

"If you had been raised like I was, then yes, you would've lied to girlfriends and lovers, just as I've had to lie to anyone who's gotten close," she told him.

She touched his face but dropped her hand when he flinched. "I've never lied to you."

"*Never?* Not all those times we found Eddie in our pool?" he ground out. "How about the downtown goat incident? Not then either?"

Alastair took exception to Coop's temper. "Tone, boy. You'll want to watch it."

Coop was in no mood to be threatened. "Condition one, remember, old man?"

Summer froze. Goddess, this was about to get ugly.

"Okay, and on that note, it's time for us to go!" she said, infusing a false brightness into her tone.

Coop stormed from the restaurant without a backward glance.

Her stomach clenched, and her heart fell to her toes.

A hand rested on her shoulder. "Give him time, child. He'll come around."

"I don't know. He's had an aversion to me being a witch from the beginning." She faced Alastair. "Now, add the fact my father is powerful enough to wipe this little town he loves so much right off the map, *and* the fact that I've lied…" She trailed off with a shrug.

Heart heavy, she didn't resist when Alastair pulled her into an embrace. He rested his blond head atop hers and sighed. "Give him time. He loves you. It's in his every action."

Of their own accord, her arms came up and wrapped around Alastair's midsection. He smelled of exotic spices and cinnamon. Not unpleasant at all.

When he pulled away, she experienced a sense of loss.

"He's waiting for you in his vehicle."

"How do you know that?" she asked.

"He's parked out front and is glaring at us through the window."

24

"You've been a bit of a dick for the last four days. Are you done sulking?"

Coop lifted his head to find Summer in the doorway of his office. "No."

"Fair enough. I've brought you lunch."

As she unpacked her canvas bag, she held up a candy bar. "Chocolate for your PMS."

He bit back a laugh.

"Cake to sweeten your disposition."

He did grin then.

"Pomegranate."

"Why pomegranate?"

She paused in unloading the groceries. "It helps with erectile disfunction."

Someone snorted in the outer office.

Coop glared through the window leading to the pit. *"I do not have erectile disfunction,"* he bit out.

"I know that. But we don't want to take any chances in the future."

He narrowed his eyes. Was she trying to hide a smirk? The little troublemaker.

"Avocado is an aphrodisiac." She waved the fruit in the air before placing it in line with the other food.

"Summer."

She looked up from the stash of food, all wide-eyed and innocent.

"Come here."

"Why, Sheriff Carlyle! I declare, I know what that tone of voice means. I'm not that kind of girl," she teased in a Southern Belle effected tone.

"Summer Thorne, you have five seconds to get your ass on this side of my desk or deal with the consequences."

Her eyes sparkled with delight and wanton promise. "What is your intent, good sir?"

He rose to his feet and threw his pen down. "One."

She backed away and giggled.

"Two."

Summer turned to flee.

"Threefourfive!" He ran the words together and scooped her up. With his heel he slammed the door. "Now pull the shade."

"They'll know what we were doing in here!" she protested.

"What's that? Having lunch? Necking a little?"

"We both know where your little make-out sessions lead, Cooper Carlyle."

His smile encompassed them both. "And your point is?"

"No."

"Come on. You show me your point and I'll show you mine."

"You have the least pointy thing I know," she retorted.

"What the hell?" He dumped her on her feet. "Are you saying I have a small dick?"

"No!" she yelped. "I said it is the least pointy thing I know. As in it's big and thick."

And losing its hard on. His hands found his hips like an angry fishwife. "So you've seen a lot of *pointy things?*"

Disgust filled her face and voice. "You know what? I'm done with this stupid conversation. You want to sit here and wallow or find things to be angry about, be my guest. I have better things to do with my time than soothe your fragile ego."

"My fragile ego. Yeah, okay."

Great retort, moron!

"Call me when you are over your snit."

He stood in front of the exit, arms crossed over his chest. "We aren't done with this conversation."

"Do you honestly believe blocking the door will prevent me from leaving?"

And that's what it all came back to—*witchcraft*.

While he liked to think he was open-minded, it appeared he wasn't. As a matter of fact, he was the antithesis of an open-minded individual.

"I know I can't. I also know I hate it," he confessed gruffly. "I also hate that you're getting cozy with Alastair. I don't trust that fucker."

"Oh, Coop."

She closed the gap between them and wrapped her arms around his neck. His own arms caught her against him.

"You're spending an awful lot of time with him."

"I am. I think he's lonely. But it's more than that. I think he knows more about my mother than anyone is saying."

His radar went up. "Like what?"

"I'm not sure, but he never refers to her as deceased. It's odd." She rested her head on his chest. "I also think he's after an object called the Chintamani Stone."

"And that would be?"

"A rare artifact said to grant wishes. The last known documentation detailing the whereabouts of the stone was around 1920 or so. A couple held it for safekeeping. When interest in the stone gained a fever pitch, they took a trip to the Himalayas and handed it off to Buddhist monks."

"So why doesn't old Alastair pop over and get it?" Coop asked.

"He would if he could. The stone disappeared from the monastery in February of 1968."

"This wish-granting stone has been missing for over fifty years?"

"Yep."

"Who's to say it's even a real magical object?"

Summer lifted a brow and smirked.

"Yeah, strike that question. I'm dealing with witches. I should've assumed there were magical artifacts." He jerked. "Wait! Are they the type of antiquities your dad, uh, Preston searches out?"

She grinned. "You make a heck of a detective, Coop."

"I'll be damned," he breathed. He paced the length of his office as a million thoughts crowded his brain. "What does he do with them once he's found them?"

"They are safeguarded by the witches' council, of which, he holds a place on the panel."

"But where are they stored?"

She compressed her lips and dropped her eyes. A definite tell that she knew but refused to say. *Well, at least she isn't lying.*

Coop ran a hand through his hair. His mind was having a hard time wrapping around all he'd learned. Coping with the information that a whole other world of magic existed around him became harder each day. He liked his life as it had been. Sure, he'd remained ignorant of the magical family living in his midst, but he didn't have to deal with a teleporting girlfriend, two lethal warlocks who always seemed to be sizing him up, shoveling elephant dung on a daily basis, and a chimp who could go off the rails at any second and bash someone's brains in.

The fact that any of these women could wipe his memories at any second terrified the holy hell out of him.

And while the thought of Summer swollen with their child was a sweet daydream, the reality was that any child of theirs would possess powers enough to make him their puppet.

He suddenly knew what he needed to do.

"I need a break." The words were torn from him.

She smiled and gestured to the food. "I know. You work too hard."

"No, Summer." He swallowed audibly and met her brilliant eyes.

As he watched, the irises lost their brightness and turned a murky shade of gray.

"From me, you mean." A small sad smile graced her face. "It was bound to happen eventually. Only a matter of time really."

Panic gripped him. Her tone sounded final which made him rethink his decision to end things, contrary bastard that he was. "It's only a small break. A few days. A week at the most. I just need to get my head on straight."

She wouldn't meet his eyes. Instead, she painstakingly folded the canvas bag on the desk as she kept her profile to him. "I understand."

"Do you?" He didn't even know if *he* did.

She gave a half-hearted smile and nodded. With a deep breath, she lifted her head. "I have a few appointments this afternoon, so I'd better head out." With her thumb, she gestured to the food. "Eat something."

Her proud martyr routine pissed him off. "You're not my mother, Summer."

SUMMER SUCKED IN HER BREATH. *OF ALL THE NERVE!* "SORRY IF I'M trying to be adult about receiving my walking papers. Self-control is necessary so I don't fry your pansy ass."

She sneezed. Goddess!

Grown men scrambling up from chairs and screaming could be heard through the office door.

"Goddammit!" Coop swore. *"This!* This shit is what I'm talking about. I want one fucking normal day. Is that too much to ask?"

If he struck her, it would've been kinder.

The door flew open and Aimes, hair wild and uniform askew, stood panting and panicked. "C.C., we have a problem. Rats everywhere, man!"

Summer pasted a smile on her face and addressed the officer. "I'll take care of it, Randy. They must've escaped from the traps in my van. I had the windows open."

"Why would they come in here?"

She waved a hand and blew a bit of magical air in his direction. In a soft, hypnotic voice, she said, "They're here because they are hungry and looking for food. In five minutes time, they will be gone and you will cease to worry about them."

"Summer," Coop warned.

Ignoring him, she asked, "Do you understand, Randy?"

"I understand," Aimes replied.

"Excellent. You may go calm everyone else."

Randy retreated a lot more relaxed than when he entered.

She stared at the empty doorway longer than necessary to avoid the censure and contempt she was sure to find in Coop's eyes. Hell, she could *feel* the rage radiating off of him.

How easy it would be to just disappear for good. She'd been fighting the desire for most of her life since prom. Facing the townspeople now that she and Coop were over would be too much to bear. The constant refrain would be "poor Summer Thorne", and there was no way she could handle the ridicule. She didn't have the strength. Odd, how world weary she felt. Much older than her twenty-eight years.

"Goodbye, Cooper Carlyle," she whispered past the lump in her throat. "It was a fun run while it lasted."

She closed her eyes and concentrated on the property she'd secretly purchased on the Tennessee-North Carolina border. Concentrated on the sound of the gusty afternoon breeze rustling the branches of fat Fraser firs. She could smell the scent of pine and fresh, uncontaminated air. And then she was there. Her and dozens of rodents of every shape and size.

When she opened her eyes, she took in the breathtaking sight of her new mountain home. "I think we're going to like it here, gang."

The chattering of mice filled the clearing. Huh, maybe she'd cussed a wee bit harder than she thought. The number of rodents staggered her.

"I guess Randy Aimes was right to be frightened. You are a pretty intimidating group." She smiled as they twitched their noses.

To block out the pain of her breaking heart, she scouted out their new digs. Nothing like avoidance.

"What kind of barn should we build, gang? Obviously a large, heated one for Eddie. Maybe an indoor pool? He'd love that, wouldn't he?"

The bevy of rodents chatted away and gave her suggestions. Mostly they consisted of a place to burrow. She'd have to make her own floor plan.

In her mind's eye she cleared the timber from the land. When she had what she thought was a large enough area, she paced it off and mentally staked it out.

"I think this is a good start for today. Y'all find a place to nest for tonight, and I'll do the same. I'm certain there's a bed and breakfast with a spare room."

When she teleported to the edge of town, her phone buzzed with all the missed messages she'd received while out of range on the mountain. Coop had left three voicemails and sent seven texts.

She deleted them all and headed for a small cafe she'd frequented on her last visit.

The dark-haired waitress greeted her like an old friend. Perhaps because she recognized what Summer was from the moment she'd set foot in town back in July.

Most witches had a glow to their aura. The brighter the glow, the more powerful the witch. Had she thought about it at the time, Summer would've realized Coop was magical by his glow alone. She'd assumed the brightness of his aura was because he was destined to be her mate. She snorted and fought back tears.

"Hi, hon. Welcome back."

"Thanks, Holly. It's nice to be back." Summer scanned the menu then held it out. "Whatever's on special works."

Holly left to place the order and returned with a cup of tea and a small jar of honey. "My friend produced the honey on her farm."

"Then I'm sure I'll love it." Summer glanced around. "Seems dead today."

"It'll pick up around four-thirty or five."

Serious blue eyes the color of the deepest part of the Atlantic Ocean studied her. "Want some company?"

"As long as you aren't going to ask me about my love life."

The other woman grinned and sat. "I bet Pete that you had man troubles. Recognized the shell-shocked look."

"Who's Pete?"

"Cook."

Summer nodded and glanced toward the serving window. A cagey old man with three days' worth of stubble shot her a toothless smile. She returned the greeting with a sharp nod and a lift of her mug.

"Is there a chance he's going to spit in my food because he lost the bet?" she asked in a low voice.

Holly's light laugh rang out. "Possibly, but we've never had complaints. It could only make the food taste better."

The women made small talk for a short while before Holly came right out and asked why Summer was in town this time.

"I purchased the land on Yellow Creek mountain. I'm going to put in an animal sanctuary."

"You must have some serious money for that. Land in these parts belong to one man only. Hoyt Thorne. He doesn't readily part with it. Not without getting a good sum."

"Hoyt is a distant relative. And you're right, he didn't part with it without a nice-sized check." Summer extended her hand. "Summer Thorne."

"Holly Thorne."

"Yikes, really? Holly Thorne? I should've known. You have the look of the Thorne. Am I to assume we're cousins?"

"Well, technically my married name is Holly Thorne-Hill, but I'm tryin' to unload that baggage. Paperwork takes time."

"There's a lot to be said for getting rid of unwanted baggage," Summer said. The two women shared a commiserating look and toasted with their chipped white mugs.

"Amen, cuz." The bell rang, and Holly rose to her feet. "Well, shit."

When Holly sneezed, Summer almost laughed. She waited for the tell-tale sound of rodents, but no such sound happened. Instead, there came a pecking at the front glass window.

Summer spun in her seat. "Goddess!"

"Yeah, it happens every time I swear. Only one man gets me mad enough to do that."

The elegantly dressed man in the black suit addressed her waitress. "She wasn't referring to the birds, child. She was referring to me."

"Hello, Alastair. Welcome to my new neck of the woods. I'd ask how you found me, but…" Summer shrugged and sipped her tea. It only took a minute or two to divine a location.

"Summer. I see you've met your sister."

Her jaw dropped in sync with Holly's. Before long, she was laughing hysterically. "I should've known. The sneezing gave it away."

"I must say, you're taking this well," Alastair said as he unbuttoned his suit jacket and sat.

"What can I say? I like her. And with you, the surprises just keep coming. I've got to roll with life's punches or never get up." The last little bit referred to Coop, but he didn't need to know that. "I am a little pissed that she got birds and I was cursed with mice. I suppose it's too late to swap now. But really, what was with the Alfred Hitchcock scene at the window?"

"I believe the birds around here are mentally challenged," Holly supplied.

"How so?" Summer asked, curious despite herself.

"Well, for one, they don't know how to add ribbon to a dress."

"Ah, well my mice aren't any brighter. They don't sing or sew either."

The two women shared a laugh.

Even Alastair chuckled.

His amusement sobered Holly. "I suppose you want a cup of coffee?"

"Please."

Silence reigned until Holly had retrieved a cup and the pot of brewed sludge. She plopped both in front of him. "Help yourself."

He surprised Summer when he poured his own coffee and saluted Holly with his mug. "Thank you." He acted as if a customer pouring his own beverage was usual.

"Did you seek me out, or were you visiting your other offspring?" Summer frowned and narrowed her eyes. "How many of us are there?"

He didn't answer, but merely sipped his coffee.

"Who's older?"

"You, by four minutes."

"We're twins?" the two women chorused.

Holly's legs gave out, and she sank into the chair next to Summer.

Because she couldn't comprehend the magnitude of the statement, couldn't wrap her brain around a long-lost sister, Summer ignored the discovery to focus on the facts. "How is that possible?"

"About a month after you were born, Aurora came to see me. She claimed whenever Preston came within two feet of Holly, the babe would scream the house down. Apparently, he'd had enough."

"Dad made Mom give up her child?" Summer asked, horrified by such a ghastly act.

"Actually, he didn't. The decision was hers." Alastair stared into the black liquid as he inched his mug in a circle.

Seconds ticked by, and Summer thought the explanations were at an end.

He shook off his memories and took another sip of his coffee. After he set the cup down with precise movements, he said, "I believe she thought giving Holly to me would ease the loss."

"The loss?"

"The loss of Aurora. Of you."

"This is blowing my mind. Every story I ever heard was how much my parents were in love."

Alastair winced before he fiddled with the knot of his tie.

She wanted to yell at him to take the damned thing off if it bothered him so badly.

"You don't believe a person can have more than one love in a life-time?" he asked, distracting her from possible reasons he stayed buttoned up tight.

"Family rumor states a Thorne doesn't. Aren't you living proof?" Summer countered, not unkindly. "You've been mourning the woman for the past twenty years."

"Not mourning," he stated softly. "Besides, your mother wasn't a Thorne. She was a Fennell.

"Not to rain on your pity party here, Alastair, but did any of y'all think about me or Summer?" Holly demanded. "Did y'all think about how two sisters would miss out on growing up together? How bitter we'd be when we finally found each other after nearly thirty years? Because I'm here to say, I'm feeling a whole lotta bitter right now."

Alastair shoved aside his coffee. "What's done is done. You harping on the why will change nothing," he stated coldly.

Holly snorted and stood. For the span of a few heartbeats, she said nothing and continued to study Alastair. Finally, she asked what appeared foremost on her mind. "Why are you here? You only stop by when you want something."

"I can't come to check on my daughter?"

"Which one? Because you barely paid me any attention growing up, unless it was to criticize my 'training' or to send me on a wild goose chase after one of your precious artifacts," she sneered. "Whatever. I guess I don't really care." She faced Summer. "It was nice meeting ya, Summer. But be careful of this one's motives. He'll use you and cast you aside."

Alastair stood abruptly, sending his chair skittering back. "Do not presume to know my motives, Holly Thorne. What did I do so wrong? I saw to your well-being. I paid for your every want. Made sure you had the best education." His cold features turned downright arctic. "What did you do with it? You marry a waste of good space and throw everything away to waitress at a dive in the middle of nowhere. If you're unhappy with your lot in life, you have no one to blame but yourself. You've had ample opportunity to become a daughter I'm proud of."

Uh, oh. Wrong thing to say. One thing Summer knew growing up in a household of siblings was that you didn't compare one unfavorably to the other.

Holly's face turned the shade of a boiled lobster. Her hand rose and the liquid of all the drinks on the table started to bubble and create steam. From the kitchen, the sound of rushing water and liquid boiling over onto the hot burner could be heard along with Pete's swearing.

Summer sent up a small prayer of gratitude to the Goddess that they weren't on a beach because her twin would've decimated them all with her tidal wave of fury.

"Let me guess," Holly said between gritted teeth. "You're proud of *her*?"

"I am."

Unable to take another second, Summer rose to intercede. "Stop! Just stop!" To Holly, she said, "I only found out he was my father five days ago. He can't be proud because he had no hand in raising me." To Alastair, she said, "What I see when I look at her is a smart, confident woman filled with compassion. She didn't have to sit and try to cheer me up when I walked in today, but she did. As far as her husband, we can't choose who we love. I'm proof positive of that. You owe her an apology, Alastair."

"I don't want one. I just want him to leave me alone—*forever*!"

"I can't do that, child. I need you, with the help of your new sister, to find me another object."

"The Chintamani Stone," Summer said.

"The Chintamani Stone," he confirmed.

"I'm done running your errands, Alastair. Do it yourself," Holly growled.

"You aren't doing it for me. You're doing it for your mother," he replied smoothly.

His little declaration took the wind from Holly's sails.

"Coop said my relationship with Alastair was going to bite me in the ass. I didn't believe him."

Alastair had long since disappeared, but the women were dealing with the fallout from the bomb he dropped. They were to perform a major scavenger hunt to find the object able to bring their mother back. Oh, and not back from the dead. Apparently, she was playing the role of Sleeping Beauty waiting for Prince Charming to wake her with a kiss— and the Chintamani Stone could do this. A stone that had been missing for the last fifty years.

"I can't believe this. All this time, she's been alive."

"It's been almost twenty years!" Summer shook her head. "He has to be lying, right?"

Holly shrugged as she stared moodily out the front window over the main street of Fontana Village, a town boasting less than a hundred residents. "Why lie when he can threaten, intimidate, or con you into doing what he wants?"

"Did you know her?" Summer asked softly, well aware that her twin was suffering.

"I did." Other than Holly's darker coloring, her sister's actions were like watching herself in a mirror. The casual shrug and raised brows were Summer's go-to gestures when she tried to appear uncaring. She was usually anything but.

"Did you get to see her for your whole eight years before...?" She couldn't bring herself to say 'her death' now that the possibility existed Aurora was resting in stasis.

"Eight? I was thirteen when she disappeared."

Thirteen? She'd been told her mother died when she was eight. Initially, the story was that Aurora was injured while she and Preston were traveling abroad. Later, after the last of the Thorne sisters turned eighteen, Preston and GiGi sat them down and told them Alastair was responsible.

Now, to find out that nothing she'd been told was the truth, made the reality difficult to absorb. Her mother hadn't died. She had, in fact, continued through life without once bothering to visit her other four children for five additional years before her coma.

The walls were closing in around her. "I have to go."

"Summer." Had the entreaty not been in Holly's voice, Summer would've teleported back to her mountain. But her twin's pain spoke to her own. "Will you come back?"

Loneliness. It hung around Holly's neck in the heaviest of chains.

"I'm the screw up of the family," Summer found herself saying. "I can't seem to perform more than a basic spell without it going awry." Unable to meet the compassionate understanding in eyes so eerily similar, she stared beyond Holly to the street outside. "I've loved one guy for an entire lifetime. Today he told me he can't handle what I am. It isn't the first time he's objected to my abilities, but somehow it was the worst, because I thought we were happy."

She hadn't realized the tears were falling unchecked down her face until Holly gently wiped them away.

"Coop was right. Other than my sisters, I have no friends," she whispered. "Or, no friends that aren't animals."

"Being what we are means we can't have friends. At least, that's what mother always told me," Holly said, her voice and expression far away, as if she were remembering. "She said, I can only trust myself and needed to listen to my heart."

"But?"

Holly smiled and met her inquiring gaze. "But I didn't listen. I believed I *could* have friends and they would be okay with what I am." She drew aside the V of her waitress uniform. A jagged scar ran from collarbone to breast on the right side of her chest. "Courtesy of my best friend and my husband."

Summer's hands flew to her mouth. "Oh, Holly!"

"They wanted to be together but were afraid of me. They thought if they killed me, I wouldn't have the power to exact revenge for their affair."

Tears poured faster. The suffering her sister must've endured ripped Summer's heart out from the inside. "I'm so sorry."

"It's the past."

"Please tell me they are in jail."

"He's dead. Until now, I'd only kept Beau's last name to remind me to make better choices." She shrugged. "I started the paperwork to change it back to Thorne. As for my ex-best-friend Michelle, she's in an institution somewhere, babbling about a man who appeared from nowhere and set Beau on fire." Holly's smile was pure evil satisfaction. "Of course, she was tried for his murder and found guilty. I do have one thing to thank our father for, I suppose."

Unable not to, Summer reached for Holly and pulled her into an embrace. "I can't imagine what you must've gone through. I'm sorry."

"It's ancient history."

"No, I'm sorry I wasn't there to light the match that set that fucker on fire."

Summer waited for the sneeze that never came from her curse word. She drew back and glanced around then turned stunned eyes on Holly. "I didn't sneeze."

Holly's blue eyes flew wide. "You didn't!"

"Do you think it's because you were a buffer? Because I was hugging you?"

"It's possible. Try it without." Holly backed up and gave her an encouraging nod.

"Do you really want mice to fill up your restaurant?"

Holly shrugged. "It's just us and Pete."

Summer cast a wary glance over her shoulder in the direction of the kitchen. "Does Pete know what you are?"

"Yes. Alastair assigned him as my protection. But the man doesn't possess an ounce of magical ability and falls asleep while chopping vegetables. If I didn't, you know..." She wiggled her fingers. "... I'd have nothing to serve the customers."

"Okay, here goes." Summer drew in a breath. "Damn," she said and promptly sneezed.

A small scurry of mice appeared at the edge of the room.

"Now again but hold my hand," Holly urged.

Summer gripped her sister's fingers. "Damn." Nothing. "I can't believe this. You try!"

"Shit," Holly said. No sneeze.

They laughed as one and took turns coming up with creative curse words.

"Well, isn't this a sight," drawled a deep I-could-do-you-all-night voice.

The girls screamed in stereo.

"Quentin Buchanan! You mangy cur! You can't just sneak up on people like that." Holly scolded the man with the mussy dark hair and milk chocolate bedroom eyes who sat on the counter.

His amused chuckle brought to mind endless hours of making love.

He jumped off his perch and sauntered to where the sisters stood. His walk was pure seduction.

"Dear Goddess," Summer breathed. It was hard to imagine anyone sexier than Cooper Carlyle, but this man had Coop beat hands down.

Her eyes shrugged off her brain's command to rein in her inappropriate sexual thoughts and continued to eat him up.

The slow knowing smile that spread across his face created a tingling in her lady bits.

"You're a warlock," Summer blurted.

"I am. And you're a witch..." He nodded toward Holly. "... like her."

"I am."

His hot gaze swept a leisurely path from the top of her head to the tips of her toes. The returning journey paused on all her woman parts. His appreciative smile grew wider.

"You certainly are."

Her ovaries fired up and caused a wave of heat to encase her entire body.

"Why don't you two get a damned room already?" Holly snapped. *Achoo!*

Crows landed on the sill outside.

In a move which shocked Summer speechless, Quentin swept an arm around Holly and buried his head against her neck. "There's no need to be jealous, my love. There's enough of me to go around."

"Get off me!" Holly snapped.

Quentin ignored her to run his tongue up the side of her throat and nip her ear. "I love it when you play hard to get."

As suddenly as he grabbed Holly, he released her and focused on Summer.

Feeling like a deer in the headlights, she froze as he stepped to where she stood. "Hello, gorgeous. And who might you be?"

"Mine," growled a voice she'd recognize until her dying day.

There was no need for her to check to know who stood behind her. What she didn't know was how the hell he'd teleported here. She assumed Alastair until she heard Autumn add, "But I'm definitely single and willing."

Fury at her sister's disloyalty boiled inside Summer. She'd sent Autumn a text to explain the situation when she'd first arrived at the restaurant. For her to show up with Coop in tow was a betrayal of the sister code.

But for now, Summer would take one issue at a time. She whirled and pinned Coop with a glare.

"Yours? Pfft." She stormed to where he stood ten feet away. "Correct me if I'm wrong, but weren't you the one who said he needed a break…" She consulted the clock on the wall. "…less than five hours ago?"

Her fist found his chest. The impact made a satisfying thud so she did it again. "You can kiss my ass!" Her sneeze brought more members of the rodent gang scrambling into the room.

"I'll be damned. It happens to her, too," Quentin laughed.

Coop shot him a shut-the-hell-up glare then addressed Summer. "You blinked out of my office without a by-your-leave, and then don't answer a damned call or text? What the hell is up with that?"

"You said we were over," she enunciated as if he were hard of hearing.

"No, I didn't. I said I needed a few days. You assumed we were over."

"I am not your plaything to pick up and put down when you get bored, Coop," she seethed. "You can go fu—!"

His hand clapped over her mouth. "Based on the emotion behind that word, we're going to have the entire rat population of North Carolina here in under a minute."

Summer shoved his hand away and clamped her jaw shut.

Cooper wasn't finished. "It turns out, I didn't need a few days. I didn't even need a few hours." He softened his tone and ran his thumb over her lower lip. "I only needed two seconds after you disappeared to realize I'd just pulled the second most bone-headed move of my life."

She knocked his hand away and took a step back. "I'm not accepting your honeyed words this time. When I said goodbye, I meant it."

"Bravo!" Quentin cheered. "Holly, my love, doesn't this scene bring back memories? Remember, just last—"

"Shut up, you tool," Holly snapped. "My sister is experiencing a moment of triumph, and you're ruining it."

"Sister?" Three heads whipped back and forth between Summer and Holly.

"Yes," Summer confirmed. "Seems dear old Mom gave birth to twins, then thought it would be a great idea to separate us and give Holly to Alastair to raise."

Autumn stumbled forward. "You're our sister?"

Holly nodded and reached for Summer to pull her close.

"How long have you known?" Autumn's temper, when riled, was a thing of beauty. She'd perfected an icy demeanor. In this, she was more like Alastair than either Summer or Holly.

"I found out less than an hour ago," Summer said.

Autumn's anger fizzled out, and she cast an apologetic glance

Summer's way as she stepped up to Holly. "Sister." She nodded. "Now it makes sense. When Summer was about six months old, I started dreaming there were two of her, but one went missing. I'd wake up crying. Dad would hug me and tell me it was all just a dream. That the other Summer was my imagination." She stroked a hand down Holly's arm in wonder. "You really do exist. The other Summer."

As Coop looked on, the tear-fest started for the three women. Quentin let out a disgusted snort, mumbled something about needing a drink, and disappeared in a swirl of light.

Another warlock.

"Great," he muttered under his breath.

Those bastards were popping up left and right faster than Coop could process the fact they existed in the first place.

The desire to escape the unfolding emotional scene was upon him. But he feared the moment he set foot outside, Summer would disappear again. Not that he could stop her if he *wasn't* outside, but he could at least attempt to reason with her to stay and work through their issues.

He'd been the idiot everyone had been calling him lately. Coop had told the truth when he told Summer it had only taken moments for him to regret his urge to take a break. What type of man ran in the face of a little adversity? A coward.

Coop wasn't a coward. Not by a long shot. But he'd been thrown into another world, one where people had the power to alter your mind, to make you forget, to disappear at will, to electrocute people with a bolt from their hand, to create tidal waves, and to freeze time with a curl of their fist. It was enough to shake even the most stout-hearted and make them freak the fuck out.

He moved away to give the women space. As he stared out the window, he noticed a male watching the restaurant from across the street. Coop took special note of his appearance; tall, maybe six-three or four, large build, but leaning to the trim side. The guy couldn't be more than thirty or so because he still retained the look of youth about him. His clothes had a look of quality, as if they were from the finest department store or tailor made. His shaggy blond hair fell across his eyes and made it difficult for Coop to get a bead on their color. In the guy's hand was a gold coin that he worked through his fingers and across his knuckles—not dissimilar to hustlers in a movie.

But what struck Coop as odd was the air of sullenness mixed with sadness. Coop followed the guy's line of sight to the three women. He knew one of them, that was for sure. Or at the very least, he wanted to.

As if he sensed Coop's regard, the man shifted his head by slow degrees until he spotted Coop off to one side of the large window. He straightened, ducked back into the shadow of the doorway he'd been loitering in, and in a quick flash of light, the guy was gone.

That made two new warlocks in less than thirty minutes. They were multiplying like rabbits in these parts. It couldn't be a coincidence.

Coop would be happy to see the last of this town.

———

"WHAT DO YOU MEAN YOU'RE STAYING?"

Coop was fit to be tied. Reasoning with Summer was like trying to change the gravitational pull of the earth—not impossible, but highly unlikely.

"Exactly what I said, Coop. I'm staying." Her stubborn chin shot into the air.

His fists clenched with the desire to wring her neck. "Summer, you have a home and business back in Leiper's Fork. I have my job as Sheriff."

Her lip curled in a semblance of a sneer. "You and your job don't figure into my plans, Sheriff."

"Why?" he demanded. "We love each other, and if you could see my side of this for one damned minute, you'd see that, while I made a mistake, it wasn't done to hurt you."

"Yeah, you keep saying that. You should have it tattooed on your forehead. Maybe then you wouldn't need to sound like an annoying song on repeat."

He stepped in close but didn't touch her. "Thornes only love once."

"So when we draw the short straw we should count ourselves lucky and go with it?" she asked nastily. "Tell me, Coop, if you can't handle

209

me as I am, how are you going to handle any kids we might have? Goddess forbid they break one of your millions of rules or let an elephant swim in your pool. Let's not even touch on the subject of one of them levitating their fork through the air in front of a stranger. Ooohhhh, we might have to alter a memory so witnesses forget what they've seen. Ooohhhh, we'll have taken their free will." She waved her hands about to emphasize her point.

He swiftly lost his temper. Because he didn't have an answer about hiding any future children's magic, he zeroed in on Eddie. "That elephant is a pervert and wants to mate with my prize mare."

"That!" she yelled and pointed at his face. "That right there is what I'm talking about. You think if things are of two different species, they can't be together. Like you and me. I'm a witch and you're powerless."

"I'm a warlock according to Alastair."

"Pfft. You can't even say the word without going green. Even if you were, which I doubt, you'd be a piss-poor one at that."

"Now you're just *trying* to tick me off," he snapped.

"We both know what happens when you get mad. The gloves come off and the weapon comes out. You gonna take out your gun and shoot me again, Sheriff?"

Breathing became difficult and sweat beaded his brow as her words took him back to the day he'd shot her. Coop cupped his palms over his eyes in an effort to regain control. Coming to terms with his actions hadn't happened yet. Perhaps it never would. Because had GiGi not arrived when she did, Summer wouldn't be alive today. And every single time he thought of his life without her, he became ill.

"That last bit was below the belt, Coop. I apologize."

He lifted his head and lowered his barriers. "I love you."

"It's not enough."

"It is. It can be. We can make it be." The raw emotion in his voice left her in little doubt of his sincerity, and yet, he could tell she wasn't moved.

"Go home, Coop."

The finality in her tone almost broke him. But he wasn't above begging. "You want to move here? To start over? Then we can do it together. You and me, Summer. I'll give my whole focus to being your partner in every way. I'll let Alastair train me. I'll help you build your business and the new rescue center. I'll even shovel elephant shit for the rest of my days."

"It's a pretty speech. Tempting to watch you try. But you'll start to question if it's worth it. Preston was right, you know. You don't have what it takes to be a witch's mate." Her irises darkened to stormy gray. "*Go home, Coop.*"

26

*C*oop spent the next six days parked by his pool in a drunken stupor and contemplated the mating habits of elephants. One elephant in particular.

Today he watched his prize mare with the traffic cone on her head. The stupid thing should've been removed months ago. He was stuck with a damned unicorn wannabe on his hands. Now, when anyone tried to remove the contraption from her forehead, the mare pitched a fit. Started kicking stall walls and refusing to eat.

Chloe insisted the mare felt more comfortable with it on. At some point, she'd decorated it with gold spray paint and glitter in order to make the mare, Macy, feel pretty. How she knew was anyone's guess.

He jerked upright and weaved a bit in the process. How did she know?

"Midget! Midge!"

"Yeah, Uncle Coop?"

"Where were you? I thought you were in the pool."

She grinned, and her brown eyes twinkled with mischief.

Were her eyes brighter than normal?

"Never mind that. How do you know the mare likes that infernal cone?"

His niece dropped her gaze, shrugged, and swept her foot back and forth along the pool deck.

An ingrained instinct told him she was worried if she told the truth, he'd think she was lying. "Midge, do you have something you want to get off your chest?"

She shook her head but didn't look up.

While not one-hundred percent sober, Coop's buzz was quickly wearing off. "Chloe, come here, sweetheart."

She inched closer but still refused to meet his eyes.

For a split second, her actions reminded him of Summer's when she was afraid to tell him the truth.

"Chloe, I won't be mad. Can you tell me how you know the mare wants to keep her cone? Is it because she kicks the stall and refuses to eat?"

His niece shook her dark head. "She told me."

"You know what," he said gently. "I believe she did."

Her head whipped up and her eyes grew round as saucers. "You do?"

"Yep. Can you tell me how it's done?"

"I saw Miss Summer do it one day when she was here. It's easy, Uncle Coop. You just put your hand flat on her head, and Macy tells you everything."

"How does she tell you?"

"She shows me pictures."

He sighed and scrubbed his hands over his jaw.

"You don't believe me," she said.

When the light brown of her irises faded a marginal amount, Coop groaned.

Chloe was a witch.

Alastair hadn't lied about magic in his line.

"I'm sorry, Uncle Coop," she said tearfully. "I made it up. Don't be mad at me."

"I'm not mad, midge. But I don't think you made it up." He smiled and willed her to see he was being honest. "In fact, I know you didn't."

"You do?" Her tears dried up, but her forlorn expression didn't change. "My friends don't. They called me a liar and don't want to play with me anymore."

His heart pinged.

Summer and her family knew what it had taken him forever to realize. Magical children weren't isolated for the outside world's sake. They were isolated for their own. To protect them against fear mongers and ridicule.

"I do believe you, sweetheart. As a matter of fact, I'd like to see what else you know how to do."

The sparkle returned to her eyes, and they brightened to their normal light honey shade. She glanced around as if ready to impart a secret.

He leaned forward to provide his undivided attention.

"Watch," she whispered.

She waved her hands.

Nothing happened that he could tell.

"Did you see it?"

Christ, he was reading into things that weren't there. She was only a child with an active imagination.

"I'm afraid not. I must've had too many beers, midget."

She laughed and tilted his head skyward. "Now watch, Uncle Coop."

She waved her hands again, and he *did* see.

He saw the breeze pick up and the trees sway before the wind died back down.

"Chloe, are you making the air move the trees?"

"Yes!" she cried excitedly. "Isn't it cool?"

"It certainly is."

"Wait until Dad finds out!"

Keaton! In his own personal angst, Coop had forgotten to mention any of this to his brother. Not the fact they were descended from witches, or the fact the two of them had most likely had any power bound at a young age.

Once Coop got his head out of his ass, he intended to train with Alastair. That wouldn't go over well with Keaton either.

"How about we keep this to ourselves until I've had a chance to speak with your dad?"

"Do you think he'll be mad?"

"No, midge, but it's not every day you find out your beautiful little girl has a superpower. These things need to be finessed."

Her eyes flew wide and her mouth opened in a perfect O. "Do you think I can fly, Uncle Coop?"

Because he didn't know and the thought caused him to break out in a cold sweat, he said, "I'm going to put the kibosh on flying until you're older. I don't need to go gray before my time."

She giggled and hugged him. "Okay."

An idea came to him. "I know some people who might be able to help you figure out if flying is possible."

"Yeah?"

"Yeah."

"The Weird Season Sisters?"

He frowned. "That's not a nice thing to say, Chloe."

"But everyone calls them that."

"They aren't weird. In fact, all the sisters are nice, funny, and extremely intelligent."

"Not Miss Autumn. She makes Daddy mad."

He lifted a brow in warning.

"I'm sorry."

"It's okay, sweetheart. Just promise you won't repeat it."

"I promise."

"Good. Now how about you pick up around here while I go talk to your dad? What do you think?"

"You have an awful lot of beer cans."

He tugged her ponytail. "I'll pay you a quarter a can."

"Deal!"

"When you have a chance, do you think you could ask Macy how she feels about Eddie?"

She giggled. "I already know."

"Care to spill the beans?"

"I think she likes him. She has lots of pictures of him in her head."

"Thanks, midget."

"You're welcome, Uncle Coop."

Coop went in search of his brother. It was time for the talk.

"WELL, DAMN, SIS. THAT WAS SWEET." HOLLY WIPED THE STRAY TEAR from her cheek.

"It was, wasn't it?" Summer sighed as she covered the mirror on the table in front of her. Little moments like these made her believe she'd misjudged Coop.

"You should give him another chance."

"Not you too!" Summer groaned. "I've had to hear this from everyone. Even Alastair, if you can believe it."

"Based on what you've told me, I expected Coop to freak out on the kid. But did you see how he encouraged her?" Holly grabbed a handful of popcorn and fell back into the plush red chaise in the corner of Summer's new attic. "I'd lay odds he intends to talk to her dad in order to pave the way for her to learn from our sisters."

Summer brought the bowl to the chair and gestured Holly to scoot over. She climbed onto the chaise beside her and offered up the bowl.

Today had been the first day she'd given into the urge to scry and spy. Oddly, she was glad she had.

Holly had arrived after Coop had opened his first beer and toasted the absent Summer aloud. Her sister had claimed she had a sixth sense that he would have a revelation. And when Holly produced the popcorn to enhance their viewing pleasure, Summer had laughed.

Her new sister was similar to Autumn in temperament. Hanging with her twin eased some of the homesickness being away from her sisters created.

"Part of me doesn't want you to go back to him," Holly confessed. "Because then you'll leave here."

"This is my home now. The animals are settling in, and I've taken out an ad to establish my business name. Once I sign the lease on the little blue two-story you found on the edge of town, I'll be able to set up an actual office for patients."

"Dear old Dad won't be happy. You'll have no time to chase after his damned objects."

Because their arms were touching, Holly didn't sneeze.

Summer suspected Holly had planned it that way. They'd made a game of it when they were alone.

"I don't care what Alastair likes or doesn't like. I'll run my life as I see fit."

"I wish I could be the same way. But he saved my life." Holly flopped her head back on the pillow. "I owe him."

"No, you don't. He's your father."

"But—"

"No, Holly. His saving you should've been done out of love or duty, not to gain a minion."

"You're right," she sighed. "I know you are. Yet, I can't seem to tell him no. Not if it's going to bring Mom back."

"I wonder if that's even possible," Summer mused.

"Enough about all that. I think you should go see Coop. Forgive him, have all kinds of wild monkey sex, and be happy."

"Until the next time he decides he's fed up." Summer rested her head on Holly's shoulder. "I don't know what to do."

"Such is love, dear sister. Such is love."

"Speaking of, we never discuss *your* love life. What's with that hot warlock?"

"Quentin?"

Summer got warm just thinking about all that yumminess. "Yeah, Quentin." She sighed.

Holly shoved Summer's head off her shoulder and sat up. "Are you lusting over Quentin?" she demanded.

"Ha! I *knew* you wanted him."

"Well, duh! Look at the man. Who wouldn't want him?" Holly settled back on the pillows. "But he's a grade A player, and I can't trust him as far as I could throw him."

"You think it's because of your past experiences, or is it the man himself?"

"If I'm being honest, probably a combination of both."

"So why not just have sex with him? See if all the buildup and angst is worth it. He could be a dud."

The sisters shared a look and laughed.

"Yeah, okay, so we both know sex with him will rock your world. But there's nothing written that says you have to marry the guy."

Holly winced.

Summer cringed inside. "I'm sorry. I wasn't thinking."

"No worries. Besides, I already had sex with him—a long time ago."

"*What?* I want the deets!"

"I'll say he was amazing and leave it at that. One day, I promise, I'll tell you the whole story."

Summer studied her sister and slowly nodded.

Holly held her cards close to her chest, and Summer could appreciate her reservations.

"Okay. And on a different note, I want you to come work for me."

"What?"

Summer laughed at her sister's dumbfounded expression. "I want you to come work for me. But only if you want to." She held up a hand when Holly would've interrupted. "Look, I know you don't want to touch the Thorne money. I get it. But waitressing can't bring in all that much. As my office manager and assistant, you can earn a decent living." She smiled. "And best of all, we get to spend more time together."

"You might hate me once you get to know me. I'm outspoken and likely to piss you off."

"Doubtful. And you can even live here if you want. There's more than enough room, and you don't have to pay rent."

"Yeah, you certainly got carried away designing the place," Holly laughed.

"Confession? I might've designed the whole right side of the house with you in mind."

"Is that why it has its own kitchen?"

Summer recalled making the glass room that separated what was essentially two residences. The floor-to-ceiling glass walls looked out over the property. With a thirty-foot-high pitched roof that boasted eight large skylights, it resembled more of a conservatory or greenhouse. The room was massive and required a thirty-five-foot catwalk to join the two homes by way of the individual attics.

To give the room warmth, Summer added dwarf ever-bearing fruit trees and lined the interior walls with bins of strawberry bushes. It was like an indoor orchard.

The glass room was Morty's favorite place to paint.

"Yes."

"I, for one, love this place," Holly told her.

"Then say you'll move in with me."

"I'll move in on the condition you give Coop a second chance."

Summer jerked to her feet to pace. "That's asking too much, Holly. I want you here, but not at the expense of setting myself up for heartache again."

"You never intend to take another chance on anyone?"

"I don't know."

"Summer, you'd be foolish not to give him another chance. He loves you."

Because thinking about her pathetic love life would require making a decision, Summer wanted to avoid this discussion at all costs. "Can we let it rest? At least for a little while?"

Holly grimaced and nodded.

"Good, now when do we move you in? I need to call our sisters for some magical muscle."

27

"Now that I have you all here, we need to discuss Alastair's revelation about Mom," Summer said as her sisters gathered around her kitchen table.

Autumn shoved aside her breakfast plate. "Look, I know you trust him. He's claimed he's your father, made a few promises, and you suddenly believe everything coming out of his mouth. Well, I'm sorry. I don't." She gestured to Spring and Winnie. "They don't either."

"I'm not sure I do. Not one-hundred percent," Summer confessed and took a sip of her coffee.

She struggled with the words she wanted to say. "I intend to have him take me to where she is kept. I want to see for myself if he's telling the truth."

Protests rose around her. She held up a hand. "I'm doing this. If there is a chance she's alive, a chance she needs a magical trinket to bring her back to us, I'll do whatever I can to retrieve it."

"Summer!" Spring protested.

"I don't need you all to get on board this insane scavenger hunt. But I do need you to understand why I'm doing it. I also need one of you to stay here and take over the day-to-day rescue operations."

"I'll do it," Autumn said.

"Thanks. I'll make sure you have the feed schedules and—,"

"No. I mean, I'll go to see her. Then I'll retrieve whatever is needed for her recovery."

Summer opened her mouth to argue, but Autumn cut her off a second time.

"I have the least to lose." She shrugged. "You have all of this. Your animals need you. Coop needs you too, whether you care to acknowledge it or not. You also have a new twin to get to know."

"No, Tums. We can't know who or what might hold the item. I can't ask you to do this."

"You didn't ask. I volunteered."

Summer turned to her silent sisters. "Say something, you three. Tell her she's being stubborn."

Winnie shook her head. "She's right. You, of all of us, have the most to lose." Winnie grasped Summer's hand between both of hers and rubbed. "You also need to repair this rift with Coop. He's sorry, sister, and he's miserable. As are you."

Irritation spiked Summer's temper. "Have all of you forgotten what he's done? Are we all so desperate for a man that we'll take whatever asshole comes our way?"

Spring was the most even-tempered of all five sisters. However, she shocked everyone when she snapped, "Your nastiness is uncalled for, Summer." She sighed and softened her next words. "You think you're the only one to have her heart ripped out, but you're not. Tums has close to ten years on you. But if she's encouraging you to patch things up, then maybe you should listen."

Autumn stood and circled to where Summer sat. "I hate seeing you miserable. It's needless because you both want the same thing."

She wasn't saying anything Summer hadn't thought in the dark hours of the night when she'd lie alone in her bed. But her sense of self-preservation wouldn't let her lay her heart on the line again.

"He's hot and cold. I can't take the back and forth, Tums."

"He's a guy. Guys don't know what they want until they screw it up. When they realize the best thing that ever happened to them walked out the door, they implode," Winnie added.

Summer received the impression her sister spoke from experience, but she'd never heard a word of any major romance in Winnie's past.

"Winnie?" she questioned.

"That's another story for another time." Winnie smiled softly. "This is about you and Coop."

"I thought it was about an ancient artifact," Summer countered to skirt around the issue of her relationship or lack thereof. "Can we get back to that subject? Please?"

Three of her four sisters shared a speaking look.

"What?" Summer threw up her hands. "Just come out with it already."

"Fine. You told us you needed to find something called the Chintamani Stone."

Summer nodded.

"I've done some additional research." Autumn opened the laptop in front of her.

Envy—not quite full green but a shade in that general color wheel—hit Summer. Just once she'd like to be able to teleport with an electronic device larger than her smartphone.

"Earth to Summer."

"Sorry," she mumbled. Gah! She had to stop with these little side flights of fancy and focus on the subject at hand. She'd have to remember to ask Winnie if she made a homeopathic equivalent to Adderall.

"You mentioned it was last in the safekeeping of a couple called Roerich. Their intent was to deliver it to a monastery in Tibet."

"That's correct."

"Everything I've read indicates that this couple never reached Shambhala. In fact, it's a mythical city," Autumn informed the group. "One written account claims they did make it as far as Shigatse which is located in the Tsang province of Tibet. There is an old monastery there that fits the description of Helena Roerich's diary entry."

"You found this all in just a few days? Impressive." Holly lifted her coffee cup up in salute.

Autumn grinned. "Research and finance are my strengths."

"What's the plan? Start with the monastery and backtrack?" Winnie asked.

"We're talking fifty years here." Autumn shook her head. "I can't imagine a relic as powerful as this one is reported to be will still be there."

"You think this is a wild goose chase," Summer stated flatly.

"I do. However, I did find another something interesting in the margin of Helena's diary."

"Wait! Are you saying you found her original diary?" Summer asked, incredulous and awed by her sister's mad research skills.

"I have. Or I should say, Aunt GiGi has."

"What's this something interesting?"

"She only wrote four words with a question mark: *Only couples in love?* I think perhaps she was making a note to herself about the stone. Although, I don't know how to decipher it." Autumn shrugged and grimaced. "If it's what I think, and only an actual couple can retrieve the stone, then it leaves all of us out."

"Not necessarily," Summer argued. "Technically, Coop and I are in love. But he has no magical ability. For that matter, you and Keaton could be considered in love as well."

"Don't be ridiculous. Keaton doesn't love me. We have a better chance of matching Winnie and Zane or Spring and Knox than we do me and Keaton."

Both sisters in question sputtered and flushed.

Interesting. Summer intended to dig deeper into their love lives when this was all done. Turnabout was fair play.

"So it has to be me and Coop." She thunked her head on the wood table. "That conversation is going to go over well. 'Hey, Coop, I'm no longer interested in a relationship with you, but do you mind jaunting off to the Himalayas with me? I have an object to retrieve for the father who terrifies you. Why yes, it will give him unlimited power.'"

"When you put it that way, I don't see how he can refuse," Holly quipped.

Winnie, the voice of reason, piped up. "I think we're getting ahead of ourselves. First, Helena Roerich could've been making a note about dinner party attendees for all we know."

223

The siblings all exchanged glances. Winnie had a point.

"Second, I still believe either myself or Autumn to be the best candidate to go. No offense, but we are the ones with the greatest abilities." Her face was apologetic when she said, "I'm sorry, Summer, but you could potentially trigger an avalanche or some other crazy natural disaster on that mountain."

Summer scrunched up her face but patted her sister's hand. "No offense taken. You're not wrong."

"I'll go, Winnie. You have a business to run," Autumn declared. "It will be a simple matter to pop over to China, ask some questions, and pop back."

They were all in agreement that any "popping" would wait until they discovered the whereabouts and condition of their mother.

"I'm with Dad on this, I don't think any one witch or warlock should possess an object with such power," Spring said. "I think if, or when, we do find the stone, we let the witches' council decide."

"All in favor?" Summer asked half-jokingly.

Heartfelt "ayes" flew around the room.

"Is this the way all major decisions get made in your family?" Holly wanted to know.

"*Our* family," the Thorne siblings chorused.

"You're our sister too, Holly," Autumn said with an arched brow.

The tears brightening her twin's eyes caused Summer's own emotion to well up.

"I'm so glad you found me," Holly choked out.

"Aww hell! Group hug," Autumn declared.

C oop shifted his stance and sent the mare he was training in a different direction. When the bay shied and reared, he checked over his shoulder for a visitor.

Summer.

He curbed the urge to rush over and sweep her into his embrace. Instead, he chose to corral the mare and hook the lead.

"Hey."

"Hey."

Their eyes connected across the distance of the round pen before she dropped her gaze.

If he didn't know better, he'd assume her look of uncertainty indicated she feared her welcome.

"How's the new sanctuary?" he asked as an ice breaker.

A genuine smile graced her lips. "Perfect. Eddie's barn is magnificent. I've added a pool."

Coop forced a smile in return. "That should make him happy."

"Yeah, they all seem to be settling in well."

"Good."

Small talk out of the way, he didn't know what else to say.

"Coop, can we talk? I mean, after you're done training or work or something."

"I'm finished for today. Let me put Sadie in the paddock and check on Macy then I'm all yours."

"I'll check Macy, unless you'd prefer Dr. Parsons."

"No, I prefer you," he said.

Her surprise was apparent.

"I know you can see the images in the horses' minds, Summer. It gives you an advantage. You're also a damned good doctor who cares about her patients." He gave a short nod. "So yeah, I'm cool with you checking on Macy. But don't be surprised by the colorful cone. Chloe has your Dr. Doolittle ability to speak to the animals and has sworn Macy wanted something prettier than the florescent orange."

Summer's wide smile was brighter than the morning sun.

He cleared his throat of the emotion building. "I'll meet you in Macy's stall after I'm done."

She nodded and headed for the barn.

As he watched her walk away, he let hope seep back into his chest. If she wanted to try again, he was going to grab on with both hands and never let go, no matter how freaked out he got by whatever magic he happened to witness.

Five minutes later, after he'd released the mare and washed his hands, he halted in the aisle by Macy's stall door and rested his arms along the top of the wood.

Summer murmured something to the mare, and the horse responded in animal speak. "She seems to be doing well," she said. "I'm impressed with her recovery. You know she doesn't need the cone for balance anymore, right?"

"Yeah, but Chloe insists Macy likes it." He unlatched the door and shifted to let her out. "She also says Macy misses Eddie's visits."

Summer cast a glance over her shoulder at the mare. And damned if the horse didn't nod her head.

"I have room at the sanctuary for her if you'd like me to take her."

Coop rubbed Macy's neck. "You'll have to ask her. I'd miss her, but whatever is best for her peace of mind works for me."

"You could visit, too."

He stopped the action of stroking the long column of the horse's throat. "What are you saying?"

"I'm saying I'm sorry."

Coop faced Summer. The dark circles under her eyes matched the ones he'd seen in the mirror lately. "You're not the one who should be apologizing, sweetheart."

"I pushed you into accepting what I am instead of easing you into it, Coop. If I'd have given it any thought at all, I'd have realized it was too much, too soon."

"I'm not going to lie and say it wasn't a lot to wrap my head around, but I could've, and should've, handled it better than I did." He tugged on a lock of her brilliant blonde hair. "I love you, Summer Thorne. I will until the last breath of air leaves my lungs and until the last thud of my beating heart. Then I'll spend my time in the afterlife loving you even more."

With a shaking hand, he thumbed away the solitary tear from her petal-soft cheek.

"I love you too, Coop. Until the last breath of air leaves my lungs and until the last thud of my beating heart."

"Sounds like you two just exchanged wedding vows," a wry voice inserted.

Coop hung his head. "Christ, Knox. Ya think your timing could be a little better?"

"It's better than catching you in the middle of doing the dirty, isn't it?"

Summer laughed and threw herself into Coop's arms.

He hugged her tight and whispered, "I'd never admit it to him, but yeah, it sounds like we just committed to each other. You in?"

"I'm in," she confirmed.

"You may kiss the bride," Knox quipped.

"I'm going to kill him," Coop told her while he attempted to ignore his smirking cousin.

She bit the corner of her lip. "I don't know. I think he has a good idea. You should totally kiss me."

"Sweetheart, when I start, I don't intend to stop. I don't want an audience for that."

Pink stained her cheeks. He laughed and bussed her brow.

Without releasing her, he looked at Knox. "What's up, man? Was it something important, or are you just here to bust my balls?"

"Can't it be both?"

Coop raised a brow.

"River's Run is selling off stock. I want to go check out a few of their stallions as possible additions to our herd. You cool with that?"

"Of course. What do Keaton and Zane think?"

"They're on board."

"When do you leave?"

"There's a flight out to Colorado this afternoon," Knox informed him. "I'd like to be on it."

"Okay. When you get back, there are a few things we need to discuss," Coop said. He drew back and glanced down at Summer. "Family matters."

"It might be a few weeks. My mom isn't faring well. I got the call last night."

"Anything we can do?" he asked, concerned because Knox hadn't spoken to or about his mother in years.

"I'll let you know if there is." Knox stepped forward and held his arms out to Summer. She went into his embrace.

Coop experienced a flare of jealousy and possessiveness.

"Congrats, beautiful," Knox said softly. "I wish you both a long and happy life together." To Coop, he said, "Take care of her, or I'll kick your ass."

They shook hands, and Coop couldn't help feeling he was sealing a deal. "I intend to."

After Knox left the barn, Coop gathered her close. "I thought he'd never leave."

She giggled and lifted her face for his kiss.

LATER, AS THEY WERE IN BED, SUMMER BROACHED THE SUBJECT SHE'D had with her sisters a few days before.

Coop stilled. He hated the suspicion that clouded his mind, but he had to ask. "Did you come here to gain my help for the stone?"

Her body tensed against his side.

He sat up and turned his back to her. "God, I'm so stupid."

"No, Coop. I mean, yes, I would like your input. But no, I'm here for me."

He didn't dare hope she spoke the truth.

As if she read his mind, she said in a low voice, "I love you, Cooper Carlyle. It's no secret that I always have. I think by now you know me. Know who I am deep inside." She paused, and he glanced over his shoulder.

She knelt in the middle of his bed, naked with arms spread wide. "You know what you see is what you get. I don't know how to be anything but myself."

"Why now? Am I to believe you've suddenly had a change of heart?"

"That's exactly what I expect you to believe because it's *true*." She dropped her arms. "Three days ago, as I sat around the table with my sisters, I was of the mind that you and I were done. But the more I thought about it, the more I remembered how happy we were for the brief time we were together, the more I realized how stubborn I was being."

Summer inched forward and wrapped her arms around him from behind, her forehead pressed against his spine. "You came to me first. You apologized and were willing to try again. How could I ignore that?"

He felt the movement as she slowly shook her head.

"I sent you away because I was afraid, Coop. You have the ability to wound me like no one else. What does it say about me that all you have to do is smile my way and I'm willing to forgive you anything?" she asked on a whisper.

Coop twisted and tugged her into his lap. "I'm sorry," he said raggedly. "I don't know how to say it enough."

"You don't have to. You've said it, and I know you mean it. Please know I mean it, too."

"You're not the only one afraid to trust. You've never given me a reason to doubt you, but I think I'm jaded after all these years in law enforcement."

She cupped his jaw. "Despite how much I love my new home, there's one thing missing... *you*."

He closed his eyes. "My job and my stables are here."

When the silence went on too long, he opened his eyes.

She wasn't upset. In fact, she appeared downright mischievous with her glowing sky-blue eyes.

"Well, Sheriff, it's a good thing I can move between places in the blink of an eye. During the day, I'll work at my practice, alternating it with the sanctuary. If you'll have me, I'll spend nights here with you. No different than any normal person's evening commute."

"If I'll have you? Oh, sweetheart, I'll have you any damned way I can get you," he said with feeling.

"That's what I was hoping," she laughed.

"Okay, let's figure out what to do about this damned stone."

29

*A*lastair arrived at the Thorne estate two mornings later. Summer and her sisters were on hand to meet him at the agreed upon time they'd set the night before.

"This looks like it could result in a lynching based on your dire expressions," he said dryly. He appeared unconcerned either way.

"My sisters have agreed to help me search for the Chintamani Stone. But I need to see Mother first."

Holly stepped forward and clasped her hand. "*We* need to see Mother first."

Alastair ran his impassive gaze over the group and settled on their joined hands.

"Aurora stays with me." His tone brooked no argument.

"We don't intend to remove her from your care." If Summer was sure of one thing, it was his love for her mother. "But I'm not going into this blindly, Alastair. I still don't trust you completely."

His expression hardened, and he nodded. "I know I rank last in this little family unit, child. But I do have your mother's best interests at heart."

"That's good enough for me. As long as she comes first, I'm cool with helping you." She looked to her sisters for their agreement.

Winnie and Spring nodded, but Autumn crossed her arms under her breasts and raised one perfectly arched auburn brow. She always was the more difficult sell of all Summer's sisters. Ignoring her, Summer faced Holly. "You ready for this?"

"Yep."

As one they turned toward Alastair. "We're ready."

"Hold on tight."

Before he touched them, Autumn stepped forward. "Hurt either one of them, Uncle, and I'll have your guts for garters."

Amusement twisted his lips. "You've been around my sister too long. You've developed her mannerisms." The mocking smile disappeared. "It's not always a good thing to emulate GiGi. Ask her why her beloved husband took off for the hills. You might find she isn't the saint you believe her to be."

"Fuck off, you tool. I'll trust her over you any day," Autumn snapped.

"Like I said, you've been around my sister too long." He waved Summer and Holly forward. "Come."

As Alastair clasped her hand, a surge of power pulsed through Summer. She glanced up in surprise, and he winked. Before she could question what she'd experienced, they stood outside what could only be classified as a mansion.

"What the hell? Where are we?"

"Your new sanctuary is there." He pointed to the west of their location.

Summer could just make out the top of her new home. "You're so close! I should be able to see your place from mine."

"It's cloaked." He squeezed her hand and released it. "No one knows it's here. I'm trusting you to keep quiet about the location, child. I've made my share of enemies."

The weight of responsibility hung heavily around her neck, yet she nodded all the same. "I promise."

"Come. Let's see your mother."

As they walked the maze of corridors, he spoke. "I understand you and Cooper have patched up your differences."

"Yes."

"Good."

She stopped short, surprised he approved. "What the... I thought you didn't think he was good enough for me."

"No one will be good enough for you." He glanced at Holly. "Or you." He ran a hand down Summer's hair. "But if he makes you happy, I'll let him live."

"You're a scary man, Alastair."

His deep chuckle made her lips twitch. She couldn't help it; his black sense of humor triggered her funny bone.

"Aurora is through that door." He said when they came to a stop a few minutes later. "I assume you want time alone with her."

"Thank you, F-father." It was the closest Summer could come to calling him Dad. Alastair wasn't the warm, fuzzy daddy-like figure she associated with a parent. Preston hadn't been either, but he'd been more approachable.

Alastair frowned, and his lids lowered to hide his thoughts. It was a long moment before he nodded and left.

"Did you get the impression he was overwhelmed?" Holly asked as they watched him retreat down the hall.

"Yeah. You?"

"Yeah."

"Maybe he isn't the monster we were all led to believe," Summer mused. "I think he's lonely."

"He may be. But he makes it difficult to get to know him. I've tried."

Alastair was a problem without a solution. The man was practically an outlaw in the witch community. He appeared cold, uncaring, and arrogant. Yet, on more than one occasion, he displayed glimpses of genuine humor or affection.

Summer found herself warming toward him, and it bothered her. Alastair wasn't above using her for his own ends.

"Let's go see our mother," Summer suggested as she shrugged off her dark thoughts.

The room where their mother resided in her current state was bright and airy. Classical music played on a low volume. A massive vase with dozens of fresh red roses occupied the nightstand next to the bed.

Holly's eyes followed her line of sight to the flowers. "I'm surprised the table can hold that thing."

Summer snorted. "Seems our father is a romantic at heart."

They approached the bed, one on either side.

The frail woman lying there didn't resemble the mother Summer remembered from her youth. Hints of her mother's beauty could be seen beneath the ravages of time's cruel hand. Her high cheekbones emphasized the stark, hollow areas below her eyes. Once porcelain skin was now underlined with the gray pallor of impending death. Black hair was lank and rested on the rise of her chest. It contrasted sharply with the high-necked white nightgown and pale ivory sheet.

"Goddess! She looks like a vampire," Holly whispered.

Summer silently agreed. At any second, she expected her mother to bolt upright and reveal a set of two-inch fangs.

"Think we should touch her?" Holly asked.

Apprehension gripped Summer. She didn't want to be here. Didn't want to see her vibrant mother in this condition. Didn't want to remember her like this if she never recovered.

"I can't... I can't..." The panic attack hit without warning, and she dropped to her knees beside the bed. Breathing became a chore. The sharp, stabbing pain in her chest terrified her further. If she didn't know better, she'd think she was having a heart attack.

Holly was beside her in an instant. "Breathe, Summer. In and out."

Black spots danced across her vision. "Can't," she gasped.

Oddly, she wasn't surprised when large, warm arms scooped her up and carried her out of the room. Once she cleared the doorway, her breathing came more naturally.

"I've got you, child. You're safe."

The sobs came from deep within. Big ugly gasps that contracted her lungs and stomach.

"Shhh. It's going to be all right, my girl."

Alastair came to rest in an armchair before a blazing fire in his great room. While she cried out her grief, her father held her to his chest and stroked her hair.

She could feel the words meant to comfort rumble inside his chest, but she was deaf to all but the feeling behind them. The deep baritone soothed her. How long they sat that way would've been anyone's guess, and Summer didn't care. She clung to him and absorbed his strength.

A tumbler with amber liquid appeared in his hand, and he urged it into hers. "Drink, child. You'll feel better."

Summer took a tentative sip and gasped as the liquid burned its way down to her belly.

"Again," Alastair commanded.

The second sip wasn't as fiery as the first. It went down smoother and warmed her from the inside. By her third sip, she began to enjoy the alcohol.

"What is this? I need to get some."

He laughed and hugged her tighter. "Cognac. I'll have a bottle delivered to you."

"Is it weird that I don't want to move? It's as if I…" she cut herself off.

"As if you feel our bond as father and daughter?"

She glanced up and nodded.

The bittersweet smile that twisted his lips closed her throat.

"I feel it too, child." He shifted his gaze to the dancing flames of the fireplace. "So many years wasted."

"I'm sorry."

Based on Alastair's slack-jawed expression, her apology had shocked him. "Whatever for?"

"That we didn't have a relationship. That I misjudged you."

Their eyes met and held. "Don't build me up or put me on a pedestal, Summer. I've earned my reputation."

"I don't believe you're all bad," she said softly.

"I'm not. But neither am I good. No one person is. Nothing is black and white." He cleared his throat and removed the glass from her hand.

"How do you stand looking at her like that? If it was Coop, I think I'd go insane."

"Hope is a funny thing. It digs its heels in deep and refuses to let go." His eyes lost focus, and Alastair's thoughts turned inward for a moment before he shook his head and dispelled whatever demons haunted him. "I don't live for the past. I live for the hope that one day she'll return to me."

"I think that's the most heartbreaking thing I've ever heard. And the most beautiful," Summer whispered past the emotion clogging her throat.

"I miss her laugh most of all. Do you remember it?"

"I do."

"Your mother's laugh was like the brightest star on the darkest night."

They both quieted in remembrance.

Finally, when the silence had gone on too long, Alastair cleared his throat. "Are you ready to head home?"

"Not really."

His genuine smile warmed her more than the alcohol. "Will you stay for lunch?"

"I'd like that."

He lifted her easily and set her back in the plush leather chair. "I'll find your sister and see if she cares to join us."

"Father?"

He turned in the doorway.

"Holly might take longer to come around. She resents that you kept us apart."

"For the record, that was your mother's doing. But thank you. It gives me a better understanding."

———

At dusk, Summer walked the aisle of the animal barn and checked in case Saul and the squirrel mafia had decided to spring the locks. All seemed secure, but she experienced a sense that everything was not as it should be. Something was off, and she was unable to put her finger on what or why.

The rawness she experienced when she saw her mother earlier could be to blame. Or it could be that she was here and Coop was in Leiper's Fork. She desperately needed to see him. Hold him. Hear his murmured words of love.

Her phone rang, and she checked the screen.

Coop.

It was as if he sensed her need.

"Hey."

"Hey, sweetheart. How did today go with Alastair and your mom?"

"Oh, Coop. I don't know how he stands it."

"That bad, huh?"

"I have no words."

"Are you coming over tonight?"

"I can't. Holly took off to parts unknown. She claimed she needed to clear her head after today. I'm the only one here on call for the office and sanctuary."

"I have the weekend off. I can drive there in less than five hours."

Five hours was five too many. She wanted him here with her now. "Or I can call Winnie and you can be here in five minutes," she suggested.

"Works for me. I'll pack a bag and see you soon."

They said their goodbyes and hung up. Summer shot a quick text to Winnie, who agreed to shuttle Coop.

As she glanced back down the barn's aisle, her unease grew stronger. What was she missing? Had the shadows in the back shifted?

"Who's there?" she called out.

A light footfall sounded behind her. Summer whirled around in time to duck the bat aimed at her head. From her squatted position, she visualized the interior of her house. In a second, she teleported.

As she ran to lock the door, a crash emanated from her kitchen. Perhaps her sister came back early and met up with Summer's attacker?

"Holly?"

The tall blond man who stepped into sight sent chills down her spine. In his hand was an aluminum bat identical to the one swung at her in the barn. She should know, she had an up close and personal view of it.

If he'd gotten to her kitchen that fast, it meant he had the ability to teleport. That ability screamed warlock.

"Who are you?"

Perhaps she could stall long enough for Coop and Winnie to arrive.

Magical backup was always appreciated considering she might blow her own house apart if she fucked up.

The man sneered.

"Not in a talkative mood?" she asked.

He frowned and lifted the bat.

Now, she had one of two choices. She could rush him and take the chance of getting her brains bashed in, or she could pop home to the Thorne estate in Leiper's Fork. If she missed Winnie and Coop in transit, they could be walking into a dangerous situation. But if she stayed, they could find her dead body in the living room.

"Look, I don't want to hurt you, but I will if you leave me no choice," she bluffed.

"Your left eye twitches when you lie. Did you know that?"

Huh. Maybe that's how Alastair knew she'd lied on the beach that day.

"I didn't. Thanks for letting me know. I'll work on that."

Damn! She just admitted to lying about her ability.

Her intruder's lips twitched then compressed into a flat line.

She took a deep breath and inched around the sofa as he moved farther into the room.

"Maybe if you tell me what I've done to piss you off, I can set about rectifying my mistake." Summer offered up what she hoped was a genuine smile but feared was more of a grimace.

"I want the stone." His voice was deep and husky as if he'd just sampled some of Alastair's expensive cognac.

"What stone?"

His smile wasn't nearly as nice as hers had been. "I think you know."

"I don't have it."

He frowned and lowered the bat a fraction. "You know, I almost believe you."

"You should *totally* believe me because I'm telling the truth." She pointed to her left eye. "See? No twitch."

Again, his lips spasmed as if he fought a smile. "Where is it?"

She eyed the blue bat. Her heart contracted when she realized where she'd seen it—other than in the crazy warlock's tightly fisted hands. *Morty!*

"That bat belongs to my chimpanzee. How did you get it?" Tears burned her eyes, and she blinked in rapid succession to dispel the moisture and focus on the man in front of her.

"I didn't hurt him if that's what you're asking. He's sleeping."

"As in, you put him to sleep with magic?"

"Yes."

"But he's not hurt?" She chanced a look at the stairs.

"Didn't I just say so?" the man snapped.

"Like I'm going to believe you!" she retorted. Anger built, and her power pulsed.

"What the fuck do you take me for?" He promptly sneezed.

"You sneezed!" *Nothing like stating the obvious, Summer.*

His scowl darkened when the scratching started at the back slider.

A quick glance showed a small cluster of raccoons.

"If I had to guess, I'd say you're related to me," she mused aloud.

His jade-colored eyes flew to hers.

"I'll ask again. Who are you?" Her voice was shaky, but it was with good reason.

"Don't recognize your long-lost brother, sister dear?"

"Holy shitballs!" She sneezed as violently as she swore.

Her army of mice weren't far behind.

"Mice?" His incredulous expression nearly made her laugh.

"Yeah, I think you lucked out with the raccoons if we're being honest."

He lost his fight with laughter. As he doubled over she inched toward the door.

"I'm not going to hurt you, Summer."

She squinted and curled her nose. "Um, yeah. Pardon me if I have trouble believing you. The bat arching toward my head in the barn painted a different story."

He tossed Morty's bat on the sofa and held up his hands. "It was a simple scare tactic."

Summer held out her hand and called the bat to her. When it was firmly in her grip, she breathed a sigh of relief. "Well, as scare tactics go, it worked. What if I hadn't ducked?"

"Overdramatic much?" he mocked.

The words were eerily familiar to Autumn's the day of the Great Goat Escapade. Too exact. "How long have you been watching me?"

Intelligence shone in his jade eyes, and his delighted smile told her that he appreciated she'd picked up on the clue. "Let's say the goats were inspired."

"I'm totally creeped out." If he'd been watching her all this time, what else had he seen?

"No need. I have a cosmic alert system in place." Her frown provoked a continued explanation. "It tells me when you are awake and active. I don't spy on your private moments. Not since the first kiss in the barn with your sheriff." He mock shuddered. "It was more than I cared to see."

"Not any less creeped out here. Witches have a scrying code, dude."

He shrugged as if it didn't matter one way or another. "Look, tell me where the stone is, and I'll be out of your hair."

"As much as I'd like to, I can't. I honestly don't know."

"Your eye twitched," he said dryly.

She scowled and lifted a hand to her lid. "Okay, so I may have an *idea* where it might be. But honestly, I don't have it."

"*That* I believe."

"Look, why don't we meet tomorrow morning for a cup of coffee, preferably in a well populated area, and we can discuss it then."

He studied her for a long moment before coming to some sort of decision. "I'm going to ask you not to tell Alastair I've been here. I'm not on his list of favorite people. Nor is he on mine." He snapped his hand and produced a business card. "This is my private number. Call me in the morning."

Envy reared its ugly little head. Her voice was on the testy side when she asked, "Magic comes easily to you, doesn't it?"

He didn't bother to contain his grin. "My name is Nash. I'll be expecting your call, sister."

He disappeared, and all that remained of his visit was the ivory business card on the coffee table.

Summer picked it up and turned it over. Nash Thorne, CEO of Thorne Industries. Well, he was a new wrinkle in the fabric of her life.

Her brother! How many other family members were going to crawl out of the woodwork? She needed to have a serious talk with Alastair.

She sat down heavily on the sofa and rested her head back against the pillows. Her life was never going to be the same.

30

"*W*hat did he want?" Coop demanded as he studied the business card again.

Summer wasn't sure why he did. It wasn't as if it would provide him with any more answers.

"The Chintamani Stone."

"I wish we'd never heard of that damned stone," Winnie blew out a disgusted sigh. "But another sibling? This is insane."

"Yeah, you can't make this stuff up," Summer agreed. "I couldn't say for sure, but I got the impression Nash is Alastair's son and he doesn't particularly care for our sire."

Winnie plopped on the sofa next to her. "I wonder if Holly knows about or has met him?"

All questions for tomorrow. All Summer wanted was for this day to be over. The emotional drain was off the charts.

"What did he look like?" Coop asked.

Both sisters stared at him in surprise. "That's an odd question," Summer said.

"Humor me."

"Tall. Maybe six-three? Sandy blond hair on the long side. He wasn't overly muscular or bulky, but he did have a don't-mess-with-me air about him. Nice dresser for a bat-wielding intruder." She recalled the intelligence in his gaze. "Light green eyes that missed nothing. The man strikes me as highly intelligent."

"If he's the CEO of a company, it stands to reason he is," Coop said wryly.

"True. But there was something more I couldn't put my finger on." She rubbed her hands up and down her arms. "He could've easily hurt or killed me if he wanted. And while he held the bat, I felt no real threat from him."

"Think he was testing you?" Winnie asked.

"That's what it seemed like."

A meep from the staircase caught her attention. Morty sat, rubbing his eyes and looking at the bat with concern.

Summer held open her arms. "Come here, my sweet boy."

Morty loped over and climbed into her lap. He signed the question, "Where did Nash go?"

"You know Nash?" she asked, shocked to her toes.

"He visits me," the chimp signed.

She and Winnie exchanged incredulous stares.

"What? What did he say?" Coop asked. While he'd learned some sign language, he wasn't quite fluent.

"He said Nash has been visiting him." She hugged Morty tight. It terrified her that her beloved pet could've been so easily snatched from beneath her nose.

"I thought you warded this place like the Thorne estate. How did he get in?" Winnie wanted to know.

"I did, and I don't know. My crappy skills as a witch?"

"No. I don't think so. He must not have intended to harm you or Morty. But he was definitely trying to gain information," Winnie surmised.

"I agree," Coop inserted. "Sweetheart, your magic is stronger than you realize. Remember, I've seen you in action."

"We need to see about getting your parents to unlock your powers, Coop. Then we can begin your training. I think you are going to need to be at full force when we search for that rock. Too many people want it, and I could very well bring the world crashing down around us if I attempt to protect us."

"I've got a message in to my father. The time difference between here and Italy is screwing us," he told her.

Winnie stood and stretched. "On that note, I'm going to head home, fill Spring in on what happened, and give Autumn a call. Let me know if you hear from Holly."

Summer stood and hugged her sister. "Thanks. And thanks for shuttling Coop." She cast him a side glance. "Perhaps soon he'll be able to pop back and forth on his own."

"Want us to come back in the morning for a pow wow?"

Coop embraced Summer from behind. "Not too early," he said to Winnie. "We like to sleep in."

"Is that code for morning sex?" Winnie teased.

"Yep." Coop laughed when Summer elbowed him.

"I'll text you when we are awake," Summer said.

"Later, kids!" Winnie chirped and disappeared.

"I'm starved," Summer said with a hand on her belly. Stressful situations made her hungry after the fact.

"Me, too," he said and nuzzled her neck.

"Pfft. Keep it in your pants, big boy. I need sustenance first."

Morty hooted.

"So does Sir Mortimer."

Coop released her with a sigh and clasped Morty's outstretched hand. "Come on, buddy. Let's get you fed."

Summer watched the two of them for a minute before she lifted Nash's card with shaky fingers. She fully intended to do a bit of online research tonight. Time to figure out what Thorne Industries specialized in.

THE NEXT MORNING, COOP SHOWED UP BRIGHT AND EARLY AT THORNE Industries. Because he was in uniform and layered the charm on thick, the receptionist didn't pay attention to the fact that he wasn't an official of their particular town.

The receptionist escorted him to the waiting area of Nash's private offices with a smile that suggested she'd be happy to escort him anywhere he cared to go. He offered up a polite smile and picked up a magazine from the coffee table in front of the modern black and chrome sofa. When she took the hint and left, he breathed a sigh of relief.

Once upon a time, he might have taken her up on the come-hither look, but the only woman he desired now was the zany blonde who had turned his world upside down with her magic and laughter.

A woman with purple-streaked black hair glided by him without looking up from the folder where she had her nose buried. "If you're waiting for Nash, it could be a while," she said, not bothering to spare him a glance.

"I'll wait."

The edge in his voice must've warned her he wouldn't be put off. Her head came up and obsidian-like eyes studied him. A slow, appreciative smile found its way to her lovely face. "Why do I have the feeling you aren't happy with my boss?"

"That obvious?"

"In all fairness, he's a good guy, but his social skills leave a lot to be desired."

"He tried to kill my girlfriend last night. Where does that fall on the scale of social skills?" he asked silkily.

She had no comeback. Eyes wide and mouth slack, she looked like *he* was the one who had attacked *her* with a bat—poleaxed.

"I didn't try to kill her. I was testing her reflexes," retorted the man in question.

Both Coop and the dark-eyed assistant faced Nash, who lounged in the opening of the hallway beside his office.

Coop casually strolled to the other man. He sized him up and down before his fist whipped out and connected with the bastard's jaw. "Doesn't look like your reflexes are nearly as fast as hers."

Nash shook off the punch and glared at Coop. "I'll give you that one. But I promise you, if you touch me again, you'll pull back a stump."

"Are you boys done pissing in each other's Wheaties? Because if you are, Nash and I have work to do. If you're not, you might want to take this outside," Nash's employee stated in an unconcerned voice.

Coop noted the amusement in Nash's eyes as he regarded the woman. There was an element of something more, but it was quickly banked.

Interesting. Coop filed it away for future use.

"Summer wanted me to escort you back to her house for a chat." Coop crossed his arms over his chest in a display of intimidation.

He could've saved his energy because Nash didn't seem impressed or intimidated in the least. In fact, the other man smirked.

Coop had the sudden desire to wipe the floor with the prick.

"Let me guess, she now has reinforcements in the form of her sisters?"

"You guessed it in one, asshole. And here I thought you weren't so smart."

Without tearing his eyes from Coop's hostile gaze, Nash addressed his assistant. "Ryanne, will you cancel my meetings for today? I have somewhere I need to be."

"Alastair Thorne is your ten o'clock."

A muscle worked in Nash's jaw and his eyes turned arctic. "Then I guess my father is going to have to reschedule, isn't he?" he snapped.

"Yes, *sir.*"

She said it in much the same way Lil did when she was pissed at Coop over some imagined slight. He almost felt sorry for Nash. The poor bastard was going to get the cold shoulder for the next few days.

As the fast clip of her heels in retreat tapped out her agitation, Nash's hungry gaze followed her.

"Does she know you're crazy about her?" Coop asked.

"I'm not."

"You are. I recognize the look." Curious, he asked, "Why don't you tell her? Is she married? I didn't see a ring."

Black rage darkened Nash's face. "She's not for the likes of you."

Coop held up his hands. "Whoa, buddy! I'm not interested. I'm taken and happy for it."

A grudging nod was all the answer he received. "Let's go."

Before Nash could snap his fingers, Coop cleared his throat. "Yeah, I drove here."

A look of long-suffering took the place of Nash's anger. "Of course you did." He checked his Rolex. "That's over a two-hour drive. You must've got an early start."

Heat rose in Coop's cheeks. The slur against his magical abilities—or lack thereof—was implied.

"Come, Sheriff. I'll teleport you, although you should really learn that particular skill. It comes in handy, say, when you need to protect your woman."

"I am going to delight in rearranging your face," Coop growled.

"Ah, ah, ah!" Nash waved a finger in admonishment. "No threatening the transportation. Why, I might get nervous and drop you on the side of a mountain by mistake."

"I'll drive."

"I don't have all day to wait for you," Nash said, suddenly impatient. "Come with me now, and I'll have your vehicle returned to you later this afternoon." Without giving Coop time to process the plan, Nash touched his shoulder and had them in Summer's kitchen.

Coop braced his hands on the island counter to catch his breath. "I'm never going to get used to that."

"You will when you are the one in control," Nash assured him. "Where is my sister?"

"Probably in the barn or at her new office. I don't think she expected us this soon."

A meep caught their attention. Coop spread his arms, and Morty loped over to him.

"Hey, buddy!" Coop said as he lifted the chimp. "Did Mama make your breakfast yet, or are you trying to mooch more food?"

"He's trying to con you," Nash said dryly as he cast a look around the spacious kitchen.

Coop frowned. "How do you know?"

"His thoughts."

"Ah, I should've known. Can all witches and warlocks read the minds of animals?"

"No. I know most of the Thornes have the ability, but I believe only about ten percent of the magical community in general can accomplish mind reading. The Thorne line, like the Carlyle line, is pure." Nash stopped his perusal of the pantry he was exploring to glance over his shoulder. "You'll be able to as soon as you regain your power."

"You know about that?"

"I make it my business to know everything about everyone. The dossiers I have on this family and anyone connected to it would blow your mind."

Coop grunted. He'd like to take a look at those files but didn't dare ask. Instead he went with, "How long have you been spying on Summer?"

"Spying? That's such an ugly word."

"What would you call it?"

"Spying. But still, it's an ugly word."

Coop laughed. Nash was an asshole, to be sure, but the guy's sense of humor appealed to him.

Nash set eggs, cheese, and toast on the counter. "Breakfast sandwich?"

"You're certainly making yourself at home."

Summer's brother shrugged in a very Thorne-like way. "I'm hungry."

It was the first real inclination that Nash might be nervous. The one thing Coop had noted in the time he'd gotten to know the sisters was that they all ate when they were worried.

"Sure. I'll take one."

Coop fed bites of fruit to Morty while the three of them waited for Summer to return.

"So, about Ryanne. Why don't you ask her out?"

"She's my employee," Nash said coldly.

"She's hot, and she likes you, too."

Nash's sharp gaze shot up.

Coop nodded. "Yep. I can tell."

The other man went back to devouring his meal without comment, but Coop sensed the guy was a bit more optimistic about a relationship with his assistant.

"Thornes only love once. Did you know that?" he said.

Nash grunted. "Yes, an unfortunate side effect of our genetics. Being descended from Isis has its drawbacks."

"Isis? Like the Goddess?"

"The very one."

"Well, I'll be damned."

"You might be if you stick around this family," Nash countered.

31

*S*ummer arrived to find Coop and Nash bonding over sandwiches piled high with bacon, eggs, and cheese. She snorted her disgust and shot Coop the glare o' death. "Really?"

"If it makes you feel any better, he punched me in the face," Nash informed her as he wiped his fingers on a paper napkin.

"Perhaps a little," she grumbled.

Her brother compressed his mouth in what she assumed was an effort to hide his grin. He needn't have bothered. His amusement was obvious.

"My sisters will be arriving shortly. We weren't expecting you to return this soon."

"I decided to forgo the lengthy car ride." Nash stood and cleared the table.

When he started loading dishes in the dishwasher, Summer stated her surprise.

A slight flush dusted his cheekbones.

It reminded Summer of the few times she'd caught Alastair performing a task not fitting his nature.

"I'm a bit of a neat freak," he said as he completed his cleaning duties by wiping the table.

"I'm not complaining," she assured him. "Can I ask you something?"

"Shoot." He tossed the dishcloth toward the sink.

"You made a noise before swinging the bat in the barn. Then again when you showed up in my kitchen." She met his steady gaze. "You don't strike me as the type to show his hand. You seem stealthier than that."

"I didn't hear a question."

Coop rose and crossed to the sink. "She's asking if you intentionally alerted her to the strike."

"Yes. As I told your modern-day Wyatt Earp here, I was testing your reflexes."

"I've got your Wyatt Earp," Coop growled.

Again, Nash smirked as if he found them vastly amusing.

"You have Alastair's mannerisms. I'm assuming he's your father, too," Summer said. "Do you have a different mother, or is my mother the same as yours and that was hidden from us as well?"

"Different mother. I'm older than you by about three years." Nash picked up his coffee mug and stared down into the bottom of the cup as if looking for answers. "My mother was a witch from the Gillespie line. She was a sister to GiGi's husband, Ryker."

"Was?"

A flash of grief flitted across his face before he blanked his expression. "She's dead. Fourteen years now."

"I'm sorry, Nash."

He acknowledged her words with a slight nod and drained his mug.

"Were they married? You have the last name Thorne."

"No. Alastair insisted I have his name, and Mother always went along with whatever King Alastair decreed."

"You basically said there was no love lost between you."

"Look, he's a dangerous man. Add his magical ability, and you have a lethal combination." Irritation made his tone sharp.

"What do you do at Thorne Industries?"

"My company finds and guards powerful magical objects for the witches' council. It's my job to stop people like Alastair from getting his hands on things that could reduce the planet to rubble."

"The Chintamani Stone," she guessed.

"Yes."

Summer noted Coop's troubled gaze. Did he believe Nash was lying? She shifted her attention back to Nash. Why did she feel he was one step ahead of her? It was as if he had started a game of wits and she was clueless as to the rules.

"I need that stone, Nash."

"Why?"

"My mother is knocking on death's door. She doesn't have long. I can feel it. The stone can revive her."

"According to whom? Our father?" He shook his head in disgust. "Don't believe a word that comes out of his mouth, Summer. He'll use you and spit you out like he's done to everyone who has ever believed in him."

"You included?" she asked softly.

His clouded eyes met hers. "Me included."

Damned if she didn't believe him and like him all the more for his honesty.

"What did he do to you?"

"It's a story for another day. You have incoming."

"Incoming?"

The air crackled around them, and Alastair appeared.

Casually, he moved farther into the room to stand beside her. "Hello, son."

"Hello, sperm donor."

Had Summer not been watching her father, she'd have missed the subtle flash of humor in Alastair's eyes before he fastened his standard arrogant armor in place.

"I can see you're becoming acquainted with your sister."

"Just trying to warn the poor woman about the pitfalls of being your kin."

"Summer is incredibly astute. I believe she can make up her own mind," Alastair said.

"I wouldn't be too sure of that. For some reason, women seem to be taken in by your fake charm. Personally, I find your level of smarmy gives me indigestion. But to each their own," Nash countered.

These two men were much alike in coloring and height. Even their verbal swordplay spoke of a similar sharpness of mind. But where Alastair wore an air of indifference, Nash's passion for his cause shone through.

Coop, ever the clear-headed mediator, inserted himself between the two men. "Before this conversation comes to blows, can we shelve the animosity?"

"Fine, but I get the last word," Nash said. He lifted a brow and faced Alastair. "This is said in all seriousness. You have to rethink the hair product. It makes you look like a movie villain."

Coop choked on the coffee he was sipping and required a pounding on the back by Summer.

"Why do I feel like we've been here before?" she murmured.

"I'll send you the bill for the chiropractor," he retorted.

In a self-conscious gesture, Alastair touched his hair and looked to Summer for confirmation. She wrinkled her nose and nodded.

"I only use it to keep the hair out of my eyes," he explained.

"May I?" she asked with a gesture toward his scalp.

He nodded, and she was left to wonder how he portrayed such trust when he had to be squirming inside.

With a wave of her hand, she closed her eyes and visualized a David Beckham-ish style; shorter on the sides but longer and wavy on top. She imagined his hair with subtle highlights and lowlights. When she opened her eyes, she caught her breath.

Alastair, with his modernized style, was drop-dead gorgeous.

"Oh, Dad!" she breathed.

Nerves got the better of him, and he produced a mirror with a snap of his fingers.

His grin was warm and engaging, occupying nearly half his face. "Well done, child. Well done."

She inwardly preened.

With his new do, Alastair looked almost as young as Nash. Granted, witches and warlocks aged slower than the average human which made her father the equivalent of a thirty-five-year-old non-magical human.

Nash voiced her thoughts. "No one would guess you're close to sixty."

"Because I'm not."

"What?" Summer, Coop, and Nash chorused the question in the same tone of "Are you insane?"

Alastair chuckled. "I'm closer to seventy-five. As are GiGi and Preston. Thank the Goddess for good genetics, huh?"

"If I look that good at seventy, I'm going to offer up praise every day," Summer said with complete truthfulness.

Coop wrapped his arms around her and placed a soft, honey-sweet kiss on her lips. "You'll look even better."

"I'm a little pissed you took the fun out of mocking his hair," Nash said to Summer. "I suppose I still have that god-awful suit to poke fun of."

Alastair studied Nash's clothing for a moment before he snapped his fingers.

Summer giggled when she realized he'd traded their outfits.

Nash scowled and magically changed into a clean set of clothes. "Not cool. Do you think I *want* to wear Alastair Thorne cooties?"

Laughter bubbled up and out of her. "Cooties? Are you five?"

Coop held up a finger. "Uh, babe, you do remember you used the term Rosie cooties, right?"

Her scowl matched her brother's. "Shut it."

"Incoming," Nash said.

The air crackled and three of her four sisters appeared.

"How do you do that?" Summer asked him.

His grin was lopsided and crafty. "Trade secret."

Summer greeted her sisters then took the measure of the room and its occupants. The mounting tension was a living, breathing thing.

Autumn's eyes swept Alastair before she turned her attention to Nash. "You the guy with the bat?"

Oh, hell! Big sister wasn't happy.

Had Nash not raised his brow and put on the arrogant Alastair mantle, he might've gotten away with a scolding. As it was, Nash never saw the fist coming.

He bent double and cradled his eye socket. "Sonofa*bitch*!" His resulting sneeze from the cussing brought five curious raccoons to the kitchen slider.

"I suppose we can be grateful they aren't those muscled male kangaroos like they have in Australia," Spring said with a nod in the direction of the back door. "Those fuckers are creepy."

Summer laughed so long and hard her family cast her worried looks. Life had been one major curve ball after another in the recent months. Her sanity was up for debate. But as she wiped away her amused tears, Summer realized she wouldn't change her new normal. Life had become exciting in a way it had never been before.

Her gaze rose to meet Coop's shining blue eyes. In his gaze, she found a love that would sustain her for life.

"I love you," she mouthed silently.

They stared at one another for a long moment. Then he was beside her, gathering her close. "I love you," he said aloud. "More than I ever thought was possible to love another person."

"Oh, Coop's game is getting gooooood!" Winnie squealed.

They all laughed, and an easy camaraderie formed.

"Let's get this meeting out of the way. I need to ice my eye and get back to work," Nash commented impatiently.

Alastair stepped forward and arched a thin beam of red light toward his son's injury. "Does that take care of it, or should I kiss it and make it better?"

Nash grimaced but had the good manners to mutter a surly thank you.

Summer grinned when she caught his good eye. She was going to like having a big brother. Nash didn't know it yet, but he'd just become one of their own. A Thorne in the truest sense of the word.

Coop released her with a quick squeeze. "I see Winnie brought some of her incredible cinnamon rolls. I call dibs on that top one."

Alastair put his finger on it. "This one right here?"

Coop glared. Seemed he didn't care for Alastair cooties any more than Nash.

Summer giggled as she expected Alastair intended when he winked in her direction.

Her father spread the warm icing on the bun and nodded to Winnie. "Thank you, child. I'll leave you all to your planning. Should any of you wish to see Aurora, my door is open."

Stunned silence greeted his departure.

"It's like you altered his personality with that haircut," Nash exclaimed.

"Stop! He's not the monster you believe him to be," she admonished as she accepted the cinnamon treat Coop placed on the table before her. "He has feelings like the rest of you."

The surprised expressions on her siblings had her biting back another laugh. For so long they'd all viewed Alastair as the bad guy, but perhaps the true story still needed to be uncovered. But before she included her new brother in the planning stages to retrieve the Chintamani Stone, she needed to be sure he was on their side.

"Nash, you're either with us or against us. I'd like you to be with us. The stone is important to reviving our mother." She swallowed hard and forced back the image of her beloved mother's corpse-like body. "You said you lost your mom at an early age. Wouldn't you do anything possible to have her back?"

Nash's somber jade-green gaze studied her at length. "I would."

She smiled her relief, but it died when he held up his hand.

"But I won't help Alastair."

She dropped her gaze to the maple-wood table to hide the effect of his words. To say she was disappointed was to put it mildly. She'd hoped he was on board to save her mom. "I see."

"I don't know if you do, Summer." Nash pulled out a chair, flipped it around, and sat beside her. With arms along the top of the chair back, he rested his chin atop his crossed forearms. "I'm sorry. If I could help you, I would. But I work for the witches' council. Alastair is at direct odds with the council. He flaunts his power and butts heads every chance he can."

"But this isn't for him, cousin," Spring said in her beautiful, modulated voice, the one designed to bring men to their knees. "It's for us."

His troubled expression said he was considering the request.

"Will you at least think about it, Nash?" Summer urged. "You don't have to decide today. We still need to determine the whereabouts of the Chintamani Stone."

With a slight grimace, he surveyed the group. "All right. I'll think about it. Perhaps if we can utilize the power of the stone without letting

Alastair get his hands on it..." He trailed off and shrugged. "We'll talk more soon."

He patted Summer's arm and rose to his feet. "I have to go. Mr. Carlyle, do you wish to go back to retrieve the vehicle?"

"I'll go," Winnie said. "Coop, you enjoy the rest of the weekend with Summer. I'll be back Monday morning to return you home."

After Nash and Winnie teleported, Autumn sank into the nearest chair. "I don't trust him."

"You don't trust anyone," Summer countered.

"True, but I *especially* don't trust him or his father."

"Agreed," Coop said as he swung a leg over Nash's abandoned chair. "Although, they both have a certain charm that sort of grows on you."

Spring joined the trio at the table. "I say we find the artifact we need and don't let either of them know until it's time to revive Mom."

"I think that's a good plan. We also need to get busy on Coop's training if he is to accompany me to China," Summer said. "Tums, will you consider training him?"

Autumn thunked her head on the table. "Ugh! That means I have to return to Podunkville."

"Just for a while. Please?"

"What about Winnie or Spring?" Autumn hedged.

Spring shook her head when they all faced her. "Can't. I'm too busy with all the weddings coming up this fall. Between the shop and getting bulbs planted for the spring, I don't have a minute to spare." The cagey look in Spring's emerald eyes was suspicious at best, but her excuse sounded plausible enough. "I believe Winnie will have the same problem with filling her internet orders. That leaves you, sister," Spring said to Autumn.

"Fine. I'll do it," Autumn grumbled as she lifted a bun from the basket. "Anything else?"

Summer took a deep breath and blurted, "Yeah, you'll need to train Keaton too."

"Fuck. No."

"We may need him before this is done," Coop said.

"I don't see how," Autumn argued. "We've done fine without him until now. There's nothing a novice warlock like Keaton can do for our family."

"Tums, I never ask you for anything. I'm asking you now. Please help me train Coop and Keaton," Summer pleaded. "I originally asked Alastair, but I don't want to be indebted to him if I can help it."

"I'll think about it," her older sister grumbled. "No promises. But first things first, Coop. You need to get your parents to remove their original spell. Until then, any training is a moot point."

"They fly home this week. I'll talk to them then."

"This means you're determined to go after the rock by yourself?" Autumn asked Summer.

"I think we have to give weight to Helena Roerich's diary. If it's true that only a couple in love can retrieve the Chintamani Stone, then that's me and Coop. But we need to wait until he is at full force."

"How long do you think Mom has?" Spring asked.

"Six months? A year on the outside. I got the feeling Alastair is desperate."

"Okay. Then we do this thing the Thorne way," Autumn said.

"What's the Thorne way?" Coop asked.

The sisters shared a wicked smile. Summer was the first to answer. "Similar to the three musketeers but it's more of a witchy quartet version."

"Oh, lord."

He was right to be concerned. When the sisters joined forces, trouble was sure to follow.

EPILOGUE

ONE MONTH LATER...

*C*oop's gaze swept the aisle of the barn before coming to rest on the scurry of squirrels in front him. If anyone caught him trying to talk to the animals, he'd die of embarrassment on the spot.

"Okay. Let's do this thing."

He concentrated on the raw power that wove its way through his veins. With a concerted effort, he visualized the magic forming into a centralized ball. Once he held the sphere in his mind's eye, he directed the magic to each cell in his physical makeup. His hands glowed bright, and he shot a triumphant look in Saul's direction.

The leader of the squirrel mafia didn't look impressed. If a squirrel could shrug its shoulders and roll its eyes, Saul would be that squirrel.

As the yellow glow shifted color to a darker more orange tone, Coop's triumph turned to unease. The power built faster than he could contain it. The orange light shot toward Saul at the same time Eddie's trunk reached through the bars of his pen to scoop the furry rodent out of the path.

Luckily for Saul, Eddie had quick reflexes. Otherwise, Summer's familiar would be charred to a crisp. Also, Coop had the good fortune for his electrical bolt to have ground out in the dirt of the breezeway.

"That sonofabitch nearly cooked my goose! Did you see that, Rocco?"

Coop frowned and glanced around. Had someone left a television or radio on for the barn animals?

"Thinks he can throw freaking magic around all willy-nilly like some fucking David Copperfield or some shit," the guttural voice complained. "I should freakin' show him what happens to warlocks who think they—*did you just sniff me?*"

"Can't help it, Saul. You smell all nutty and delicious. Like a peanut butter sandwich," someone replied in a contrite tone.

Saul? Surely it was a coincidence. Coop's wary gaze shifted to where the squirrel faced off against the elephant.

"You don't fucking go 'round sniffing another man's junk! Stupid big-assed, saggy-skinned, perverted mutherfucker!" Saul paced back and forth in front of the elephant pen. His tail hair stood on end as if he were fearful or, in this case, enraged. His stubby little arms waved about in the air like an old Italian mama scolding her young. "You know what I'm gonna do? I'm gonna teach you a fucking lesson, is what I'm gonna do. Touch *my* junk?" The furious squirrel faced his more laid-back rodent companion. "Get me de knife, Rocco."

"Uh, boss, I don't know if it's such a good idea. The boss-lady might get pissed, ya know," Rocco tried to reason.

"Do I freakin' look like I care?" Saul demanded. "I'm going to castrate me a mutherfucking elephant, that's what I'm gonna do."

Dumbfounded and speechless, Coop watched the drama unfold. Damned if Saul didn't remind Coop of a squirrel-like Robert DeNiro, right down to his little New York street-thug accent.

"Saul, think about this, man. Eddie's balls are three times your size," Rocco said with a skeptical look at the elephant's scrotum. "You'll need a knife bigger than you could possibly carry."

Eddie stroked his trunk down Saul's puffed up back.

The squirrel turned positively rabid. "Don't you freakin' touch me you mutherfucker! What did I tell you about touching me?"

Saul stomped off, and Coop figured he'd heard the last of the threats until the squirrel returned, dragging a rusted vintage razor blade circa 1889 or earlier.

"Grab some bale twine," Saul directed Rocco. "We're gonna tie him up."

Things just got real in the animal barn.

Coop had heard enough and whipped out his phone.

Summer picked up on the first ring. "Hey, Coop."

"Yeah, I need back up in the barn. Shit is going down."

He heard the wheels of her office chair roll back along the hardwood floor.

"What kind of things?" she asked.

"It's Saul. He plans to castrate Eddie."

Her laughter echoed around the barn as she instantaneously appeared beside him.

"It's not funny, Summer. I don't know how to disarm a squirrel without one of us getting hurt. You see what he's packing?" Coop demanded as he thrust his cellphone back inside his pocket.

She doubled over, and tears streamed from her eyes.

Irritation flitted through him. Here he was, trying to get her help to defuse an escalating situation, and there she stood, laughing so hard she sounded like a wheezy asthmatic.

"What the hell?" he demanded.

When she could finally keep a straight face, she wiped the moisture from her eyes. "He threatens Eddie at least three times a week. Poor Eddie can't keep his trunk to himself."

"Macy is going to be heartbroken he is cheating on her."

Summer's giggles erupted again. He noted the exact moment she realized he could hear the animals.

"Coop! How… what… you…?"

With a sheepish grin, he told her what he'd done.

Instead of the anger he'd expected, she laughed and clapped her hands. "Well done!"

"You're not mad?"

"I might've been had you burned down my barn, but no, I'm not mad. I'm proud of you." She embraced him and laid her cheek against his chest. "Extremely proud."

"Babe?"

"Mmm?"

"How about we teleport into the hayloft?"

She laughed her delight. "I knew you were the one for me the moment I saw you, Cooper Carlyle. I'm glad you finally came around."

"I'm slow, but I'm not a complete idiot." Coop lowered his head and captured her mouth with his. The languid kiss rocked them both. "I love you, Summer Thorne."

"I love you too, Coop."

ALASTAIR THORNE SMILED AT THE IMAGE OF THE COUPLE IN THE mirror. He waved his hand and gave the two of them their much-needed privacy. After he placed the mirror on the bedside table, he perched on the edge of Aurora's bed.

"It took them long enough, but I think those two crazy kids are going to make it." He smoothed back her black hair and traced her delicately arched brow. "You'd be proud of our daughter, my love. She has your temperament."

He straightened the already perfectly aligned buttons on her nightgown. "I suppose our next project is Autumn. She's going to be a tougher nut to crack. But I won't give up. I made you a promise, and I intend to keep it."

Alastair looked away from the pale face and out the floor-to-ceiling window of her room toward the setting sun. He blinked away the building moisture and smoothed a hand down his already pristine tie. The remaining words he wanted to say were trapped in his throat. None of them mattered. He'd spouted them all before. Promised her the moon and stars to return to him—all to no avail.

But he could, and would, follow through on those promises. He would see that her children were happy—even if he had to manipulate her daughters to make it so.

* * *

Love what you've read? Turn the page for an excerpt from **AUTUMN MAGIC.**

AUTUMN MAGIC EXCERPT

NINE YEARS AGO...

*T*oday was the day.

Today, she intended to confess her deepest, darkest secrets to Keaton. It was past time. After all these months together, he deserved to know the truth.

Stomach in knots, Autumn Thorne cut through the dense woods between their family estates. In the clearing between the two adjoining pieces of land, Keaton would be waiting.

"Keaton," she said with a sigh. Her forever love.

Family legend held that any born of the Thorne bloodline would only have one true soulmate. No other love would they take. It didn't matter, because Autumn had found hers, and she was more than content. She was blissful.

Ten months earlier, they both had returned to Leiper's Fork from their respective colleges. Full of dreams and high hopes for the future, she had uncharacteristically agreed when her best friend, Diane, suggested a casual graduation celebration at the local restaurant.

Keaton Carlyle had been seated at the long, glossy pine bar with two of his friends and his cousin. With his shaggy dark hair, eyes the shade of the aquamarine waters of the Caribbean, and a quick-to-flash sunny smile, he'd made many women's hearts flutter.

Autumn had been no exception. The moment she entered the over-crowded room, Cupid's arrow had lodged in her heart with a resounding thwack. From that very second on, she'd only had eyes for Keaton.

And he for her.

She laughed in remembrance of their initial meeting.

Both had been struck dumb in the presence of the other.

Wine flowed freely as they hid in the dark corner of the room and ignored everything and everyone. The magic of the alcohol had done its trick and eased them into a flirty conversation. Within twenty minutes, they'd set a time and location for their first date.

That night had been the beginning of a beautiful relationship. One that far exceeded anything Autumn could've dreamed. Keaton was an attentive lover who catered to her every whim, and she adored the very ground he walked on.

"True love," she murmured. Rare and precious.

Last night, he'd hinted at a future together, going so far as to ask what type of stone she wanted should he choose an engagement ring. The answer was obvious: aquamarine to match his incredible eyes.

When she at last reached the clearing, she found him half asleep on a blanket under the large oak tree. For a moment she stared, unable to catch her breath. He was beautiful in all the ways that mattered, and he was hers.

"Hey, babe," Keaton greeted with a lazy grin. He held out his arm, and she curled into him.

She rested her head on his chest and listened to his steady heartbeat.

"Keaton?"

"Mmm."

"Were you serious last night?"

"Mmhmm."

She lifted her head and met his sleepy gaze. "Why are you so tired?"

"Late night. One of the horses was colicky." He rolled on top of her and pinned her arms over her head with one of his hands. The other quickly found its way under her sundress and explored the waistband of her panties. He inched his fingers beneath the lace and touched her most sensitive area. "But not too tired to make love to you." He grinned and lowered his head to capture her lips.

Autumn broke their kiss before they became too heated. "Keaton, we need to talk."

He lifted his dark head to judge her earnestness. "Can't we talk *after*?"

"No. I need to tell you something."

"So serious!" he teased, flaring his eyes wide.

She smiled despite herself. His fun, laid-back attitude was easy to adopt.

"Will you promise me, whatever I tell you doesn't leave this clearing?"

"Of course." He sat up and pulled her to rest between his long legs.

"I've thought about how to say it a million times. I don't know how."

Keaton ran his index finger along her temple and tucked a stray lock of hair behind her ear. "Just stay it, babe. It can't be that dire." He grew still. "Unless you plan to break up with me. Is that what this is about?"

"No! Goodness, no. I love you, Keaton, and I want us to be together for always."

He sighed and hugged her tight. "For always."

Because there was no way to soften the words she needed to say, she blurted, "I'm a witch."

"Pardon?"

"I'm a witch."

He laughed.

A sick ball of dread formed low in her belly. *He thought she was kidding.*

"Keaton."

Her serious tone penetrated his amusement.

"Babe, there's no such thing as a witch."

She shifted to kneel in front of him. "There *is*."

"Is this like a Wiccan thing? Where you worship the trees and shit? I'm cool with that; just don't tell my mother. She might flip."

"No, it's not a Wiccan thing. They aren't witches in the real sense of the word."

"Autumn, come on. I'm too tired for game playing today."

A demonstration was in order. "Watch."

Autumn held her hand out flat and concentrated. She pulled from her element and created a beautiful, glowing fireball. The orange-red flame pulsed and danced in her hand. Smiling, she shifted her gaze to Keaton and froze.

His horror-filled eyes were locked on the flame.

Her earlier dread returned with a vengeance. "Keaton?"

"You're a witch," he croaked.

"Y-yes." She balled her fist and extinguished the fire. "I've wanted to tell you so many times. I—"

With his gaze still locked onto where the flaming ball had been, he asked, "Do you cast spells and things like that?"

"Yes. But only—"

"Love spells?" he demanded, expression hardening.

Her nervous laugh came out stilted and uneasy. "No. There's no such thing as a love spell."

"What about an obsession or desire spell?"

His angry intensity unnerved her. She had no idea where he was going with this.

"I suppose there are spells like that, but—"

Once again, he cut her off. "Remove it."

Autumn swallowed past her suddenly parched throat and wet her lips. "Pardon?"

"The spell you cast on me. I want you to remove it."

"Baby, I never put a spell on you."

He scrambled to his feet. "You're a liar!"

"No! I'm not lying. There's no spell."

"This explains so much," he ranted as he paced. "God, I'm stupid!"

She stood and tentatively approached him with her hands held out. "Keaton, it's me. I'm still the same person. I love you. And I promise, there is *no* spell."

Hands tucked behind his back, he skipped out of her reach as if her touch were contagious. "*Don't fucking touch me!*"

Shocked by his behavior, Autumn's own turmoil bubbled inside. His attitude had become completely unreasonable. "Why are you behaving like this?" she demanded.

"Because I don't like having my free will taken from me." He gripped his scalp and shook his head. "Christ, this explains so much," he repeated.

"What? What exactly does it explain?"

"My obsession with you. You're always on my mind. Even my dreams are filled with you." He pointed to her face, and his countenance hardened, growing ugly in his rage. "*You* did this to me. I don't know whether you thought it would be funny, or whether you honestly believed this is a way to tie a man to you, but the game is *over*, sweetheart." His tone was scathing and bitter at the same time.

Shock held her immobile. Speechless and hurt, all she could do was stare.

"If you won't remove the spell, I'll find someone who will. When I'm through with you, your name will be worthless in this town. No man will come near you."

Tears seeped from her eyes. She swiped at them in a vain attempt to hide her devastation. "Why are you being nasty? There's no spell."

"You want to play it that way? *Fine*. Don't say I didn't warn you."

"Keaton, you promised me you wouldn't say anything," she cried. "You promised."

"You remove the spell and stay the fuck away from me, and I'll *consider* keeping quiet."

Pressure built in Autumn's chest. *This must be what if felt like to have a heart attack.* The inability to take a deep breath, the sheer agony of the heart struggling to beat, the knowledge that the end of something precious was imminent.

The breeze picked up, and the trees around them began to sway. Back and forth they bent under the pressure of the howling wind. Branches cracked and plummeted to the earth with loud thuds. The blanket swirled up from the ground, caught against his legs, then whipped free to disappear on the air current.

Keaton lost his tan. "What the fuck?"

Lightning struck the ground on the opposite side of the clearing.

"If you're doing this, Autumn, knock it off!" he shouted over the building elements.

Words whispered through the tree and spoke to her. In her mind's eye, she pictured the athame from her altar. When it appeared in her hand, Keaton jerked in fear.

She didn't have time to cast a circle. He would bolt by then. Improvisation was required, and with the wickedly sharp tip, she scored her palm. "I bind thee, Keaton John Carlyle."

"What the fuck are you doing? *Autumn!*"

"I bind thee. Never shall you reveal the truth about me or any of the Thornes. Not in word, not in writing, not in gesture, not in deed. I bind thee from revealing the truth." She lifted her face to the sky and spread her arms wide, palms facing upward. "Goddess hear my plea. Grant me the power to bind this man's speech."

Lightning zipped sideways across the sky and struck the tree behind Keaton's back. His involuntary yell echoed around the clearing.

"You crazy bitch!" His words ended in a gurgle, and he clawed at his throat. Fear filled his bulging eyes, and his face turned an alarming shade of purple.

For a brief moment, Autumn's own throat seized in response. Young witches couldn't always control their power, and she worried her impromptu spell may have collapsed his larynx. When his face returned to a more normal shade, he cursed again.

She breathed a sigh of relief. While she might be angry with him, accidentally killing him would've left her devastated.

He stormed to where she stood in the center of the clearing. "What did you do to me?" he rasped.

"I neutralized your threat."

Wide-eyed, his gaze shifted to the bloody knife in her hand. "You stay away from me. Do you hear me?"

Keaton beat a hasty retreat and ran away as fast as his legs could carry him.

Energy depleted, Autumn stumbled to the flattened grass where their blanket had been. Kneeling, she ran her hand over the indentation their bodies had left. How had it gone so wrong so fast? How was it possible to feel such an aching hollowness inside, to feel on the brink of death, and yet continue to breathe?

She placed a hand on her lower abdomen. She'd never had a chance to tell him about the baby they'd made. Based on his reaction, another revelation was out of the question for the moment. With a silent prayer to the Goddess that her binding spell would remain solid, Autumn curled into a tight ball on the ground.

Grief caught up to her. Harsh, hiccuping sobs shook her frame, and all she could do was give herself over to the pain. Hours passed, and the sun set. Still she remained unable to drum up the energy or will to move.

She stared at the overhead stars peeping through the branches of the mighty oak. Oh, to be there! Far, far away from the hell she was experiencing here on Earth.

A beam of light settled on her face.

"Autumn?"

She turned her head toward her sister's voice.

Winnie rushed to her side. "Sister? What's wrong?" When she noticed the smattering of blood, she freaked. "Tums, where are you hurt? Where is the blood coming from?"

Autumn opened her mouth to speak. All but one word eluded her. "Keaton," she rasped.

"Is it Keaton? Did something happen to him?"

The tears she thought had dried up flowed once again. Warm, loving arms wrapped around her and pulled her close.

"Tums, talk to me. Was Keaton hurt?" Winnie asked urgently.

"No, but I can't talk about it. I just want to go home."

"Okay. Hold on."

With a quick incantation, Winnie teleported the two of them back to Thorne Manor.

"Why don't you go lie down. I'll bring you a sandwich and a cup of tea," Winnie suggested.

"Honestly, I don't think I can keep anything down right now." Autumn hugged her sister and drew in some of her warm, healing energy. "But I love you for offering."

As she trudged upstairs to her room, she wondered if she shouldn't try to speak to Keaton one more time. Surely, he must've calmed enough to see reason?

She called his cell phone but received no answer.

Tomorrow. Tomorrow she would visit him and tell him about the baby. They could decide where to go from there. If he still didn't want to be part of her life, she'd raise their child on her own.

She'd been wrong to blurt out her secret without feeling the waters first. But she could afford to allow Keaton time to adjust to the shock. He would see this was all a misunderstanding. Keaton was level-headed and calm in most situations, and Autumn had no doubt he'd see reason.

WHEN MORNING DAWNED AND BROUGHT WITH IT A GLORIOUS SUNRISE, Autumn stood on the front porch step and absorbed the sun's rays. The warmth fed her soul and restored her faith to full power.

With a cleansing breath, she borrowed a page from her younger sister's book of optimism and headed to the Carlyle estate.

As Autumn pulled into the drive, a strange foreboding took hold. Diane's yellow VW Bug was parked outside the Carlyle house, and Autumn couldn't help wondering why her friend would be here this early. While Diane had made no secret of the fact she'd be happy to hook any of the Carlyle brothers or cousins, she hadn't had any luck in gaining their interest.

Keaton's brother, Cooper, answered her knock. "Hey, Coop. Is Keaton home?"

His handsome face took on an unhealthy shade of green.

"Coop?"

"He... uh, now's not a good time, Autumn."

Nausea churned in her stomach. As her unease grew, she worried she might lose the half muffin she'd managed to choke down this morning.

The truth was written on Coop's face. The pained sympathy. The distaste for what she was about to be put through.

Without another word, she shoved by Coop and raced for Keaton's room.

PRESENT DAY

"Word on the street is that you are the most skilled witch to train us," Keaton said by way of greeting.

If asked, Autumn would have said the only way Keaton would've given her the time of day was if she were the absolute last woman on earth, especially after their tumultuous history.

However, everything had changed a few weeks ago when Keaton learned he was a warlock whose powers had been bound at birth. Now that those powers were unbound, they radiated off him. To Autumn, he appeared brighter than the sun. And like peering at the sun, it hurt to look at him.

The irony of their little meeting today was not lost on her. A little over nine years ago, he'd shunned her because she was a witch. Now he sought her out because he needed her to teach him how to use his magical abilities.

Odd how, after all this time, his deep baritone still had the ability to reach right inside her and warm her lady parts. Because her body's reaction to him irritated her, she raised a brow and placed her hands on her hips. "We can start as soon as we get your apology out of the way."

He looked like he'd eaten sour grapes. His lips screwed up, and his eyes narrowed. "I'm sorry."

"For?" she asked tauntingly.

"Can we not leave the past in the past, Autumn?"

"Same old Keaton. Can't admit when he's wrong."

"Oh, and *binding me* from telling anyone you were a witch wasn't wrong? *Destroying* the project I worked on for so long with my daughter wasn't wrong?"

"I apologized for the truck and paid for the damages." Autumn shrugged as if she couldn't care less one way or the other when, in fact, she did. The damages she'd wrought to the restored truck back in the spring was bad form. At the time, she hadn't realized his daughter had had a hand in helping him rebuild his rust bucket. She believed she was only striking out at Keaton when she set the truck on fire.

"And?" he asked as tauntingly as she had a moment before.

"That's all you get. The binding spell was cast to protect myself and my sisters."

Anger caused red blotches high on his cheekbones and altered his normally tan complexion. It didn't detract from his male beauty. *And didn't that piss her right off?*

"You made me feel as if I was losing my mind. I couldn't talk about our relationship to anyone."

"We didn't have a relationship, Keaton. We were two stupid kids exploring sex. The term relationship indicates feelings, and you had none."

"That's not true," he argued, taking a step forward.

She held up a hand. "You know what? I've changed my mind. Keep your apology. I don't want to get into this." Down that path lay heartache, and she had no intention of trekking it again. She wished she'd never brought up the apology to begin with. "Go down and get Coop. We'll start the basics."

"Autumn." His tone had changed. It warmed enough to resemble the caring man she had thought she knew nearly ten years prior. In truth, that man never existed. *Not for her.*

"If you want me to teach you, we shelve the past, Keaton. No talking about it. *Ever.*" Because if she did, it would break the fragile walls she had in place around her heart. She needed those walls to elude the charming net he could so easily cast. Needed them to keep the pain and anguish of their breakup at bay.

The intensity in his deep-blue eyes disturbed her. Made her skin itchy and tight. He'd always seen too much. Her only saving grace was that those eyes weren't the loving ones she remembered. Time and pain had darkened his irises to a deeper, cloudier blue-green than they used to be.

Changing irises were a witch's or, in Keaton's case, a warlock's tell. The closest she'd gotten to him in recent years was a few months ago when he confronted her over setting fire to his truck. Because of her own hurt, she hadn't registered the change in color at the time. Had she done so, she'd have recognized him for what he was.

His daughter, Chloe, hadn't inherited his aquamarine eyes. Hers were a warm, golden shade of honey. It bothered Autumn to think that, eventually, some dickhead would come along and hurt little Chloe, too. Her eyes would lose that stunning color.

But such was life. Getting your heart bruised and battered was inevitable. She hadn't met an adult, certainly not a Thorne, who hadn't had a rough go of it.

"You're wasting my time, Keaton. You had two hours from when you showed today. Clock's ticking, buddy."

"I don't remember you as such a hard ass."

Autumn's inability to swallow came unexpectedly. She struggled through it. "Yeah, well, we all grow up." To create distance, she moved to the stand holding the Thorne grimoire and flipped through the pages. "It was bound to happen."

Because she could feel his gaze studying her profile, she tilted her head down and removed her hair clip. Her thick locks created a curtain, blocking his view.

"Thank you for being kind to Chloe." His husky voice came from close beside her and made her jump. Despite his six-foot-three, muscular frame, he moved as silently as a damned cat.

She inched sideways. To give herself something to occupy her hands, she touched a fingertip to the candle wicks around the room and lit each one in turn.

As far his daughter was concerned, Autumn could afford to be kind. "She's lovely, Keaton. A daughter anyone would be proud to call their own." *And she might have been theirs had things not taken such an ugly turn that day in the glen all those years before.* The thought had taunted her on more than one occasion. Whenever she saw the two of them together, laughing or sharing an ice cream in town, or whenever Chloe ran toward the Thorne gardens in search of Autumn's sister, Spring, the sight would stab Autumn right in the chest.

By now, Autumn was well practiced at shoving down her bitterness and anger. A few months ago, when she'd so carelessly set fire to the truck, she realized her destructive behavior had hurt an innocent. The wake-up call caused her to pack up, leave town, and re-evaluate her life.

"I worried about her reception here when C.C. first mentioned she... we were... like you."

He stumbled over his words and triggered her first genuine laugh.

"You make it sound like some dreaded disease you happened to catch." She sobered. "It's a gift from the Goddess. You should be proud to be from a powerful line. There aren't many pure-blooded witches or warlocks left. Most have been bred out of existence. And about your daughter…" She offered some semblance of a smile. "I don't hold the sins of the parents against the child."

"Bred?"

Apparently, he chose to ignore her dig about "the sins of the parents," and Autumn was happy to ignore the topic if he was.

She shrugged. "Throughout history, pure-bloods have married non-magical humans. Any children they created would've only received diluted abilities. Like Chloe." She finished lighting the candles and brushed her hands together. "Some witches bound their children to give them a normal life, or what they believed would be normal. Not unlike what your mother and father did to you, Coop, and your cousin, Zane."

Keaton frowned. "What about Knox? He's a Carlyle."

"I've only spoken ten words to Knox in as many years. I haven't had much interaction with your family and wouldn't know."

"I should ask him."

"I can't believe it hasn't come up in the weeks since you've found out the truth," she said as she stopped a few feet from him.

"He's been away, acquiring new breeding stock for our herd, and hasn't been around."

"Gotcha." No skin off her nose either way. She checked her watch. "We're down to one hour and forty-five minutes of training time left."

"You're going to be a stickler about this, aren't you?" he said softly.

"I am. I have a busy schedule, and I don't appreciate my time being wasted."

The hard edge crept back into her voice, but she'd be damned if she could prevent it. She didn't want to train Keaton. But a favor was a favor, and Autumn had grudgingly promised her sister, Summer, that she'd teach Coop and his brother. Since Summer's own powers were hit or miss most days, it fell to Autumn or one of their other sisters. And because those sisters had actual money-producing businesses, Autumn was the one chosen to help the newbie warlocks.

"Where did the carefree girl go? The one you used to be?" he mused aloud.

Tears burned behind her lids, and resentment gnawed at her insides. She presented her back and stared out the large attic window. From her vantage point, she could see the clearing where her life had gone to hell in a handbasket. "She was an idiot. And thankfully, no longer exists." *She died with her unborn fetus.*

"I miss her."

The wistfulness in his voice triggered her outrage. Where did he get off being sweet after all this time? Livid, she struggled to keep her voice level. "I don't. Like I said, she was an idiot." She consulted the time again. "One hour and forty minutes."

KEATON OBSERVED THE TENSION IN AUTUMN'S STANCE.

She hated everything about him occupying her space. It was in the defiant angle of her chin, her harsh dismissal of the past, and her eagerness to be done with teaching him and his brother the basics of witchcraft.

He hadn't wanted to learn and had initially rejected Coop's revelation last month—*especially* if it put him in close proximity to Autumn. But when his parents had returned and removed the binding, Keaton felt the supercharged energy pulse through his body on a cellular level. Finally, he understood.

Magic was like a powerful sword he needed to learn to wield for the safety of everyone around him. If he walked around untrained, he might unintentionally let loose one day and hurt someone.

His father and mother had expressed regret for their lie, and because of who they were, because he'd known them to be loving and generous parents, Keaton's only choice had been to forgive. In forgiving them, he'd been forced to compare their actions to Autumn's. If he was honest with himself, he had to acknowledge her magical crimes against him were much less life altering.

"You wanted an apology. I'm sorry, Autumn. Truly."

She jerked as if struck.

The urge to touch her overwhelmed him, but he curbed the impulse. He didn't have the right, not anymore. He had killed her love. Maybe not with his words in the clearing, but definitely when he'd slept with Diane the same night of their breakup. He'd never had the opportunity to make it right before he found out Diane was pregnant with his child.

"Look, if your intent is to stand around jawing, then I need to get to my real work." She headed for the door without sparing him a glance. "I'll catch you later."

Before she could leave, Coop stepped into the room.

"You're late," she snapped as she shoved a lock of auburn hair behind her ear.

Coop flashed her the patented Carlyle grin. One glimpse of those pearly whites was guaranteed to set fire to the panties of unsuspecting females everywhere.

Keaton had a moment of unease when he saw the twin spots of pink bloom on Autumn's cheeks. *Was she attracted to his brother?*

He released his pent-up breath when Autumn said, "Your charm doesn't work on me, Sheriff. Save it for Summer. Tomorrow, if you aren't on time, you can find another sucker to teach you. I have better things to do than wait around for you while you flirt with my sister."

"You're warming up to me, Autumn. I can tell," Coop teased as he tapped a fingertip to her nose.

Keaton called on every ounce of self-control not to rip his brother's arm off for touching her. He didn't want to *think* what it meant that he was still territorial after all these years.

Autumn snorted. "Pfft. Keep dreaming, Coop." To Keaton, she asked, "Do you want Chloe to join us for future classes? I know she's learned a few things from Spring, but she's more than welcome to come with you tomorrow."

Her generosity surprised him and shook him out of his pique. What kind of woman would offer to help the daughter of the woman you screwed in a drunken stupor? "I'll ask her tonight."

"Great. Now, let's get started." She tapped the book on the altar. "This is a spell book, also known as a grimoire. Every magical family has one. It is handed down through each generation. These books can be hundreds or, depending on the family, thousands of years old. Your family should have one, too." She ran a hand lovingly over the binding. "Most spells are in Latin, although there are a few in our grimoire in another language that we've been unable to identify. I'm sure your family's book is the same."

"I thought a lot of people didn't know how to write in the old days," Keaton said as he inched closer to get a look at the book she held.

"The book is like a magical version of Dragon Dictation. You can speak a spell, and it will appear on the pages."

"Dude! That's badass." Coop reached for the grimoire. "May I see it?"

"No." She softened her sharp answer with a half-smile. "Not yet, anyway. I'll explain why later."

Keaton studied her as Autumn droned on about the altar and the best wood for magical purposes when creating one. She hadn't changed much. Her ivory skin was still as flawless. The deep auburn hair still caught the light and glowed red in its beam. Her lips were just as full, and her body... *God, her body.* At thirty-two, the woman had the same tight, toned body she'd had as a twenty-two-year-old.

His skin tingled in remembrance of holding that curvy body against his own. Of tasting every inch. Of being cradled between those long legs. He mentally shook himself. If he didn't stop, he'd be sitting here with serious wood popping up—and not the magical altar type.

With a suspicious glance in his direction, she went on to explain the process of casting a circle. Apparently, magic was to be done within this circle for a number of reasons. The most important was to protect the spell caster. She also explained the purification steps before a ceremony.

While Autumn answered his brother's questions, Keaton put his finger on what bothered him about her appearance. Her eyes. Once a bright, beautiful shade of light amber, they were now an average murky brown. How was that possible? It was as if all light had escaped them.

"When can we get to the good part?" Coop asked and rubbed his hands together.

"Slow your roll, Sheriff. Until you learn the rules, you don't perform magic."

"Rules?" Keaton asked, drawn back into the conversation.

"Rules," she said. "Number one, do as you will, and it harm none. In other words, magic is never to hurt or strike out at another."

Keaton's brows shot up, and he snorted. "I'd say you broke that rule."

Autumn turned incredulous eyes on him. "Are you serious right now?"

"I'm just saying, when you—"

Coop clapped a hand over Keaton's mouth and wrestled him to the floor. "Shut up, you idjit! She already hates you. Do you want her to shish kebab you?"

"Are you two done? We are down to only an hour left," she informed them. The cold tone left little doubt how much she despised Keaton's presence in her home.

"Number two, you don't use magic for personal gain." She stared directly at Keaton. "No spells or binding potions for love, revenge, or financial gain. Nothing that doesn't benefit the whole. Remember, do as you will, and it harm none."

She knelt and gestured for him and Coop to do the same. "There are other rules, but those are the most important. I'll be sure to have a list of the others for you tomorrow morning. Now let's practice meditation. It's important to be centered before starting any spell."

With the breathing techniques she demonstrated, Keaton got a good grasp on how to calm and center his inner self. These would also be useful tools for his everyday life as the small town mayor where stress and mayhem were the name of the game.

Autumn went on to discuss ways to draw out their magic, the importance of discovering their individual elements, and the need to obtain a familiar to boost their spell-casting power. "You are to try nothing on your own. Is that clear? *Nothing.* Not even the smallest spell. I will tell you when you are ready. All spells should be cast in a dedicated circle. That is tomorrow's lesson. I'll see you at eight a.m. sharp. Don't be late, or we're done."

FROM THE AUTHOR...

Thank you for taking the time to read *SUMMER MAGIC*. If you love what you've read, please leave a brief review. To find out about what's happening next in the world of The Thorne Witches, be sure to subscribe my newsletter.

Books in The Thorne Witches Series:

SUMMER MAGIC
AUTUMN MAGIC
WINTER MAGIC
SPRING MAGIC
REKINDLED MAGIC
LONG LOST MAGIC
FOREVER MAGIC
ESSENTIAL MAGIC

You can find my online media sites here:

Website: www.tmcromer.com
Facebook: www.facebook.com/tmcromer

TM Cromer's Reader Group: bit.ly/tmc-readers
Twitter: @tmcromer
Instagram: @tmcromer

How to stay up-to-date on releases, news and other events…

✓ *Join my mailing list. My newsletter is filled with news on current releases, potential sales, new-to-you author introductions, and contests each month. But if it gets to be too much, you can unsubscribe at any time. Your information will always be kept private. No spam here! www. tmcromer.com/newsletter*

✓ *Follow me on BookBub. If you are into the quick notification method, this one is perfect. They notify you when a new book is released. No long email to read, just a simple "Hey, T.M.'s book is out today!" www.book-bub.com/authors/t-m-cromer*

✓ *Follow me on retailer sites. If you buy most of your books in digital format, this is a perfect way to stay current on my new releases. Again, like BookBub, it is a simple release-day notification.*

✓ *Join my Facebook Fan Page. While the standard pages and profiles on Facebook are not always the most reliable, I have created a group for fans who like to interact. This group entitles readers to "fan page only" contests, as well as an exclusive first look at covers, excerpts and more. The Fan Page is the most fun way to follow yet! I hope to see you there! bit.ly/tmc-readers*

AFTERWORD

According to Buddhist and Hindu legend, Chintamani Stone is a wish-fulfilling jewel that fell from the sky. This may be an indication that the stone was a piece of a meteorite. And while the Chintamani Stone was rumored to have actually existed, the object did indeed disappear around the 1920's.

Were Nicholas and Helena Roerich in possession of the stone? Possibly. It ties into the time the Roerich family spent in the Himalayas.

But the bottom line? I took a bit of creative license with the stone's power and with Helena's journal—*as writers are wont to do*—as I will also do with the artifacts listed in the coming stories for the Thorne sisters. I mean, that's the great part about being an author, isn't it?

If you care to learn more about Nicholas and Helena, you can find a link for the museum dedicated to the couple here: www.roerich.org.

ALSO…

Vestibular is a real medical issue for animals. I had two cats contract this disease. One went deaf, and the other retained the head tilt the rest of her life. They both eventually grew accustomed to their disabilities and learned to function like a normal cats.

The cone idea for Macy is made up. I've never heard or read of anyone attaching a counterbalance to an animal's head. It just seemed like a fun element to add to the story that would irritate Coop.

Made in the USA
Las Vegas, NV
02 July 2022

51027981R00164